The Sinner Detector

BY KATHLEEN A. MURPHY

DORRANCE
PUBLISHING CO
EST. 1920
PITTSBURGH, PENNSYLVANIA 15238

Dorrance Publishing Co
585 Alpha Drive
Pittsburgh, PA 15238
Visit our website at *www.dorrancebookstore.com*

ISBN: 978-1-6491-3461-5
eISBN: 978-1-6491-3814-9

The Sinner Detector

A special thank you to my daughter Lisa
for her constant encouragement and belief in me...
and
to my granddaughter Jessica
for always being on call as my IT girl.

Chapter 1

PRESENT

My shift didn't start yet, but here I am on a beautiful autumn morning waiting for my partner to pick me up. As I bend to pick up some trash someone threw out their car window, I notice Cully's SUV barreling down the road.

As he came to a semi-stop, I jump in and ask, "Who called it in?"

"Jeb Landis," As he stated the name, we both rolled our eyes.

"Mary Lou, the dispatcher said he was screaming something about finding a body in the woods. Kept saying naked lady, naked lady…so I thought we had better check it out."

Jeb Landis is sort of our town drunk and has, on many occasions, dragged us around on his drunken fantasies.

As we tore through town with lights and sirens blazing, I asked Cully to slow down and dump the siren.

"Christ, Vinny, I never get to use the siren, so leave me be. Jeb just might have seen something. Maybe we finally have an actual crime around here."

We drove four or five miles out of town to a wooded area called Blackwood, with lots of dirt roads veering off into the woods.

I asked Cully if he knew which one and he said, "The one where all the school kids go to screw." His having been one of those school kids not too long ago, I gave him a silent nod.

I have been the Chief of Police for many years, and at times I feel the clock inching up on me. Cully has been out of the police academy only four years now and has already surpassed my tech knowledge. It seems every day there is a new connection to the ether world. Despite our ages, we have a good working relationship. We treat each other with respect and as equal peers, and besides, I like the boy.

As Cully follows the dirt road about a mile in, we see Jeb sitting on a rock holding his shot gun. He is rocking back and forth and what seems like wailing. We come to a halt, get out of the truck, and approach Jeb carefully. Jeb has been known to hit the bottle just a little too hard starting early morning, then decides to take his gun for a walk. He hears us coming and jumps up with a start.

"Vinny, Vinny, I didn't do it, I found her and I didn't touch her, I swear. I watch those crime shows and I know not to touch anything. But, Vinny, I never seen anything like this, it's horrible, that poor girl, why would anyone do that?"

As I take the shotgun from Jeb, I say, "Calm down, Jeb, show me where you found her." As we follow Jeb down a deer trail, I notice some broken branches and called out to Cully. "Keep a watch for footprints and other evidence." As we came into a clearing, there she lay. My first thought was to cover her up, but I knew better, and despite the obscenity of what I was looking at, I thought again of this beautiful autumn day.

I asked Cully if Mary Lou was contacting the coroner and he said, "Not yet, but I'll get right on it."

Jane Doe lay among the colored leaves, birds were angered at our disrupting their quiet and were chattering noisily. She could not have been put there too long ago. There was some decay where nature was claiming her as its own, but she would still be identifiable. She lay face up, naked, except for the arrow standing upright out of her heart. It looked like her knees were positioned up, but because of the time and elements, they collapsed outward showing something inserted in her vagina. Her eyes were closed, but someone painted eye makeup on the lids in a hideous fashion and smeared lipstick across her mouth. Her breasts did not sag, which led me to believe, "implants." Perhaps a way to identify her. On the tip of the arrow was a tag with words written on it. It had deteriorated somewhat due to the weather, but you could see the letters: J-e-l. The rest was washed away or smudged.

I told Cully to take Jeb back to the SUV and get the crime scene tape and then wait for the coroner.

"Call the crime unit if Mary Lou hasn't already done so. We need to get pictures and collect any evidence from the body before that jackass Will gets here."

Will Strauss is a self-serving egotistical jackass who thinks because he got elected coroner, his shit doesn't stink. A real officious bastard. Vinny and Will butted heads the hard way when he acted like there was something suspicious about how Vinny's wife Lily died two years ago. Lily and Vinny were married sixteen years, and she died of natural causes. Will wanted to make it look like foul play on Vinny's part.

Cully called out, "Frilly Willy is on the way, as well as the crime scene guys."

"Cully, don't let Will hear you call him that."

"Come on, Vinny, everyone knows he's gay. What's the big deal? It's not like he's the only one in town."

"I know, but keep it professional."

I took some time to examine as much as I could. I noted the pose and the definite symbols surrounding our Jane Doe's death. I looked closer, and after the first horrifying sight, I began thinking like a detective. The first thing I noticed was her breasts were taped to give them a "perky" look. I don't believe there are implants. She looks to be between thirty and forty. No jewelry but a tan line on the ring finger. A wedding band or engagement ring? Missing now. I will have the police scour the trail to see if it dropped off while she was being transported here. She has pierced ears but no earrings, and it looks like maybe a piercing on the right nipple, again no ring. As I continued examining her, I heard the rest of the homicide team arrive.

As the crime crew and the coroner came traipsing into the area, everyone got about their jobs. Crime guys took photos, removed the arrow, and started examining the girl close up.

Will spotted Vinny and yelled, "Did you get a hard on, Vinny? Probably the first naked lady you've seen in some years…HA!"

"Show some class, Will, our Jane Doe died a horrible death, you could show some respect."

"Why? She can't hear me, and besides, whoever did this showed no respect. Hey, Eddie, what's that sticking out of her pussy?" The crime tech Eddie just shook his head and removed the object. It was a small plastic statue of the Blessed Virgin Mother.

Will went to take her liver temp and examine her decomp and decided she had been dead for at least five days.

Will Strauss is thirty-four-years-old and still lives with his mother. Will does not see this as odd. He likes the good life, and with his salary as coroner and having to not pay for his living arrangements, his money goes to more hedonistic pleasures. The house he grew up in is paid in full, his mother, Irene, has a more than comfortable income. Both of Will's parents were doctors. His father passed away seven years ago from a massive coronary. Dr. Strauss senior, Art to his friends, was seriously overweight and he, too, enjoyed the good life. Golfing, cigars, booze, pornography, and high-priced call girls. Art enjoyed the fruits of his labor.

Will was still in medical school when his father died and his plan was to move home after he graduated to help fill the huge home and be company, of sorts, to his mother. Will knew from an early age he was gay. His mother suspected but never asked. His father suspected but denied it. Now Will was free to live his life out in the open, although society demanded he be discreet if he was to be accepted as a medical doctor and coroner. And discreet he was. For as large a man as his father had been, Will was just the opposite. A slight man some would say and some days more effeminate than others. Will kept himself in good shape, for he enjoyed the attention he got at gay bars and social events.

Will enjoyed his life, his toys. Always the latest, most expensive cars, suits, shoes, accessories that cost a working man's yearly salary. He established himself as a doctor in the community and was well liked due in part to his parents and their connections to the country clubs, charities, and social circles. Will found himself in the position of running for coroner. He was surprised when he won, and as most young people, power went to his head. He became officious and demanding of his staff. His first autopsy was of a local woman in town by the name of Lily Hayden Miller, age thirty-six, white, attractive, and a school teacher at the local high school. Will could not determine the cause of death, but for some reason, her air-passage became clogged and she died of asphyxiation. Will wanted to go after the husband. Seems he is the Chief of Police in town, and Will was sure he did something to hasten her death. Because of his arrogance, he ended up with a split lip, courtesy of the Chief of Police. And now the working atmosphere was indeed strained.

Detective Vincent Miller and Office Cully Andrews left the scene and headed back to the station. It will be up to the crime techs and the coroner to give them the direction in which to head. As they came into the squad room, Captain Ritter called them into his office. Like all government offices, the Captain's was typical. It is painted a drab color, uncomfortable chairs, and ratty file cabinets. Among all this drabness was a sparkling, clean window. It is said that Captain Ritter personally cleaned it, so when the sun shone its rays through the window, it would land directly on a glass cabinet holding miniature crystals, which would send rainbows of color dancing all around the room. The display of colors would only last fifteen to eighteen minutes a day, but if you were fortunate to be in his office at the right time, it was a sight to behold.

Rumor has it that when Ritter was in college, he was known as Harry "Hurricane" Ritter and quite the football star until one game, someone cleaned his clock and sent him to the hospital. He remained in a coma for several days. One day a nurse came into the room and saw all these flashing rainbow lights dancing all over the room, and as she looked to see where the colors were coming from, Harry "Hurricane" Ritter woke up and said four words.

"It was an angel." As the nurse turned toward him, there on the nightstand was a small crystal angel. To this day no one knows who put it there, it just appeared. So all these years later, Harry's collection of small crystals stays close by to remind him of miracles.

"So, Miller, what have we got? I hear it was a brutal murder. Bring me up-to-date." After a short briefing, Captain Ritter told the policeman to start checking through databases to see if there were any other deaths in the surrounding counties and to even go as far as checking other state records. "This crime has too many distinct markers, Vinny, we may have come across the work of a serial killer."

CHAPTER 2

YEAR 1998

"Hey, Mom, I'm going over to the school gym to shoot some baskets. What time should I be home?" Grace Dougherty called back to her son Nick that he should not be later than 5:30 P.M. Grace was a busy mother of five children and the wife of Mark. They were a happy family, close knit, and she has been fortunate enough to be a stay-at-home mom.

It was a beautiful day. Fall not wanting to let go and winter nipping at its heels. Grace was baking on this beautiful afternoon, getting ready for the bake sale to be held at St. Jerome's Catholic Church on Saturday. The Dougherty family were devout Catholics.

Alice, their sixteen-year-old daughter, came into the kitchen complaining, "But, Mom, it is just not right."

"Alice, we have been over this. Nick wants to attend his Winter Snow Ball dance. It is his senior year."

"Yes but, Mom, he's taking Sarah Warner and you know he doesn't like her!"

"Alice, of course he likes her."

"Aw, Mom, you know what I mean. He doesn't like her like that...Sarah would die for Nick."

"I am sure Sarah knows Nick is only going with her as a friend. You know your brother has committed himself to God. He wants to be a priest and has already been accepted at St. Borromeo's Seminary. As his mother, I am so proud of him and a little vain to be able to say I have a son who is a priest. Maybe Pope some day! And, Alice, Sarah knows this."

"He's crazy, why would he want that? How can he fight off all the girls? He is gorgeous and could have any girl he wants."

"Alice, ever since Nick was little, he leaned towards the spiritual. He would rather be in church praying or helping Father Hughes with the tasks at the church and rectory than going on dates with girls who will never claim his heart the way God has."

"Now enough of this, I need you to walk over to Mrs. Nye's house and collect your brother from his piano lesson."

"May I take the car?"

"No, you may not. The walk will do you good. Maybe a few prayers along the way will help you accept your brother's decision."

As Alice stomped down the steps and onto the sidewalk, she mumbles under her breath, "You would think I was their maid, live-in slave, Alice, do this, Alice, do that. Well, maybe Nick wants to waste his life, but I am not going to. I plan on having boyfriends and go to parties and have a career. Maybe I will become a movie star." As Alice was mumbling, she heard her name being called.

"Alice, Alice, where are you going?" Alice looks across the street to see Austin raking leaves. Austin Harding is Alice's nemesis and neighbor. He worships her, but she only sees him as a friend, although Austin won't give up. He is certain that someday Alice will change her mind.

"Hi, Austin, oh, I have to pick up Tristan from his piano lesson. Want to come along?"

'No, I have to rake up these leaves. We are expecting company for Thanksgiving and my job is cleaning up the yard."

"What is it with our parents?" Alice complains. "We are nothing but cheap labor. Well, gotta get going. See you later."

As Alice continued on her way, Austin stares after her, wondering what it must be like to have so many brothers and sisters. Not to mention the parents. Always doing charity work, going to church, which seems every second of the day, and having a son becoming a priest. Austin's mother and father are blue collar workers, and the family struggles just to stay above water. There will be no fancy college or cars in Austin's future. He will work hard to just to go to the community college. Austin's sister, Marcelene, went to beauty school and is working in a local salon. She still lives at home at the age of twenty-two and contributes to the household. Austin's family may not be super religious and entertain the parish priest every week, but they are a loving, happy family, and some day Austin is certain he will be able to support and love forever Alice Dougherty. Austin watches as the sun catches the golden highlights of Alice's hair as it sways down her back determined to one day steal her heart.

With an assuredness he doesn't really feel, he proclaims to himself, "I am going to ask Alice to the Snow Ball Dance."

Tristan is sitting on the porch steps waiting for one of his brothers or sister to get him. Tristan is eight-years-old and feels he is entirely too old to need someone to walk him home, so he is in a bad mood because his family thinks he is a baby. He sees Alice coming down the pavement and is glad to see her and not Patrick. Pat is four years older and does nothing but tease and aggravate and make him cry.

"Hi, Tristan," Alice calls and sees his face all scrunched up. Alice knows he hates having to be picked up but sees the relief when he sees it is her and not Pat. "Want to race home?" Alice asks.

"Ok, bet I can beat you this time," and with that, Tristan takes off. Alice is finding it harder and harder to stay up with him. Someday Tristan will be a great runner.

As they turn the corner, Tristan spies Austin and hollers a hi. Tristan likes Austin. He always treats him like a big kid.

Austin yells back, "Hurry this way, we will hide in the leaves." As Tristan tackles Austin, they both fall into the pile of leaves laughing, and as Alice finally catches up, she, too, dives in and enjoys the carefree fun of youngsters enjoying life.

When the laughter dies down, Alice tells Tristan he has to go home now. Mom is waiting on him.

"Ah, darn it, Alice, we were having such fun."

"I know, but you have to get cleaned up for dinner. Father Eric is coming, so we can all sit around and worship 'St. Nicholas,' the perfect son, brother, and future priest."

As Tristan scampers across the street and Alice is picking leaves from her hair, Austin turns to her, reaches up, and helps with the leaves and asks, "Alice, will you go to the Snow Ball Dance with me?"

CHAPTER 3

YEAR 2014

Larry pulled into the parking lot ready to go to work, despite having one hell of a hangover. As he gathers his gear and lunch, he keeps going over and over the night before.

"Oh, man, that Linda was some piece of ass. I can't wait to tell Jimmy all about it." Larry is twenty-eight-years-old and works for a small town in Bucks County. He is an underachiever and does only what is required and charms his way through the other sections of his miserable life. As he gets out of his car, Jimmy pulls in.

"Hey, man," calls Jimmy, "you look like shit!" Larry looks across the roof of his car and decides to banter despite the hangover.

"Yeah, but wait till I tell you why, what a night!"

Jimmy and Larry have clean-up duty today. They must walk the entire length of the train tracks and clean up trash and brush that may have blown on to the tracks. It is usually an easy job, but the weather today is bitter cold and neither man is excited about pulling this duty. The two men get their gear ready, put on the gloves, and with tools in hand, decide on what tactic they would take. They would walk one side down to the park area, take a break, then walk the other side back to where they parked. There they would have lunch, drive to the park, and finish the second section using the same pattern.

As they start down the track, Larry spares no details of the conquest of Linda the night before. He encouraged Jimmy to get a taste of "sweet Linda" because according to Larry, Linda would do anyone. Jimmy is not interested. He has a wife and kids and figures one woman is plenty. As they approach the park and start looking forward to their cigarette break and a rest, Larry spots something farther in the bushes. It looks like a stick with something white attached. He calls to Jimmy to join him to check it out. As they walk into the brambles and thick bushes, they come across a horrific sight. There laying in a small clearing is a naked woman posed with her knees in the air and an arrow sticking out of her chest with a tag on it and some writing. Her blond hair was chopped off unevenly, a clump here, a clump missing there. Her eyes were painted garishly with make-up, and there was lipstick smeared across her lips.

As Larry and Jimmy stood staring at the once lovely woman, Larry's night of hard drinking took its toll and he lost it in the bushes. As he fell to his knees, Jimmy got out his cell phone and dialed 911 and went to see about his friend. As he knelt beside Larry, he noticed there was something sticking out of the woman's private parts...

CHAPTER 4

Outside of a farming town in a field, neglected for years where brambles and weeds grow at will, the wind picks up and blows trash from one section to the other, swirling in the air only to settle a few feet farther in the field. Among the trash being blown about is bone dust from the corpse which had once laid behind an abandon outbuilding. The bone dust comes from what use to be a young wife and mother and is now part of the land. Parts of her body have been carried off by small animals to lay in gullies and be buried beneath the ground, and time and weather have claimed the rest.

Someday in the far future, the land may be developed or perhaps a child set upon having an adventure will stumble upon the outbuilding, which now lay in shambles, strewn about like match sticks. While exploring the landscape, the developer or that inquisitive child will kick over a rock or a plank and there in the dirt will be a small statue of the "Blessed Virgin Mary" and wonder where in the world did that come from; they will pick it up and put it in their pocket. The child will take it home and put it in a special place where all secrets are kept. A developer will take it home and show it to his wife where they will both wonder and perhaps look upon it as a good omen.

No one notices the strange stick, which looks like just another broken weed and the message, which was affixed to it, is long gone.

CHAPTER 5

YEAR 1998

Nick is laying on his bed reading his bible. The Christmas vacation is almost over, and he is anxious to get back to school, finish up his senior year, and head off to St. Borromeo Seminary in Philadelphia. Unlike a typical eighteen-year-old, Nick's bedroom walls hold posters of Saints, past and present Popes, and his bureau resembles a Catholic Church's alter. Oh, there are some sport figures and dirty clothes laying around. Nick may have a calling, but he is still a boy. He loves basketball and his secret pleasure is to dance. He was so glad Sarah agreed to go the Snow Ball Dance with him, and even though Sarah did everything in her power to temp him, he enjoyed dancing with her. His chaste kiss on her cheek when he took her home seemed to finally convince Sarah they would be nothing but friends. But oh, how she could dance. After Nick received his First Communion and was confirmed into the Catholic faith, he told his mother one day that he kept having a recurring dream.

Each night when he would fall asleep, he would see this light that looked like a bright star with sparks flashing all around it, and he would hear a voice calling, "Follow me." As a child, the dream scared him, but as he grew older and the dream stopped, Nick was totally convinced that it was God himself. From that time on, Nick devoted himself to God and his church. He was rock solid in his faith sometimes to the annoyance of his family. He had only one goal in mind and that was to follow God as a priest.

It was the end of Christmas week, and Mark was looking forward to getting home and do some relaxing before the New Year celebrations. He was glad that the New Year was falling on a Sunday. Mark has taken some much-needed vacation days. The TV station where Mark was a meteorologist was very good to him, and he was living his dream. Thoughts like this brought him back to agonizing over his eldest son's decision to be a priest. Of course he is proud, but he thinks of all the things his son will miss. And he must admit, he is so glad the holidays are soon over and they don't have Father Eric at the door every day. Nick has secured his spot at the Seminary and is counting the days. Mark marvels at how dedicated his son is.

Mark pulled in the driveway of their lovely home. He sits in the car for a while thinking how fortunate he is. While other couples are cheating on their spouses and divorcing, he prides himself in the fact that he and Grace are as much in love now as when they first met. As he gets out of the car, he glances across the way and sees Austin struggling with the garbage cans.

Mark calls, "Hey, Austin, could you use some help?"

"No," he replies, "Mom says it will give me muscles. Ha!"

Mark agrees and says, "I could use some of those muscle doing chores myself." Mark notices Tristan coming up the road on his bike hurrying to greet him. Mark thinks at least he has other sons who will hopefully have lots of babies to carry on the Dougherty name. The sun is going down and he hears mothers calling for their children to come in now, dinner is almost ready. The trees are bare and some snow still remains in piles. A few snowmen have carrot noses and mother's scarves. Mark likes this time of year. As a meteorologist, he sees and hears things others do not. Tristan catches up to him, drops his bike, and gives him a big hug.

"Hi, Dad, are you on vacation now?"

"Sure am, son, and I am looking forward to doing some fun things."

"Like what?"

"Well, maybe you and I can go into town to the batting cages one day and see if we can improve on that stance of yours."

"Wow, Dad, that would be awesome, and maybe Nick would come along and I could show him how good I am."

"Well, we shall see," says Mark and ruffles his son's hair.

Grace is in the kitchen preparing dinner and greets Mark with a kiss, one that Mark realizes tastes very much like wine. "Wow, that was some greeting, wife, into the wine a bit early, aren't we?"

"Oh, Mark, it is the holidays and soon a new year, don't spoil things by being a stiff shirt. Living with one 'holier than thou' is all I can take right now."

"I'm sorry, Grace, is Nick sermonizing again?"

"Yes, and I will be so glad when he is off to the Seminary. Does that make me a bad mother?"

"No, I am on the same page. I know you are as proud as I but, Grace, I am so tired of Father Eric and all his promises of how Nick is going to be Pope someday!"

"Yeah, me, too," says Grace and pours them each a glass of wine.

Nick is so anxious to get back to school and finish this year. It seems his life is in limbo. He knows what he wants, he's prepared and doesn't know why it must drag out five more months before he graduates. As he jumps into his car (something he has to give up), he waits patiently for Alice. She is a junior this year, and even as a brother, he sees she is going to be a beauty. He secretly hopes she continues to confide in him, even when he goes off to the Seminary.

"Sorry for making you wait, Nick, I couldn't find my cell phone."

"That's ok, teachers are always lenient the first day."

"By the way, Nick, you never told me how your date went with Sarah? Did you dance or just sit there looking all priestly. "

"Don't, Alice, you know I don't like you insinuating things."

"Yeah, but did you kiss her goodnight, do a little feel here and there?"

"Alice, that is disgusting!"

"Well, once you are a priest, you'll never find out stuff like that."

"Alice, you of all people know where my heart is, now stop the trash talk."

Life in the Dougherty house continues without incident. Grace is happy to have four of her kids in school. She will now have so much time to devote to Catherine, her three-year-old. She is such a pleasant, eager to please child. Mark is back to work looking more handsome than ever on the TV screen, and Grace always makes sure to watch his section of the news cast.

Grace is a stunning woman, even after five children. She has kept her shape, stays current with the news, and at all times knows what is happening with her children. Right now Nick's behavior is baffling her. He has become a bit sullen, lost that excitement about his future. He still talks about the Seminary but not with quite the enthusiasm. Grace is aware but not too concerned; after all Nick has planned his life since he was born, so it seems. Perhaps it is just nerves. Graduation is only three and a half months away.

Nick is indeed in turmoil. He just got back from seeing Father Eric, who was no help to him at all. Nick came through the front door, barely said hello to his mother, and went straight to his room and is now on his knees praying for guidance. Father Eric says he is just being tested by God, but Nick knows that is not right.

On his knees, he laments, "God, I have wanted to serve you since before I was born. You have been my light, my strength, why would You test me? I don't need testing, take this temptation from me, please God," he prayed. "My plans are made, my family has sacrificed for me, I must not waiver."

When Mark came home that evening, Grace said, "You have to talk to Nick, something is going on with him and he will not confide in me."

"What has he said?" asks Mark.

"Nothing, except he will work it out," comments Grace.

"Should we not let him do just that? He will be off to the Seminary soon and won't have us then."

"Ok, but if this continues, you must try to find out the problem."

There is a problem all right…at the beginning of February while Nick is engrossed in his third period literature class, the door opens and Principal Father Kirk walks in with the most beautiful girl Nick has ever laid eyes on. Nick has never paid attention to the beauty of girls. Girls have always been unimportant to him. His heart belongs to God.

As Father Kirk approaches Sister Madeline's desk to introduce this new student, Nick pays attention to how her hair is piled on top of her head in some messy fashion. His mother would call it a bun. There are wisps sneaking out and trailing down around her face, and Nick thinks a beautiful face. She walks demurely behind Father Kirk with her eyes downcast. Father Kirk turns to the class and introduces Mary Ellen McGrath. As she looks up, an electric shock jolts Nick as he looks into the eyes of his soul mate. They are deep brown, not just brown but a rich coffee brown, and he feels he is lost forever. Nick regains his senses as Mary Ellen says hi to the class, and as Father Kirk directs her to a seat, he tells her he will see her later, don't forget.

Father Kirk is about to take his leave when he turns and says, "Nick, meet me in my office after school."

CHAPTER 6

PRESENT DAY

Mary Lou Stratton has worked for the police department for almost twenty years. She is a wonder when it comes to the computer, and this new technology is absorbed quickly. She loves retrieving information and searching the net for all kinds of things. When Chief Miller asks her to do a search for similar crimes in the area, she is anxious to get started. With several bangles on her rather oversized wrist, you can hear her doing her search way down the hall. As Vinny and Cully head out the door to the morgue, Vinny calls to Mary Lou to notify him, no matter what, if she finds any connections.

When the two policemen arrive at the morgue, Will has already begun his examination and autopsy. They grabbed some gowns and masks and watched as Will goes about his job. Despite Vinny's dislike of the coroner, he is the first to admit Will does good work.

"What have you found so far, Will?" Vinny asks.

"Quite a lot actually. Our Jane Doe did not die of an arrow through her heart, but the arrow looks as though it was stabbed in her chest, not shot using a bow. Another thing I found puzzling was her hair."

Cully seemed intrigued and asked, "What about her hair?"

"It's been chopped off here and there, like someone wanted to make her look ugly. Same with the make-up on her face. I took samples and sent it to the lab to see if we can identify the brand. If we identify her and the make-up isn't her brand, we will know the killer brought it with him or her. Our killer could be a woman caught up in jealousy."

"What about the statue we found?" asked Vinny.

"Common, could be purchased in any religious store. I have no idea of the significance of it; also this tape used to tape up her breasts…weird. Again,

I sent all this to the lab. Perhaps they will find prints or maybe even semen if this was a guy jerking off or a rape."

As Cully and Vinny stood around watching Will at work, Vinny's cell phone buzzed.

"Yeah, Vinny here. What have you got, Mary Lou?"

"I think you should come back to the office, so I can show you. Seems like some backwater town in Buck's County had a similar find."

"Be right there."

Upon hearing this, the civility between Will and Vinny went by the way side when Will told Vinny, "I am sure some smart detective somewhere will solve this crime for you." Vinny gave him the finger and stormed out listening to Will's girlish titter. When they got back to the office, Mary Lou was on the phone with the detective in Warrington. She put her on hold and gave the phone to Vinny while mouthing it is Detective Gail Arnold.

"Detective Arnold, Vinny Miller here, I understand you have a murder case similar to one we just caught. What can you tell me?"

"Well, yes, we had a case in 2014, when some maintenance men came across a young woman lying in a clearing in a wooded area along some railroad tracks. It looked as though she was shot through the heart with an arrow. There was some sort of message attached to the arrow, but most of it was gone."

"Detective Arnold, did your coroner do an autopsy?"

"Of course, we may be a small burb, but we do good police work."

"Oh, I am not suggesting you don't, but I was wondering if the autopsy showed the arrow being pushed in and not shot by a bow?"

"I don't know that," says Detective Arnold, "I will have to check."

"Please," says Vinny, "it is very important, was anything else found that was unusual?"

"Yes, but we are keeping that under wraps, we did not go public with it."

"Will you tell me what?" Vinny asks.

Detective Arnold says, "You go first."

Vinny answers, "The Blessed Virgin Mary!"

A very quiet yes comes across the wirers.

"Detective Arnold, I think we may have stumbled on to a serial killer. Will you send me all the records you have and please include the autopsy report and any lab findings, and I will do the same for you. Did you identify the woman?"

"Yes, a local woman, her name was Suzanne Cunningham. Married to a service man. He was overseas at the time. They had no children."

"Thank you, please let's stay in touch." He turned to Mary Lou and said, "Good work, now set up a crime board for us and continue your search for more murders similar to ours. We are going to hunt ourselves a serial killer."

CHAPTER 7

YEAR 1999

Nick had a hard time concentrating the rest of the day. He went through his classes like a comatose patient. He did not understand the impact those brown eyes had on him, and he was concerned about meeting with Father Kirk. Has something gone wrong with his admittance to the Seminary? Nick literally jumped when the last bell rang. It was shrill and unnerving; never before had he even been aware of it, but now it seemed to rattle his whole being. He could not help but think of Poe's line, "The bell tolls for thee." Nick gathers his books and heads out to the Principal's office.

"Whoa, Nicky," his friend Charlie says as they work their way to the door. "Hey, Nick, what do you think of the new girl?"

"What's there to think, Charlie, she seemed nice, but we only had one class with her. Besides, girls are not in my future, you know that."

"Man, you don't know what you are missing. I am going to charm the pants off that cute little bird. She won't know what happened until she's screaming for more of Charlie Sullivan."

"Enough, Charlie, see you later. I have an appointment with Captain Kirk."

"Yeah, well, say hi to Spock for me!"

Nick arrives at the office and the secretary, Ms. Webb, tells him to go right in. Nick opens the door and comes face to face with Mary Ellen McGrath.

"Come in, come in, Nick," Father Kirk beckons. "I know you already met Mary Ellen, but I brought the two of you together here because, Nick, I want you to be Mary Ellen's mentor for the rest of the school year. She will graduate on time, but you can show her the ropes and help to bring her up-to-date on her classes and what she will need to graduate. Spend time tutoring and get Mary Ellen to feel like she belongs here at St. Jerome's. I expect you to meet her in my office in the morning. She will have most of the same classes. Good, that's settled. Any questions? No, ok then. Mary Ellen, see you in the morning. Nick, please stay a few minutes." As Mary Ellen leaves the room, Nick remembers to breathe; he thinks to himself that the tingling he is feeling must mean maybe there is a storm brewing. He has no idea how right he is.

"Nick," Father Kirk begins, "I know this is an awful lot to ask of you. I may be a priest, but I know what a girl like that can do to all this male testosterone in this school, and with you off to the Seminary in a few months, I know I could trust you to treat Mary Ellen with the respect she deserves. Understand?"

"Yes," Nick stammers, wondering what he is to do with her. "I can't even talk when she's around me, how am I to tutor her?"

Thus begins the predicament in Nick's life. He meets with Mary Ellen the following morning and escorts her to class. He introduces her to his circle of friends and can see what Father Kirk meant. His male friends are drooling, and some of the girls are so mean and jealous. The first two weeks go smoothly. Nick is chaste and business-like, but one evening, they decide to go to the park to study. It is one of those balmy days that surprise you in the middle of winter. Nick planned on sitting at a picnic table, but Mary Ellen brought a blanket, so they could lay on the grass. There is a sweetness in the air. Only a light jacket is necessary this evening, and even that is taken off and placed beside the young couple. Nick is reluctant to lay down on a blanket with a girl. He feels very uncomfortable, but it seems that Mary Ellen has such a way about her that it just seems so right. As they sit side by side, they slump and shoulders touch. Nick jumps up so fast, the book goes flying.

"Nick, what's wrong? Come sit back down."

"I don't know," says Nick, "let's go over to the picnic table. I am not comfortable trying to read sitting on a blanket."

"Ok," says Mary Ellen. She reaches out her hand for Nick to help her up. He takes her hand and thinks in that split moment what it would be like to kiss those luscious soft lips…and then it happens. They come together in the sweetest, most innocent kiss, and for Nick, he sees bright stars and sparks and hears a voice that says, "Follow and be with me." Only it is not God's voice but Mary Ellen's. Instead of being horrified at what he did, Nick looks into those chocolate brown eyes and declares his love for her.

A few days later, while the family is gathered at the dinner table all talking at once and enjoying the coming together after their days' happenings, Nick clears his throat, looks at his mother, and states, "I am not going to be a priest, I am in love with Mary Ellen McGrath."

CHAPTER 8

PRESENT:

Vinny reserves one of the conference rooms and asked Mary Lou to get the room set up for their use while he gets on the phone with the Captain to see what officers he can pull to help in this investigation. As the phone was ringing, Vinny kept going over in his head who he would ask for to form his task force. He had to convince Captain Ritter they were on to tracking a serial killer. The murder of our Jane Doe was not an isolated case.

"Captain Ritter here."

"Captain, it's Vinny. I need to meet with you as soon as possible regarding our Jane Doe."

"Come right up, Vinny, and tell me what you have."

As Vinny entered the Captain's office, he was again struck by the beauty and brilliance of Captain Ritter's crystal collection.

"Well, Vinny, convince me we have more than a single murder on our hands."

"Mary Lou has been surfing the internet, or whatever it is she does, and has come up with at least nine unsolved murders throughout our section of our state that has more than enough similarities to believe we have a serial killer on the loose. The connection that Mary Lou discovered so far are these women have all been found naked and staged with an arrow piercing their heart. The strange thing is that the arrow was stabbed into their heart and not shot with a bow. Some still had a tag with words, but so far none have been complete. Weather and conditions of the elements have destroyed the wording but not completely. Also, Cap, a statue of the Blessed Mother has been found with six out of the nine."

"Well, Vinny, you might really be on to something. What, or should I say whom, do you want to work with you?"

"I'd like to put together a task force, and I would like to hand pick them."

"Who do you have in mind?"

Vinny has already made up his mind as to whom he wanted and slid a list across the desk. The Captain picked it up, looked it over, and didn't seem to have any objections until he saw Mickey's name.

"Mickey O'Hara is a hot head. I am not sure you could get along with him being you can be a hot head, too."

"I thought about that, Captain, but Mickey can go places and get results better than anyone I know, and I think he knows and respects me enough that we should not clash too badly. He is a hell of an investigator."

"Ok, Vinny, I will give you the go ahead and see where this leads, but you identify our Jane Doe. She has got to be top priority."

Vinny went pounding down the stairs and handed Mary Lou his list and told her to contact each person and tell them to meet him in the crime room at 2:00 P.M. today. As he takes the stairs back up to the crime solving room, he starts to formulate in his mind how he wants to go about this. He reaches the second floor and shuts the door. He goes to the bank of windows along the north wall and stares out at the scene. He cracks a window a couple of inches and lights a cigarette. His thoughts drift back to his wife Lily. When they got married, she nagged and nagged for him to quit smoking, and he finally did only because he loved her so much. After she died, he went back to them. He stares out the window and watches the people scurrying around, going about their business. Thanksgiving and Christmas are just around the corner. Surely someone is missing this once beautiful young woman.

He heard his first member of his squad before he saw him. Lucas Marino, a thirty-three-year-old handsome Italian, sing-songing compliments to the women on the force. He just manages to stay under the wire when it comes to sexual harassment. Don't know how he does it. The women love him!

"Hey, Chief. Am I early? I want to thank you for putting me on your task force. I am going to work my ass off for you."

"Thanks, Luke, I think this is going to be a tough one."

The other members of his group file in at different times. Luke is busy making coffee, and Vinny is still focused on the scene outside. Christmas decorations flood the street. Every store has some enticement to shop and spend. He sees parents out while their children are still in school. People walking their dogs. Life going on without any knowledge of the monster just around the corner.

Finally, his team has arrived. Once everyone gets coffee and settles in, Vinny looks around the room and is satisfied with his choices. There sits Max, known to a few as Maxine. She is a black woman, 5'8", and weighs a good 200 pounds. Vinny chose her because she is an excellent interrogator. No one messes with Max Dixon. And despite her fearful appearance, Max is so girlie. Bangles on her wrist, ears are pierced several times, very subtle eye make-up, and has a voice like a cat's purr. Sitting beside her is Cully Andrews. The contrast is startling. Cully is Vinny's favorite. Calls on him to drive and keeps Vinny on track. Cully is a dwarf beside Max, but he is sharp and Vinny sees him advancing quickly. Although the youngest of the group, Vinny has a lot invested in him.

Mickey, his time bomb, is already arguing with Lucas over who makes better coffee. Mickey is a quick to anger Irishman. But Vinny thinks he can keep him in check. Mickey is a seasoned investigator. Goes places others can't. Has contacts in every back alley and gin joint in the city. Vinny needs him and intends to keep him focused. Standing looking out the windows on the left side of the room is C.J. C.J. is a thin, black man, 6'2", and reminds Vinny of Morgan Freeman. Christopher Robbins Jackson, AKA C.J. His mother was so into Winnie the Pooh stories when C.J. was born, she hung that monitor on him. Through his childhood, he was teased and bullied unmercifully, and instead of lashing out, he grew inward, not sullen and bitter but quiet, thoughtful, and had the insight at a very young age that with a name like that, he was meant for greatness. It is his quiet, reflectiveness, and intense need to know that Vinny chose him.

Vinny turned from the window and said, "It's a little after two. We can get started and hope Jet shows up." With that the door opens.

"Sorry I'm late, Chief."

"That's ok, we were just getting started." Vinny watched as Jet sat and set up her computer. She was going to be his link to the ether world. Jet Jones is a pixie of a woman, petite with jet black hair. She reminds you of Peter Pan, only she is into the Victorian era. Long skirts, high ruffled collars, and sometimes, her speech reflexes years gone by. But she is a computer whiz and highly sought after by other departments. Known as J.J., she is excited to be counted as one of Chief Miller's task force. It means she will be working with that hot-tempered Irishman. Jet may look Victorian, but her attitude towards sex is not.

Vinny goes up to the white board and officially starts the investigation.

"Ok, people, here is what we have. A Jane Doe. Our first priority is to identify her. Jet, get on the missing persons lists. Do at least a five county search."

"Why five counties?" asks C.J.

"We have ourselves a serial killer. My snooping around has come up with a possible nine to twelve murders of similar M.O. I took the info to Captain Ritter, and that is why we are now a task force." Vinny goes up to the white board and starts listing what he knows. "Ok, I have listed the names and places of the victims we know about. Victim one, Tammy Reed, white, female, age thirty-six, and married. Three children. Found along a popular swimming hole in 2008 near Maple Glenn. Close to Horsham. Died from an arrow to the heart. Not shot but stabbed. Small statue of the Virgin Mary found. Rings missing. Hair hacked off unevenly.

Victims two and three, both found in 2009, fifty miles apart. Both females. One a twenty-three-year-old black woman found in Bethlehem, and victim number three, a white woman, possibly forty-five to fifty, found in Tobyhanna. Again a statue found with both women. The twenty-three-year-old still had traces of the garish make-up, but victim three was too decomposed. No jewelry found with either woman.

Victim four, could have been killed in 2009 but not discovered until 2010. Very little evidence. The police thought her to be a prostitute, so they did little to solve the murder. Being she was naked and no identification. She was found in Philadelphia."

Lucas interrupts Vinny and asks why he thinks these crimes are committed over such a wide area. Vinny tells Lucas he will get into that but wants to finish listing what he knows about the victims.

"Victims five and six, two more victims in 2010. Also women. Both identified. A young Hispanic woman. Only twenty, named Rosa Gonzalos, just married before her husband was deployed overseas and she was found near Harrisburg. A place called Penbrook. He is in the Marines. The second woman, white, age around thirty. Found near Camp Hill. Married, no children. Her name is Stephanie Kuntz, and her husband is also a soldier but is stateside. He works for the Department of Defense. According to the investigation, he was the prime suspect. Seems Miss Stephanie was cheating, but he has an airtight alibi, and once we put together the facts of this and the other murders, he was ruled out.

Victim seven, Victoria (Vickie) Bartlet. Born and raised in New York but died in Scranton. Ms. Bartlet was divorced twice and was planning to marry number three in two months. Has adult children that says Vicki was loved by all. Same M.O. No jewelry, clownish make-up, and an arrow through her heart. No statue was found. Could have been picked up by one the CSI thinking it was not connected. The question is being asked. The M.E. thinks she was killed in 2012.

Victims eight and nine. The most recent victims were found in 2014. Two more women. Both white. Believed to be killed within months of each other. Both professional women. Victim eight, Anna Serento, a defense attorney in an up and coming firm. Smart, educated, and street smart. Found behind some dumpsters. Posed the same, arrow, but this time the paper clipped at the top spelled out 'Jezebel.' The other writing was too weathered. The interesting thing here is the writing is cursive, not printed. Keep that thought in mind. She was dating a service man. She was found in Reading.

Victim nine. Another professional woman. A physician's assistant. Claire Harrison, also found in Reading. She was just discovered in the woods by some hunters. With this victim, we have a real good clue. The tag on the arrow had slipped under some rocks when the arrow tilted, and there is more of the message. On the paper attached to this arrow was written, 'Jezebel – Satan's Whore!" She is married to a doctor who is a surgeon in the Army. Now we can fill in more of what we know of the victims as we go. I want some input from any of you. Lucas, any thoughts?"

"Yeah, Chief, seems that there is not a type other than women. We have young, old, white, Hispanic, and black."

Max interrupted, "There seems to be a connection to service men. The ones we identified are married or were married to service men. Do you think that's a coincidence?"

"Let me add that to the board," says Vinny. "Ok, we have no specific type and a possible link to the military."

Cully chimes in with a question, "Were any of the victims abducted, or does it seem they went willingly?"

"Good question, Cully. J.J., get those magic fingers of yours working and see if any cars were left abandon, or were there any witnesses that think these women went missing due to foul play?"

You could hear J.J. pounding away at the keyboard and just then a knock, and Mary Lou comes through the door waving papers, saying, "Chief, they found that missing Caitlyn Thomas who went missing from that truck stop."

"How do you know it is Caitlyn Thomas?" asks Vinny.

"The detective in charge is following our investigation and called. Told me he was sure she was killed with the same M.O. and asked that you call him. His name is Morrison up near Williamsport. The missing person report is a resident of that county. They identified her by the tattoo. Seems the M.E. found a tattoo of a semi-truck inside her thigh headed to the canyon with lights on, if you know what I mean?"

C.J. called out to Lucas, "Anybody you know, lover boy?"

"No," said Luke, "but sounds like I may have missed out on something."

"Enough," Vinny says very quietly, "she is someone's daughter."

Mary Lou hands Vinny the paper and Vinny reads the report out loud:
In Williamsport it was reported that one Caitlyn
Moore Thomas did not show up at her night time shift
at the "Rest and Relax" truck stop last month. It was
thought she traveled to Maryland to be with her husband
of two months. Her car was found at the bus station.
No foul pay was suspected. The landlady of her apartment
 building heard her cats crying and went to investigate.
The cats were thought to be abandon. After
reporting the information to the police, a search was
conducted. Anyone with information is asked to contact
your local police. Caitlyn is 5'2", 110 lbs., blond, and blue
eyes. She has a tattoo of semi-truck on her body.

"Well," says Mickey as he walks to the evidence board and adds her name as victim number ten. "We at least have some evidence to go on. J.J., would you see if her husband of two months is in the service?"

Vinny walks away from the crime board and watches out the window with his back to his crew.

As he sees the sky spitting bits of snow, he says to no one in particular, "It's going to be a long winter."

CHAPTER 9

Year 1999

After weeks of tears and threats and prayers and pleadings, Nick and Mary Ellen have "sort of" become an accepted couple. The first part of February is over, and the couple have settled into a comfortable routine with each other. Mary Ellen is the dominate of the two. She knows that Nick is so in love with her, he cannot even look at her that he is not all over her.

The scandal has died down, and even Nick's mom, Grace, feels she can go about town again without comments, albeit sincere comments, that this must be what God wants. Mark is feeling a little bit guilty. He is pleased to have his son be a man and not a man of God.

After the Valentine Day dance, Mary Ellen and Nick have driven to their favorite secluded spot to do some necking. The very same spot that nineteen years from now, the body of a Jane Doe will be discovered by a town drunk named Jeb Landis. The kissing gets hot and heavy, and Nick (after much tutoring from his friend Charlie) tries one of the lessons. He starts sneaking his hand up under Mary Ellen's sweater. His only thought right now is to touch and maybe, just maybe, if Mary Ellen relents just a bit, he can take one of those spectacular breasts into his mouth and suck until there is no tomorrow.

Nick feels himself getting hard as he inches closer and closer, and all of a sudden, Mary Ellen says, "No, stop, Nick. You must not do that. That is a sin!"

"Oh, Mary Ellen, how can just wanting to feel your flesh be a sin when I love you so much?"

"I love you, too, Nick and maybe when we have been together longer, I will let you at least look at my breasts, then later maybe touch them."

"I can't stand it, Mary Ellen, I want you so much."

"I know, Nick, but I want to save myself for marriage. Don't you want me to be a virgin on our wedding night?"

Nick mumbles a no under his breath but says out loud, "Let's get out of here." He drops Mary Ellen off at her house and heads home. Thanks a lot, Charlie, he thinks, your lesson didn't work. In his bedroom, as he masturbates while looking at his posters of saints and the Pope, he decides he needs to change his décor. "Damn that Mary Ellen."

The next day after church, every one is gathered around the dinner table. Grace insists on this one family meal without guests. It gives time to each child to tell their parents the happenings of their week. Alice is anxious and excited to tell her parents she is going to try out for track. Her coach is sure she will be an excellent runner. As she goes to speak up, her mother over talks her and asks Nick what college he has finally decided on. The tension is thick, and Nick's parents want to know his plans now that the seminary is no longer an option. And with that question from Grace, Alice explodes!

"Did anyone at this table even hear me? Mother, don't you realize that you have other children who have dreams and are dying to share them with you? But no, it's always Nick, Nick, Nick. He has given up his dreams for that saucy tart. Can we not stop making him the center of the universe? Mom, he doesn't care about anything." And with that, Alice storms out of the room.

Nick yells at his mother, "See what you have done? Leave me alone. Mary Ellen and I are working out a plan, and when we are ready, I will tell you what it is!" And with that, the second Dougherty child leaves the table.

Mark has had enough and slams back his chair, scaring the younger children, and flies up the steps to Nick's room. Grace asks the two older boys to please clean up and keep an eye on Catherine. She, too, leaves the table and seeks the comfort of her sitting room off the master bedroom.

Mark does not stop to knock and barges into Nick's room, "What the hell are you thinking, Nick? How dare you talk to your mother like that. I don't care what you are going through right now, but don't you ever treat your mother like that again, and before this night is through, you had better see that she gets an apology." Mark leaves with the same anger as when he arrived.

Pat and Tristan are quietly cleaning off the table and putting things away. Tristan is visibly upset, and tears are in his eyes.

Pat sees that Tristan is trying hard not to cry, and instead of bullying and making fun, he says to Tristan, "Don't worry, T. I am scared, too, but this will blow over. Lots of families fight, and they make up."

Tristan appreciates this side of Patrick, and as he goes to comfort Catherine, who is oblivious to all this, he says, "What do think that was all about?"

Pat says, "It seems Pope Nicolas has finally shown his true nature."

Nick is smoldering in his room over the tongue lashing he got from his father. He knows his father is right, he should never have attacked his mom like that. He will give it a bit of time, then look for her and apologize. When Nick feels enough time has passed, he goes through the hall in the direction of his mother's sitting room. As he walks the hall, he stops and gazes at his mom's photo gallery. Every possible inch of the walls are covered with family pictures. The one he stops in front of is his parents' wedding day. They were married at Disney World. His mom was truly a princess. She had a job during the summer while she was in college as Cinderella. The story his father tells is how he took one look at her and fell in love. Why can't they understand that is what happened to him?

Nick knocks softly, and his mother says, "Come in." Nick opens the door, and the first thing that hits him is how this room smells just like his mother. Subtle, clean, if the scent was a color, it would be Celestial Blue. Nick always thought that is what heaven will smell like. He looks to where his mother is sitting on her chaise lounge holding a box of tissues. This memory of how he made his mother cry will haunt him all his life, and in that split second, he vows never to ever again be responsible for tears shed by his mother.

"Mom, can we talk?"

"Of course, Nicholas, come over to me." With those words, Nick bursts into tears himself and folds himself in his mother's arms. After ten or so minutes, Nick composes himself. "Mom, I am so sorry I made you cry. And yes, you do need to know what my plans are. Mary Ellen has been accepted into Bryn Mawr, the all-girls college near Philadelphia. I plan on going to our local community college and take some basic courses until I decide what to pursue. I never had a plan B. We will see each other every chance we get and let our love grow and mature."

"Have you any ideas as to what you might want to do?"

"Well, I would like to find myself helping others. Perhaps social work, working with the poor and homeless."

"Nick, that sounds like you are at least thinking about your future, but I don't think Mary Ellen is going to be content living that kind of life. You do know she is terribly spoiled."

"It's not so much she's spoiled, Mom. Remember, she never had a mother. Her mother died when she was only three, and her father has made her his whole life. Once Mary Ellen and I are married and raising a brood of kids like you and Dad, we will be fine. She really is so very special."

Nick and his mother hugged, and Grace forgave her son. She tried so hard to have faith in believing this would work out, but in the deepest part of her heart she has this gnawing; things are not going to turn out well.

CHAPTER 10

PRESENT

"Ok, gang, it's going on 7:00 P.M., and I want you all to take copies of every crime. I had Mary Lou prepare folders for all of you. Tomorrow we meet back here at 8:00 A.M. Be ready to give ideas, possible connections, and where we go from here. I will also be assigning a few of you to go to some of the crime scenes to see what we can learn."

As the task force picked up their folders and talked with each other going out the door, Mickey walked over to the coffee station and started cleaning up.

"You can leave that for the cleaning crew, Mickey," Vinny says.

"I know, but my Ma, bless her soul, always taught us to clean up after ourselves. Cleanliness is next to Godliness…you know the saying."

"Yeah," says Vinny. "And speaking of Godliness, do you see any kind of religious connection here? You know with that little statue being shoved into their woman parts?"

"Woman parts! My God, Vinny, can't you even say vagina?"

"Sure, I can and will if necessary, but answer my question."

"Well, has it been established that any of these women were raped? Any semen found? If once we get into the investigation and find answers to that question, and if the answer is no, they have not been raped, then yes, I think it is a possibility. Now my cleaning duties are finished and I am out of here. I have a date with some woman parts!"

As Mickey goes laughing down the hall and out the door, Vinny puts his papers away and he, too, heads out the door. Unfortunately, since his wife's death, he hasn't seen too many woman parts himself. He had that one encounter with that Mrs. James over in Blandon. Don't know why he blurted out would you like to go to dinner with me? Susan, that was her name. He had taken his car in for inspection and she was waiting for her car to be done, too. They struck up an easy conversation, and before you know it, they agreed to a dinner date. Man, thought Vinny, what a fiasco that was. After a most pleasant dinner and getting to know each other, Susan invited him back to her place for coffee and dessert. Little did he know, being out of the dating scene, which seemed like forever, that she was going to be dessert! They no sooner entered her house and got their coats off she was grabbing his crotch, unbuckling his belt while stripping off her blouse. And wham, she had his prick in her mouth and was doing some righteous stuff. It had been so long since he had any sexual activity that he came within minutes. It startled her and she pulled him out, spraying all over her face and chest. Vinny was mortified and kept apologizing while wiping at her very ample chest.

"Oh, Vinny, look what you did." Susan stood up, and instead of being upset, she took his hand and led him into the bedroom. She finished undressing down to a pair of thongs, then started undressing him. While she was working on getting him hard again, he was so thoroughly enjoying sucking and rubbing those humungous breasts. Unfortunately for Vinny, he was a "come once" kind of guy. He suggested he leave, and Susan did not stop him.

Leaving the station, he shuddered remembering his embarrassment. He hasn't tried since, but his urges are definitely getting stronger. Perhaps I'll leave that door open, he thinks, no telling what might walk in. Just thinking about Susan's tits got him excited.

The next morning, Vinny arrived at 7:30 A.M. only to find his crew already there in the crime room. Drinking coffee and eating donuts while discussing the different files on the victims, J.J. and Mickey were over in one corner being very animated, and it occurred to Vinny that maybe the woman parts that Mickey had a date with last night belonged to J.J. He will keep an eye on that, it is not good to have members of your squad fraternizing.

"Glad to see you are all here. Let's get started. I will throw out a question, and feel free to jump in. First, anybody come up with any ideas that could connect these women. C.J., you look like you might have an idea."

"Well, boss, the pattern seems to be no pattern. We have women of all ages, blonds, brunettes, Hispanic, white, black, so I don't think our killer is going after a particular type of woman but something they all do."

Lucas chimes in, "What, like they all Zumba or parachute?"

"Yeah," says C.J. "Something they all do, no matter where they live. Victim one gets her nails done in Cleo's Salon while victims two through ten also get their nails done there also. I think it is something like that that connects them."

"J.J." Vinny looks in her direction, "Get busy with your voodoo and cross reference the lives of the women we have identified. See what pops up. Also, check the internet for references to Jezebel. Max, I want you and C.J. to make arrangements to go to Reading. Once there check in with the local police. I want you to go to each crime scene, talk to anyone who knew these women and when they were last seen."

Max interrupts, "Chief, enough already, me and C.J. know how to investigate."

"Sorry, Max, I am just really pumped. I am itching to get started. Never worked a serial killer case before and I don't want to mess it up."

"Understood. Come on, C.J., we got some planning to do," says Max, and they head out the door.

"Cully," calls Vinny.

"Yeah, Chief, what can I do?"

"I want you to gather every autopsy report and study them over and over. Make a chart, so we can cross reference every detail. Piercings, tattoos, and find out who did the semi-truck on our latest vic. If any of the autopsies show tattoos, do the same. And most of all, I want to know their stomach contents. Might tell us where they had their last meal."

"On it, Chief," and Cully gets to work.

"Oh, one more thing, Cully, if any coroner gives you a hard time, let me know, but start with the police files. Autopsy reports should be in the file, if not, then contact the morgue. Work it hard."

"I'll go to Williamsport and check out our Ms. Caitlyn. I want nothing overlooked. This one happened close to home, and I think if we get a handle on this one, the rest will fall into place."

"Jet, I have made a list on the crime board for you to also research. See if the arrows are traceable, check with Max and C.J. to see if the Reading police still have theirs. We should have our arrow in the evidence room. Find out if they match. I want to know the brand of make-up used, too. Was it the victims, or did the killer bring it with him, and find out as much as you can about those damn little statues. Cully, while you are at those autopsies, find out if the victim's hair was cut with a scissors or hacked off with a razor or other tool. That could be important."

The rest of Vinny's day was spent in the crime room going over each file and frustrated that the evidence is so sparse. Now that all the police departments where these murders were committed will acknowledge a serial killer passed through their district, they will amp up their efforts, too. Vinny could hear the muffled sounds of computer keys while J.J. and Cully went about their work.

Around the noon hour, Mary Lou announced she had a lunch date and headed out. By this time, J.J. and Cully had left, too. Vinny was thinking about doing the same thing when his phone rang. It was the department receptionist.

"Chief Miller, I have a call from a Detective Kristoff from Berk's County, and Mary Lou is not answering her phone, should I put it through to you?"

"Yes, Cindy, I will take it. Chief Miller here."

"Good afternoon, Chief, I am Detective Martin Kristoff over in Berk's County, and I think we found another victim of your serial killer. Ever since we saw the notification come through to watch for certain markers, we have been keeping an eye for anything that could link any of our homicides to your serial killer. A woman's naked body was found several days ago in a cemetery. Her name is Candice Upkoff, people around here call her, or called her, Candy because of her red hair. She's thirty, just had a birthday, one child, a little boy, about five. Husband's in the service overseas. We found that statue that was mentioned. An old man came across her when he came to pay respects to his deceased wife."

"Sounds like one of ours, Detective. Thanks for calling. Have you done the autopsy yet?"

"Yes, it seems she was strangled but had an arrow through her heart. The doc found no sexual activity."

"Would you send everything you have to my office, especially the autopsy report, and if I am not stepping on anyone's toes in your department, I would like to send one of my crew over to question witnesses and try to establish her last whereabouts."

"No, Chief, that would be fine, just have your man report to me."

"I'll be sending Detective Lucas Angelo. He'll be there as soon as possible, and Detective Kristoff, thanks."

Vinny got off the phone and walked to the crime board. As he is listing the name and information on Victim eleven, Candice Upkoff, Jet and Cully return from their lunch.

"Seems we have another victim. List her as victim number twelve. I called Angelo to go over to Shillington and see what he can find out. He is going to interview her friends and family. As soon as I am done here, I am going to see Captain Ritter. We have really got ourselves a serious situation. Jet, get those fingers moving and see what you can find out about our latest victim, Candice Upkoff."

Vinny headed up to see the Captain taking two steps at a time. He felt the urgency in his gut. Someone is killing young women. He felt so responsible to find out who.

Vinny knocked on the door, and Captain Ritter yelled, "Come in." If Vinny wasn't so engrossed in his own thoughts, he would have noticed the Captain's gruff response. As Vinny entered the Captain's office, Harry Ritter was staring out the window with his hands clasped behind his back. Before Vinny could say anything, the Captain started talking. "Have you ever thought of retirement, Vinny? I have."

"Oh, come on, Cap, you still have a few good years yet."

"I know, but my wife is starting to lay some ground work. Seems she would like to travel and do things with me before it is too late. We often talk about you and Lily. Bet you didn't know that."

"What about me and Lily?"

"How you lost Lily, and she being so young. My wife reminds me as to how fleeting time is. Well, anyway, sorry for the diatribe. What's up?"

"We caught another murder. It's over in Berk's County, and I got the call a few minutes ago. We seem to be pulling some evidence together, but the bodies are piling up faster than we can write their names. We do have a few links. Most of the women we have identified seems to have a military connection. They all have either been married to or divorced from someone in the military. All the husbands or ex-husbands have been cleared, so we are trying to find some other link. Also, not all of the men have been overseas. Some are stationed in the states. There also seems to be a strange but vague connection to religion. All the women were or had been Catholic. The one link we can't seem to establish is why the victims are spread out over such a large number of counties, and this has been going on for years. This is the first time we or anyone has connected them."

"Any sexual activity?"

"No, that's another anomaly. The women are naked, posed, humiliated, and degraded, but there doesn't seem to be a sexual motive."

"Well, Vinny, you have a good team and I will do anything I can do to help. We need to stop this monster."

"Captain, do me one favor?" asks Vinny.

"What's that, Miller?"

"Don't leave until we solve this case. I ask for selfish reasons, Cap. You understand what we are up against, and we work well together. It would be a hardship on me and my team to try to work with another Captain who might not agree with what we are doing."

"Well, Miller, I don't want to make promises, but I don't think I'm going anywhere just yet. Annabelle and I haven't even sat and discussed finances or anything. It is just a thought at this time. Now get out of here."

When Vinny returned to his office, there was a call from Will, the coroner from Hell. The note read to come over to the morgue as soon as possible. Vinny got to the morgue as Will was cleaning up. He had finished the autopsy and looked up as Vinny entered.

"What did you find?" As Will turned, Vinny was aware that even in the morgue doing autopsies, Will was dressed to a T. His shoes alone would equal Vinny's monthly pay. The man even had on cuff links visible under the plastic gown. Here is a man who would never apologize for who he is, and despite the bad feelings between them, Vinny admired him for that.

"Come over to the work table." As Vinny approached, Will was paging through his notes. "I found some interesting clues when I went back over the autopsy again. You know I like to be thorough. As you know, Chief Miller, I miss nothing."

"Aw, Will, cut the crap. What is different?"

"I found a strange substance in her stomach, along with the meal of oatmeal and rye bread, which makes me believe she was killed shortly after breakfast. I could not identify it, so I sent it out to the crime lab over in Philadelphia. They have a more sophisticated lab than we do. Also, there was some foreign sticky residue on and around her forehead. Again, I had to send it out. Now it could have come from whomever bagged her, or even the bag itself, but I found it odd."

"Any guesses?"

"No, but I do think it is important. I will let you know when I have the results."

"Do you have any idea when?"

"It will be a while; the labs take things in the order they get them."

"Ok, keep me posted, and Will, thanks."

When Vinny left the morgue, he contacted Angelo to see how the interviews were going. Angelo told him he is almost finished and would meet him back at the station by 5:00 P.M. He then contacted Max and C.J. and they, too, were almost finished and would report in when they got back to the city. Vinny realized the crew all have different time schedules, so he calls them back and tells them not to report back to the squad room until the next morning at 8:00 A.M.

As Vinny enters the office, he sees Jet and Cully working on the computers. They both look up and nod. Vinny sees that the crime board has been updated. Cully has listed the stomach contents of the women that were not too decomposed. One thing stood out. They were not all killed after breakfast. Something else jumped out as well. In two of the other victims, an unidentified substance was listed. Just like what Will discovered.

"Hey, troops, looks like you two have been working non-stop. Time to call it a night and enjoy your weekend. I want you to finish up, turn off those computers, and head home. Monday, we meet at 8:00 A.M. and everyone will be brought up-to-date."

As the final members of his crew close up for the night and leave, Vinny goes into his office and sits at his desk. He twirls around, so he is facing the window. He really enjoys watching people come and go about their business. He wonders if he has some voyeurism in his heart. Ah, there is old Mr. Saunders getting into that boat of a car. He must be in his eighties, still driving and dresses like he is going out on the town. His family is worried about his driving but cannot get the doctor, who is just as old and Mr. Saunder's best friend, to sign off on his license. Vinny straightens up and looks a little harder at the pretty lady coming around the corner. He knows immediately who it is...the lovely, available Justice Channing. Looks like she is headed to work.

Justice is a waitress at the restaurant down the street. She walks with such confidence. Slim but curves in all the right places, has auburn hair, curls down her back, and as she travels the pavement, most people greet her. Justice, what a strange name, Vinny thinks. Vinny decided he is hungry and a visit to the Yellow Tree House just might be in order. Perhaps tonight he will have the courage to ask her out; after all what can she say but yes or no.

Vinny likes the Yellow Tree House restaurant. It is the first place Lily and he went after moving into town. People told them they just had to see it. So that first Friday night, they walked hand in hand into the restaurant and stopped dead in their tracks. Right in the middle of the restaurant was this huge, gigantic tree trunk holding a tree house. The trunk extended into the floor and the limbs became tables. At each table were chairs made to look like oak leaves. In the center was this enormous chandelier shaped like an acorn with acorn sconces adorning the structure of the tree house, and it was painted the yellowest of yellow you have ever seen. Lily and I just stared. It was the weirdest, most beautiful, strangest, most awesome thing we ever saw. Huge limbs reached to the ceiling covered with bunches of acorns and oak leaves. After getting our breath back, we asked if we could sit up in the tree house. Our waitress took us up this elegant spiral staircase made to look like the roots of the tree, and we entered wonderland. We were so taken by this tree house, we made a standing reservation for every Friday night. Vinny reminds himself that he has not been in the tree house since Lily died, although he frequents the restaurant often.

As Justice makes her way down the walk towards the Tree House, she is aware of passing by the police station. She is hoping beyond hope that that Chief Miller is looking out the window. Justice cannot understand why he won't ask her out. It seems he wants to… He always sits at my station, chats me up, seems interested. Maybe the next time she sees him, she will do the asking.

Justice arrives at work and starts getting herself ready to begin her shift. Veronica (better known as Ronnie) is already there and waiting to start work. Ronnie is Justice's best friend, and they chat a bit, bringing each other up to date on the their current goings on. All of a sudden, Ronnie looks over and leans towards Justice, letting her know that that gorgeous Chief Miller just came in the pub. Tall, at least 6' or 6'2". He has a camel colored corduroy sport coat over a black shirt opened at the collar. Fills out his jeans in all the right places and still enjoys the Wellington boots of yester year. Starting to get a little paunchy above the belt but only adds to his charm. Curly black hair with a hint of gray, and it is always unruly when he takes off his baseball cap.

"Oh, Ronnie, what to do? I would love to go out with him, but he seems so gun shy."

"Justice, do it, ask him. Nothing ventured, nothing gained."

As Justice approaches Vinny, he cannot take his eyes off her, and as he smiles, his eyes crinkle, and looking at him, you don't know if his eyes are green or hazel, depending on the light. His mustache is in need of trimming, but to Justice, he is darn near perfect.

"Evening, Chief Miller."

"Hi, Justice, what's good tonight?"

"The meatloaf is always a winner, and the stuffed peppers are awesome."

"Ok, you sold me on the stuffed peppers."

Justice wrote his order, and as she started to turn away, she stopped and came closer to Vinny's table.

"Chief Miller."

"Please, call me Vinny."

"Vinny, ah, er, the local vineyard is hosting a wine and cheese tasting party on Saturday. Would you like to go with me?

Vinny is left speechless and just stares at Justice, which Justice takes as a no.

"Sorry, Chief, that was forward of me. I am sure you are busy."

"No, no," sputters Vinny, "I would love to go with you."

"You would?"

"Oh, yes, I would. But I do have one condition."

"What is that?"

"You must tell me why your name is Justice."

"I will see if you can earn that privilege."

As Vinny and Justice iron out the details of when to meet and where, they are both harboring pleasant thoughts of what is to come.

CHAPTER 11

YEAR 1999

As Nick is making right with his mother, Alice has run across the street to Austin's house and just cannot stop crying. Instead of seeking out someone, Alice finds solace on the old tire swing in the Harding's back yard. As she swings and cries, nothing is making her feel better.

A car pulls into the driveway, and it is Marcelene coming home from work. As she exits the car, she hears whimpering. Setting out to find where the noise is coming from, she sees Alice, their neighbor, on the old swing crying.

"Alice," calls Marcelene, "is that you?"

Between sniffles, now finding herself embarrassed, Alice says, "Yes, it's me."

"What's wrong, sweetheart?"

"Everything, everything, everything! Ever since Nick got involved with that Mary Ellen, everyone is always angry. Nick walks around like he has the crucifix on his back bearing such guilt for falling in love, and my mom and dad are ignoring the rest of the family. No one cares what are accomplishments are!"

"No, Alice, that's not true. You have the best parents in the world, but sometimes even parents don't know just what to do. Now is the time for you to be patient with them."

"I guess, but I feel like I'm not important."

"That's not true, and you know it. Why don't you come in and hang with Austin for a while?"

"No, but could you ask him to come out?"

"Sure."

As soon as Austin learns he has an opportunity to comfort Alice, he is out the door. He goes right up to her and wraps his arms around her while she once again lets the tears fall.

"Hey, Alice, come on, dry those tears. I'll tell you what, Jimmy Sykes is having a party this Saturday. His parents are out of town, and it should be a blast. He throws some awesome parties. Come with me?"

"I don't know, Austin. My parents would never let me."

"From what you are telling me, they won't even know you are gone. Nick's angel wings will blind them to all the comings and goings."

"You're right. Ok, it's a date."

"Now dry your tears. Want to come in for a while?"

"No, I should go home and see how the little ones are doing. They were so scared."

"Ok, I'll walk you home."

Things get back to normal in the Dougherty household, and the outburst the weekend before seems to be forgotten. The children are all back in school.

During gym class, Charlie goes after Nick about coming to a party.

"Nicky boy, how's my man?"

"Doing ok, Charlie, how was your weekend?"

"You want to weep. I'll tell you. You know that hot little number Jen Bradford in eleventh grade? Well, I took her out on Saturday, and after dinner, we went to the movie. Slick old Charlie was able to get the hands under the sweater and, man, I had that chick squirming, getting hot. I suggested we leave and find some privacy, so we went up to make-out hill. Had the sweater off, then off came the bra, and my hands were full of tender, yummy softness. I got the pants down, and when I went for the overcoat, I had none...God damn it, I couldn't believe it. So no nooky for Charlie. I am not risking a pregnancy for any piece of ass."

"Charlie, is that all you care about, a piece of ass?"

"Listen, buddy, if that ice berg of a girl you have ever thaws, believe me, you'll know what I'm talking about. Which is what I was getting at, Jimmy is having a party on Saturday. His parents are out of town, and that house has lots of bedrooms. Grab the ice queen and come along."

"Mary Ellen is going to be checking out more colleges this weekend. She won't be home."

"Oh, man, that is even better. Come along, and maybe we could find you something interesting to do besides sit and drool over Mary Ellen McGrath. By the way, Nick, I don't think she is as into you as you are her. Come on, go with me. We'll have a blast."

"Ok, count me in. I don't want to sit home and watch my mom wring her hands over the loss of 'Pope Nick.'"

Saturday night comes, and Nick gets ready to go to Jimmy's party. He just got off the phone with Mary Ellen and is feeling depressed. This is the first time they have been apart for more than a day. Nick doesn't understand why she is checking out other colleges since she has already been accepted at Bryn Mawr. According to Mary Ellen, she wants to be sure in her choice. Nick is petrified that she will go to some college too far away for them to remain together. Nick comes down stairs and calls a good bye to his mom.

"Bye, Nick, have a nice time, and don't be too late. We have church in the morning."

Nick heads out the door and scolds himself for being such a prick. He has to stop being so mad all the time. He is hurting his parents, especially his mom, not to mention he is seeing his brothers shy away from him. Damn Mary Ellen, all he wants is to be with her and it is consuming him. He decides maybe a night of partying will do him good.

As soon as Nick arrives at Jimmy's party, he is greeted by several of his buddies, and Charlie is already in front of him handing him a beer.

"Hey, Nicky, glad you could make it. Now relax a bit, and let's have some fun." Charlie leads Nick over to the center of the room where some of the kids are playing a drinking game. Nick and Charlie both get into the game.

As soon as the door opened and Nick walked in, Sarah's radar went up. What, Nick without Mary Ellen. Wonder if they broke up? Sarah watched Nick laugh and decided to bide her time until Nick had a few more beers in him, then she would make her move. Tonight was the night that Sarah thought if she played her cards right, she would make Nicky boy hear the angels sing, and he would forget that bitch Mary Ellen. She would show him what he's been missing and finally he would be hers.

About an hour in, the party was in full swing when Austin and Alice arrived. It wasn't hard for Alice to slip out of the house. She just had to wait until her parents did their bed check.

At first Alice was a little overwhelmed. It seems every kid from school was here and on their way to a dandy hang over tomorrow. They made their way through the crowd and grabbed a couple of beers and started dancing. Alice was actually having a good time. Alice thought she spotted Nick but lost him in the crowd. She could not imagine Nick coming to a beer party without Mary Ellen, and that guy she saw was all over some girl. Alice excused herself from Austin, using the bathroom as an excuse to check it out. She headed over in that direction and realized it is Nick and the girl who is all over him is Sarah. Sarah had a very drunk Nick by the hand and was leading him upstairs towards the bedrooms.

Oh no, thought Alice. I've got to stop them. As she hurried through the crowd of kids, Charlie steps in front of her.

"Hey, pretty girl, where are you going in such a hurry?"

"Charlie, thank goodness it's you. You have to go get Nick. He and Sarah just headed up to one of the bedrooms."

"Yes, I know. Sarah's been mooning over Nick for years, and I don't want to stop it. Nick's my friend, and I have seen what that ice queen has done to him. It's time Nick realizes he's human and a good fuck with a girl like Sarah is just what he needs."

"No, no, Charlie, he'll regret it. Mary Ellen will find out and break up with him, and Nick will kill himself if he ever loses her. He's drunk, we must stop him."

"Oh, looky there, too late! Gone are the love birds off to some blissful screwing. Ha-ha!"

"Charlie, I hate you." Alice made her way back to Austin and said, "I want to go home."

Sarah leads Nick to the first bedroom she finds. How long she has waited for this. Her love for Nick is almost as bad as Nick's for Mary Ellen. She starts kissing him and is so joyful when he kisses her back. She has her blouse open and put Nick's hands on her breasts as she starts to unbuckle his pants.

As she reaches in to caress him, he moans, "Oh, Mary Ellen."

With that she steps back and slaps him hard across the face. It startles Nick and sobers him a bit.

"Sarah, my God, what are we doing?" Nick starts to pull his pants up. "Cover yourself up, you know Mary Ellen is my girl. What were you thinking?"

"What's the matter, Nick, aren't I good enough for Pope Nicholas? You gave up God for that bitch, why couldn't it have been me? I love you so much." Again she reaches for his privates. "Please, Nick, make love to me. I want you so much."

"No, Sarah, stop." Nick pulls away from her and heads out the door. As he comes down the stairs, Charlie grabs his arm.

"Hey, man, you don't much look like you enjoyed your fuck."

Nick shakes Charlie off and heads home. A lot more sober than he had been.

Alice heard him come in, and before he closes his door, she stormed into his room.

"What did you do, Nick? I saw you go into a bedroom with Sarah. Did you have sex with her? Mary Ellen will never forgive you."

"No, sis, I didn't, not for her lack of trying, but you are so right. I cannot nor would I do anything to jeopardize my relationship with Mary Ellen."

"Well you better make sure everyone knows nothing happened because Mary Ellen's going to find out."

"Alice?"

"Yeah, Nick."

"Why does every girl I know want to have sex with me, except Mary Ellen?"

"Because she's pure, Nick. She wants to be untainted when she walks down that isle. She wants that for you."

"Thanks, Alice, you're a good sister."

CHAPTER 12

Sunday night Nick is in his room looking over pamphlets to decide his career choices at the local college. It wasn't so long ago his future was secure. He marvels at how quickly things can change. His phone rings and his heart leaps when he sees it is Mary Ellen.

"Mary Ellen, are you home?"

"Yes, Nick, and I miss you so much. Can you come and pick me up?"

"I'll be right there."

As Nick is changing out of his sweat pants, he is going over in his mind what to tell Mary Ellen about the party.

Mary Ellen is waiting for him at the curb. As she gets into the car, she can't wait to shower him with kisses and tell him how much she missed him.

"Where would you like to go, Mare?"

"Oh, Nick, let's go to our special place. I just want to be alone with you."

After their passion dies down a bit and they settle into talking, Mary Ellen tells Nick all about the colleges she visited and reassured him that she intends to stick with Bryn Mawr. Nick is so happy and was hesitant to bring up Saturday night.

"Mary Ellen, there is something that happened Saturday night that I must tell you before rumors fly and you hear lies. It could be very hurtful, that's why I must tell you what happened."

"Nick, you are scaring me."

"I went to a booze party on Saturday night. Charlie talked me into it, and I was having a good time, but I got awfully drunk. The next thing I know, I am in a bedroom with Sarah and she is going at me until I push her away, realizing what was going on. I want you to know, despite what you may hear, I did not have sex with her. I pushed her off me and left. At all times fully clothed. I learned two things that night. First, don't get sloppy drunk, and second but most important is that even drunk, I would never betray you. I love you that much. I also think Charlie set me up."

"Oh, Nick, what am I to do when someone makes a comment about that night?"

"Just remind them that you love and trust me never to hurt you and you know in your heart of hearts I would never betray you. Everyone that matters, Mary Ellen, will never believe it anyway. Although I do believe Sarah may stir up some trouble. Do you believe me?"

"Of course I do, Nick. Now let's get some more kisses in before you take me home."

School was winding down, and there were only a few more weeks before graduation. There were a few snide remarks made concerning Sarah and Nick, but the gossip fell flat. Those at Jimmy's party knew nothing happened, and as for the rest of the kids, they really didn't care. Summer and college, work and fun loomed big in their lives, not who slept with whom.

Nick continued his mission to get Mary Ellen to make love to him before college started, and Mary Ellen held him at bay as always.

Graduation finally arrived. Nick did not want a party but asked his parents if they could all go out as a family to dinner and invite Mary Ellen and her dad. The following day, Grace called Mr. McGrath and extended the invitation.

"Oh my, Mrs. Dougherty, that would be wonderful. Are you sure you would rather not have a party?"

"No, Nick asked if we could just get together and have dinner, and please, call me Grace. I wanted a huge party to celebrate this occasion, especially after the year we have had with Nick. He certainly put us through some difficult time. I am just glad that he seems to more content now and has finally made some decisions on his future."

"Well, Grace, and please call me Shawn, I cannot think of a better celebration. After all it seems our children are headed to the altar. I do hope though that they will wait until their education is complete."

"Mark and I feel the same way, Shawn. I thought I would make a reservation at "Valentino's. Will that be good for you?"

"Yes, perfect, and you must allow me to treat you all. Your family has been so good to my daughter. I would consider it an honor."

"Well, Shawn, you can work that out with my husband. Will you be bringing a guest?"

"No, just Mary Ellen and me."

"Very good then, I will make the reservation and I will be in touch. Good bye, Shawn."

"Thank you, Grace, talk to you soon."

Two weeks later, Nick and Mary Ellen graduated on a beautiful day in May. Grace shed some tears as she realized that her first born is now headed out on his own to become the man she knew he could be. The tears were not only for Nick, but looking at her other children, she knew that their time was coming, too. Alice will be a senior this school year, and she will be sitting at a graduation again much too soon.

They all gathered at Valentino's. With Mark and Grace and all the children, plus Mary Ellen and her dad, they made for a happy, joyous occasion.

"So, Nick, Mary Ellen tells me you will be life guarding this summer while attending the community college."

"Yes, Mr. McGrath, I haven't decided yet on my career."

"When do your classes start?"

"Not until August."

"Mary Ellen must leave mid-July for college. I am so proud of her."

"Yes, I know. I hate the very thought of her being away from me."

Nothing more was said about the impending separation of these two love birds. Soon conversation began among the adults, and the kids were busy talking about all the fun summer had in store for them.

Summer life becomes routine. Mary Ellen is counting down the days until she can leave for college. She is so excited to get on with this part of her life. Nick is also counting the days, only his end day will make him very sad. He cannot imagine being without Mary Ellen. Their time alone is spent arguing. Nick insists Mary Ellen make love to him before she goes off to college, and one evening, just days before she leaves, she explodes.

"Enough, Nick, I have had it with this constant pressure from you. All summer I have had to fight you off. Now listen and listen good. I love you, I want to someday marry you, and it is my utmost desire to come to you as a virgin. Pure like the Virgin Mary, with a heart filled with love, but if this is what you are going to do every time I come home to see you or you come to visit me, I will not, do you hear me, Nick, I will not come home to see you. And If I do come home, I will see to it that we are never alone. Nick, look at me. Do you understand? Now stop this. I have fought you off for seven months, and I no longer intend to. I want you to promise right now this stops. Promise, Nick, I mean it!"

"Wow! I never heard you so angry. You would think I was asking you to commit murder instead of making love to me."

"Nick, promise."

"Ok, Mary Ellen, you have my promise, but I get to say some things, too. How do you think I feel when we are heavily engaged in passionate kisses and fondling? It drives me crazy. So if you want me to promise not to want you so much, you have to stop teasing me."

"Tease you! I don't tease you."

"Every time you let me caress and suck your breasts and your hot passionate kisses makes me believe that you are willing to take the next step. Then you freeze! Maybe Charlie is right. You are an ice queen."

"Take me home right now."

Nick does as she asks, and Nick realizes this blow up between them feels good. Maybe now she will understand how I feel for a change.

The freeze between them lasts for two days. Finally, Mary Ellen calls Nick.

"Nick, I am so sorry. I miss you so much. Please come pick me up, so we can talk. I can't bear for us to be like this. I leave in a week, and we must make this right."

Nick went right over, and there was tension in the air at first. Nick drove to their favorite spot and waited for Mary Ellen to talk. He never even tried to kiss her.

"Nick, I am so sorry. You were right. I guess I was teasing you, and I did enjoy seeing you squirm and to know that I could have such power. I am not sorry though for insisting that we wait and that won't change, but I will respect your feelings more than I had. Will you forgive me?"

"Oh, Mary Ellen, of course. I have been so miserable these past two days, and I think our relationship has just morphed into a more mature and deeper love. I, too, am going to respect you more, and I will patiently wait until our wedding day."

For the rest of the summer and into the fall, things are going smoothly. Nick has started college and finds he has a knack for the medical profession. He is undecided as to going for doctor, physician's assistant, nurse, or EMT responder. He thinks going on to become a doctor will make Mary Ellen want to postpone their plans until he is at least in residency, but studying to be an EMT will be fulfilling, difficult but rewarding. His ulterior motive being it won't take as long.

Mary Ellen is absorbed in college life and loves being away from the small town, smothering boyfriend, and over protective father. She comes home frequently at first, but as the months go on, it is fewer and fewer. Nick complains but accepts her reasons.

The Dougherty household is getting ready for another Christmas holiday. Grace is getting out the decorations and preparing for when the children get home from school. They will decorate the tree. Perhaps Nick will join in. Grace is pleased with how things have calmed down, and she feels a pleasant rhythm to their lives.

Alice calls to her mother that Mr. McGrath is on the phone.

"Hello."

"Grace, Shawn here. Do you have a minute?"

"Of course, Shawn, what can I do for you?"

"Well, it seems my company is transferring me to Oregon, and I am to be ready to move the first of the new year."

"Shawn, is this good news or bad?"

"Good for me, but I am concerned about Mary Ellen. She'll want to continue to come home to see Nick, and I'd be ever so grateful if you would let her stay with you? She will no longer have a home to come to with my moving."

"Of course she can stay with us. We love her as a daughter already, so that will be no problem. Have you told her yet about the move?"

"Yes, and I even told her that I would talk to you and Mark."

"Well, don't you worry. We will take good care of her. Shawn, we would love for you to join us for dinner some evening during the holidays before you leave. Please let me know when would be a good time."

"I would love that. I expect Mary Ellen home for the break. We can get together then. I will let you know as soon as I can."

"Wonderful, I'll look forward to hearing from you."

The holidays came and went, and Mary Ellen was extremely upset that her father moved away. She felt very welcome in the Dougherty household the few times she came to visit, but as the months went by, her visits became less and less. Nick was on the phone several times a day with Mary Ellen, and in his naivety, believed her studies and classes were keeping her at college.

Grace was not as naïve. She thought Mary Ellen was very distant but kept her feelings to herself less she upsets Nick. Something didn't seem right, but right now, Grace was excited about the upcoming graduation of her oldest daughter, Alice. When did she become this beautiful talented woman? How, Grace chided herself, how could I not know what a fantastic cook she has become. To think she will be going to Paris after graduation to study at the Le-Cordon Bleu on a scholarship. She will be leaving mid-summer, and Grace decided to devote so much more time to her.

Time flew by for the Dougherty family. Alice's graduated in June, and by mid-July, she was off on an adventure of a lifetime. Austin was sorry to see her go, but he enlisted in the Air Force and was anxious to start his adult life, too.

Mary Ellen took extra classes during the summer. She told Nick it would help her graduate sooner. Implying they would start their lives together earlier than planned.

Nick is at the computer studying and researching. His tests to complete his training as an EMT is coming up and he is excited. Grace is so pleased Nick found something that excites him besides Mary Ellen.

"Nick, will Mary Ellen be coming home for Thanksgiving?" askes Grace.

"I don't think so, Mother. She told me she was going out to Oregon to be with her dad. She hasn't seen him in a while."

"You plan on being home with the family, don't you, Nick?"

"I sure do. It may be my last chance to be with all of you. I am not sure where my EMT training will take me, and despite all I have put you through and how you have all been here for me, I want all of you to know how much I love you and appreciate you. Especially my brothers and sisters."

It was a wonderful holiday for Grace. She was in her glory making Thanksgiving dinner, having her family and only her family around her, and now that it was over, she could look forward to Christmas.

Then a strange occurrence happened. One day when the kids were in school and Mark was at work, Grace was in the living room going through the Christmas decorations when the telephone rang.

"Hello," says Grace.

"Grace, good morning. It's Shawn."

"How nice to hear from you. What I can I do for you? Is everything all right?"

"Is Mary Ellen there?"

"Why, no, we haven't seen her since before Thanksgiving. Didn't she come out to see you?"

"See me, why, no. I can't get a hold of her. She seems to be avoiding my calls. Her and Nick didn't run away together, have they?"

"No, Shawn, Mary Ellen told Nick she was going out to see you over the holiday. Perhaps Nick knows if her plans changed and just didn't say anything."

"Hell, Grace," says Shawn, "I'm worried. I've never gone this long without talking to her, and you did promise to take care of her."

Grace stiffened at that last comment and said, "Yes, when she was here, but not day and night while she is away at college. Now before I say something I will regret, I will end our call with the promise that I will get Nick to see what is going on. Good-bye, Shawn."

Grace hung up the phone and was really angry. How dare he expect me to keep tabs on that daughter of his while she is away at college. As soon as Nick gets in, I will talk to him about Shawn's call. What is that girl up to?

When Nick gets home that night, Grace shared with him the call she got from Shawn.

"Didn't you know that Mary Ellen didn't go out to see her father?"

"No," says Nick, "I thought she did. I know! I bet she decided to stay at school and get caught up on her class work. Needed some quiet time. I think I will surprise her with a visit this weekend. We haven't seen each other for weeks. I'll talk to her then about neglecting her father. I have a short day on Friday. Now I am all excited. I should have done this sooner and not listened to how much work she has. After all, a girl has to have some fun. So don't worry, Mom, I will straighten everything out."

CHAPTER 13

Sunday afternoon, and the Dougherty's are home from church, have filled their bellies from the brunch Grace made, and now they are all content. Mark is enjoying the Sunday paper, the kids are over at the neighbors', and Catherine is down for a nap.

Grace is at the kitchen sink finishing up the dishes when she sees Nick come flying up the drive-way. He jerks his car to a stop and gets out slamming the door and looks so angry.

Just as Grace is heading to the door, Nick bolts through it, screaming, "She's pregnant, Mary Ellen is pregnant!" Spittle flying from his mouth.

Mark comes out of the living room as Grace goes to Nick, saying, "Nick, calm down. It's not the end of the world. Things happen when young people are in love. You'll just get married sooner than you planned. Please, Nick, it will work out. It's not what your father and I had hoped for, but please calm down."

"No, Mother, you don't understand," Nick says with the calmest, emotionless tone in his voice. "It's not my baby! I wasn't allowed to touch her." In a high-pitched voice, Nick says, "Oh no, don't you want me to be like the blessed Virgin Mary? Don't you want me to be pure? And I fell for it. Is that how you all are, Mother? Tease and taunt, then go off and whore with someone else? Lie and cheat when the one that loves you believes you? You are all alike." And with that, Nick silently beaten down slumps off to his room. Grace starts after him, but Mark stops her.

"I'll go," he says.

Mark goes up to Nick's room to find him crying. Mark hugs him and is at a loss for words.

Soon Nick says, "It's ok, Dad, I need to be alone. It seems God and I have some things to discuss. Don't worry. I am not suicidal or have any plans to be destructive. We'll talk later, ok?"

Mark hugs him again and leaves him to his discussion with God.

Mark and Grace decide to tell the children that Nick and Mary Ellen broke up. Nick is upset and that they shouldn't bother him. They then go to the living room to talk about what happened and to comfort each other.

Nick stays in his room for all most two weeks. His parents and siblings hear him cry out, pray, and throw things around.

"Why, God? You play so dirty. It was you who put her in my path. Was there no other test you could give me?" Nick falls to his knees and asks God's forgiveness in being such a weak disciple. Day after day, he prays for guidance. Comes out of his room only at night when everyone is asleep to forage for food. He has lost weight and neglected his hygiene. One evening Mark and Grace are in the living room and there is a knock on the door. Mark goes to the door and there stands Father Eric.

"Come in, Father, why are you here?

"I had a call from Nick. He asked that I come and wants you to let me see him alone and in his room."

"Of course, Father, what has he told you?" asks Grace.

"Everything. And now he needs me."

After spending over an hour with Nick, the door opens and Father Eric and Nick come down the stairs. Nick is carrying a duffel bag and Father Eric lets Nick pass by and go outside.

He then says to Mark and Grace, "Nick asked that I tell you he is headed straight to St. Borromeo Seminary where he will finish his education in the medical field and start his process of becoming a priest. He has left a letter for you and asks that you not contact him. He wants and needs solitude right now, my dear friends. He feels he must make things right with God and get back on track to the life he was meant to have. Serving the Lord."

Mark and Grace are speechless as they watch their dearest son go out of their lives, looking like he has all the sins of the world on his back.

They retrieve the letter from Nick's room and all it says is that he will come home for Christmas and sit down with them and talk. By then he hopes to have his mind no longer jumbled and will be able to talk about his future.

CHAPTER 14

PRESENT

Vinny woke to a crisp, sun-filled spring day. For the first time in a long time, his first thoughts were not of murdered women and gruesome crime scenes. His thoughts went to reliving the wonderful Saturday he had in the company of one Justice Channing. Just thinking of her brings a smile to his face and a smile to other parts of his body, too.

Vinny picked Justice up on Saturday, and they spent the entire day together. It was so comfortable, Vinny felt he knew her all his life. They laughed, shared sad stories, and seemed to genuinely like each other. Vinny was so comfortable with her that he asked if he could see her on Sunday. Justice startled him by saying yes but only after church. Would he like to go with her? Vinny hadn't been to church since before Lily died. Despite all his misgivings about God and faith, he heard himself say yes. After a pleasant good night with several intense kisses, they parted, both looking forward to Sunday.

Vinny was up early Sunday, going through his closet looking for something to wear, like a silly school girl. He chose a light charcoal blazer he would wear with his black jean, a wine-colored dress shirt open at the neck, and a black overcoat. Upon inspection in the mirror, he felt he looked rather handsome. He arrived at Justice's house promptly at 8:30 A.M. She was taking him to St. Jerome's for the 9:00 A.M. Mass.

When Vinny saw Justice, she took his breath away. Vinny thought she was the prettiest gal in town. Justice had a suit of pale lavender with a white blouse and just the damnedest, cutest hat he ever saw. He felt so proud.

"Good morning, Chief," says Justice.

"And good morning to you, too, Ms. Channing. May I say you look absolutely beautiful," says Vinny with a slight blush as he helps her with her coat. "I had a wonderful time yesterday and was looking forward to seeing you today."

"Vinny, I had a wonderful time, too. What shall we do today?"

"You did say you like antiques, and I know of several stuffed antique stores I thought you would enjoy."

"Oh, how wonderful."

Vinny and Justice arrived at church just as the Dougherty's pull in.

"Good morning, Mark," calls Vinny. "Nice to see you ordered a beautiful day."

Mark laughs, "Yeah, I sure get a lot of God's credit."

"Say, how is that son of yours doing? Does he ever get to come home and say Mass here at St. Jeromes?

"No, Chief, we don't get to see much of Nick. It seems his superiors move him around a lot. Nick finds it difficult to stay in one place very long."

"Well, it is good to see you and your family," says Vinny.

"Yes, you, too, Chief."

Vinny has a strange feeling come over him. Mark and Grace seemed reluctant and sad when talking about Nick. Vinny thought that was an odd reaction. Soon he forgot all about it and went on to having one of the best days he has had in a long time.

After Mass Vinny and Justice went to this out of the way diner for brunch. Justice joked about needing nourishment before they tackled antique hunting. The diner was crowded, and as Justice and Vinny waited for a table, Vinny asks if she knows the Dougherty's and what is the story there?

"Oh," says Justice, "it seems Nick, the priest, has cut all ties to his family and friends."

"Why would he do that? Especially being a priest and all."

"I guess his embarrassment and humiliation over what that Mary Ellen McGrath did to him was just so devastating."

"Yeah, but aren't priests supposed to be forgiving?"

"Well, perhaps he has forgiven, but it is hard to forget."

"Enough talk about sadness, we are going to have a great day," says Vinny. "But I have to ask, have I earned the right to know why you are called Justice?"

Just then they were called to their booth.

After placing their order, Justice says, "Ok, Vinny, but you are not to ever tell anybody. It is my story and my right to tell it." Justice begins. "I have five siblings."

"Five siblings, yikes," says Vinny.

"Yes," continues Justice, "and all five are older brothers. When my mother got pregnant with her sixth child, she made the comment, 'If there is any justice in this world, I will finally have a baby girl.' When I was born and the nuns told my mother she'd had a baby girl, my mother said, 'Now there is Justice in this world.' And, that was my given name. Of course the church wouldn't acknowledge it at baptism, claiming there are no saints named Justice. So my baptismal name is Justine, but that is a fact that no one knows, not even my friend Ronnie."

"Wow," says Vinny, "what a beautiful story."

Their food arrives and conversation comes so easy to them as they tell each other about themselves. Neither wished the day would end.

CHAPTER 15

The alarm goes off at 6:30 A.M., and Vinny gets out of bed, ready to face the task of solving a serial killer's murdering spree.

He first reflects back on the wonderful weekend he spent with Justice. He allowed himself this pleasure only through his shower and cup of coffee. As he gets dressed, he starts going over in his mind how he is going to bring order and assignments to the squad room. They must make identifying their Jane Doe a priority. He was out the door by 7:30 A.M. He had scheduled his people to be there by eight. When Vinny got to the prescient, he was so pleased to see his crew already there and working.

As Vinny entered the squad room, Max calls out, "Yo, boss, seems like you have a bit of a spring in your step today, and is that a smile I see on your face?"

"Nothing escapes you, Max, does it?"

"Boss man, I am a dee-tec-tive, in case you forgot, and I do believe I am detecting some vibes of pleasure coming off you."

"Just be glad I am in a good mood because we have tons of work to do."

Chairs shift around and coffee is being poured. Jet and Mickey are rubbing elbows, and Vinny calls for them to please sit and let's get started. He approaches the white boards and is startled to see twelve victims. Vinny knows there are many, but to see them listed is unnerving.

"Ok, guys, any closer to identifying our Jane Doe? Do we have anything that leads us in finding a name?"

Cully speaks up, "Chief, there are no missing person reports filed recently. We do know she had several piercings, but no jewelry was found. No tattoos, but she does have a birth mark on her lower back towards the right. Will calls it a strawberry birth mark. We found no clothes dumped anywhere near the surrounding areas. Rain and the elements washed away any footprints, tire tracks, or prints that could have been on the arrow. We are tracing the lipstick brand and color, as well as the other make-up. So far that's it."

"I have moved Candice Upkoff's name to victim twelve. Our Jane Doe is eleven. Upkoff may have been killed before Doe, but we just learned of her. I am so very worried seeing how close these two killings are that there doesn't seem to be a cooling off period."

"Lucas, what did you learn from your interviews over in Berks County?"

"I met with Kristoff, who by the way seems to be a hell of a detective, and he took me out to the cemetery where our victim twelve was found. Kristoff says it looks like she was placed there, not just tossed. The position of her body was the same as our Jane Doe. The old man who found her, just a minute, I have his name here in my clue book, ah, here it is. An old gent by the name of Hank Simmons. Tough old bird. He is an army man served in Korea and did a stint in Nam, so I felt he was very reliable. He said he came to visit the wife, dead some ten years already, and the first thing he saw, not blocked by a head stone, was a bare leg and foot. The leg was up, bent at the knee. At first he thought he came across some lovers, but upon further inspection, discovered the body. He knew not to touch anything and immediately called the police. Kristoff dispatched his officers and they swept the crime scene as we would have. They found and bagged the statue, which may produce a finger print. The one officer, a Lloyd Purcell, recognized her red hair, which had been chopped off like our Jane Doe. They, too, are running tests on the make-up. Maybe it will match ours. I talked with Purcell, he claims this Candice, he called her Candy, and his daughter were friends. I asked permission to talk to her. Her name is Betty Purcell-Reilly. She works in a flower shop over in Laureldale."

"What about the victim's parents? Did you meet with them?" asked Vinny.

"No," replies Luke, "but I have an appointment to meet with them later. I'm going to interview the Reilly girl first, then onto the parents. Should be back around five or six tonight."

"Good, anything else?"

"Oh, one more thing, boss, might not be important. When I was talking to Hank, he said something strange. When he first saw the girl laying there, for some reason he had the impression that someone left knee prints in the grass beside her. Of course there was nothing there by the time the police got there, so he never mentioned it."

"Knee prints, that is odd."

"Yeah, I would not have mentioned it either, but this Hank is one observant old man."

"We will list it, Luke, any tiny bit of information is important. Ok, people, who's next? Cully, what have you got?"

"I've been pouring through the autopsy reports for any connections and they all read the same. One of the reports on victim eight, Anna Serento, listed an unknown puncture would in the neck. The coroner had no clue as to why it was there. Toxicology reports indicate no drugs in her system."

Vinny hears Max's bangles rattling and asks, "What is it, Max? Can you add to this?"

"Chief, I cannot get the idea out of my head that there's a connection among these women to religion, the military and estrangement. One, all these women were or are married to service men, two, they are or were practicing Catholics and all were either divorced, getting divorced, or not living with their significant other. We need to do more interviewing of families and friends for as many of these victims as we can."

Luke chimes in with one more thing our Mr. Simmons mentioned. "Our witness told me he has never seen such hatred and demeaning violence toward another person. He said whoever did this despises women beyond comprehension. His only purpose is to humiliate them and make them pay for whatever was done to him. And I agree with that after seeing what we have seen."

J.J. asks Vinny, "What have you found out about the make-up?"

"Not much, most of it was washed away and the ones we discovered who were linked to our vic never had it analyzed. But victims eight, nine, ten, our vic and Ms. Upkoff all had the same brand and color, so that means he brings it with him. The brand name is 'Joyland.' The lipstick color is 'Poppy Paradise.' The eye make-up is called 'Vixen Green,' again the same brand. Hasn't been around since the 90's. It is said to have been very popular with young teenage girls. The foreign substance in our Jane Doe's stomach and on her body has still not been identified."

"Any more luck on finding a missing person's report on our Jane Doe?" asks Vinny.

"No, Chief, sorry."

"Ok, guys, let's stop for now. It is coming up on noon. Luke, I want you to take Cully with you when you interview Ms. Upkoff's friends and family."

"Max and C.J., what did you find out on your trip to Reading? Did you talk to the coroner who did the autopsies? He may remember seeing a puncture on the necks but didn't report it. That piece of information intrigues me."

"People, we are going into the fifth month, and so far all we have is dead bodies and no closer to solving this crime than when we first discovered our Jane Doe. We need to pound the pavement, do some intense investigation. Dig as deep as possible, push witnesses. People always know more than they think. I am personally going to go over to Buck's County and meet with Detective Arnold. See what I can find out about Suzanne Cunningham. Alright, head out and start digging.

CHAPTER 16

2001

Grace lays awake listening to her husband stir. It is not quite 7:00 A.M., Saturday morning. As she lays quietly, her mind is not quiet. Nick is supposed to come by the house today to sit and talk with his parents. They have not seen nor heard from Nick since he walked out with Father Eric.

Mark starts to wake, and after years of marriage, senses that Grace is already awake and he knows she is in turmoil over her eldest son.

"Good morning, wife, how's the love of my life this morning?"

"Good morning, husband. I am both excited and terrified at seeing Nick today."

Mark reaches over and holds her. They lay silently as they watch the gentle snow fall outside their bedroom window.

Grace says, "How can a mother be fearful of her child and the things he might say? Mark, what went wrong? We were so wrapped up in keeping Nick so protected from the world because we knew he was headed to the priesthood. So we failed to warn him of what life can throw at you. How could that girl hurt him so much?"

"Grace," Mark says, "we are good parents. Maybe we don't have all the answers, but we do the best we can. Perhaps this was God's way to humble Nick. You must admit, he became so self-centered. Paid little or no attention to his siblings and look at the way he spoke to you."

"You may be right, Mark. Well, we will find out more today. I guess it's time to get up and rouse out the little ones."

Nick seems to be at peace with himself and has gone over in his mind what he is going to say to his parents. He has found some solace the past several weeks staying in the rectory at St. Jeromes. He gets up and dressed and sees that God has blessed his day with a soft, gentle falling snow. He feels this is a good omen. Around 11:00 A.M., he heads over to his house. A house that he will no longer call home. Before he sees his parents, he goes into the garage and gently caresses his beloved car. As he opens the door, a whiff of Mary Ellen's scent hits his nostrils and he is surprised at how hard the memory of her slams into his conscientiousness. He reminds himself his goal here today is to clean out the car and hand the keys over to his sister. Alice has been his rock through this and he wants her to have the car. He sits a box on the seat and starts with the glove box. Here he finds a pretty plastic container that holds some of Mary Ellen's make-up. His memory goes back to when she told him it was her "repair kit." She needed to touch up her make-up after a night of passion or sometimes after seeing a teary movie. He tosses it in to his box. Next, he finds a condom that seems 100-years-old and actually chuckles at that. He picks up a small flashlight, a collapsible water cup from when he was in the Cub Scouts. Other miscellaneous items get put into the box, and soon he is moving to the trunk. He has some gym clothes, a baseball bat and glove, and as he fills the box, he is relieved not to find anything more of Mary Ellen's. He carries the covered box with him into the house.

Nick opens the back door and calls out, "Hey, Mom, Dad, you home?"

Grace races into the kitchen and hugs Nick with all her might.

"Oh, Nick, I am so happy to see you."

"I'm happy to see you, too, Mom, where's Dad?"

"He's in the living room. We've been waiting for you."

"Mom, let me go up to my room first. I need a few of my things. I have a carton here to put them in, then I will be down to talk to you, ok?"

"Sure, Nick, your father and I will be waiting. Take your time."

Nick goes through his room taking down posters, taking some of his trophies but leaving others. He cleans out his desk and bureau drawers of personal items. For some reason, he keeps all of Mary Ellen's love letters and cards she sent him. Keeps some pictures. One of his best friends Charlie and him at a pool party clowning around. Soon he is finished and taking the carton with him, he goes to meet his parents and tell them his life plan.

Mark gets up and goes to hug Nick and tells him how good it is to see him. Mark is concerned at how gaunt and sad Nick looks but can't really expect anything else considering what the boys been through.

"Come, Nick, sit and talk to us," says Mark. "Tell us your plans and keep in mind how much we love you."

"I do know that, Dad, and I so appreciate how you and Mom have put up with me. I have been knocked down a peg or two, and I have come to realize since I have been at the rectory that I needed that. Father Eric has helped so much and I have prayed and prayed for forgiveness for being so arrogant and hurtful. I hope you and Mom can forgive me."

"Nick," says Mark, "of course you're forgiven. You are our son."

"Thanks, Mom, Dad. Now my plans. Father Eric has secured a place for me at the seminary. I will leave next month and get settled in. In the meantime, I will stay at the rectory. I need time, Mom and Dad, away from you and the family. I don't want you to contact me. I need solitude and time to get things right between me and God. Please honor this request. I promise to write on occasion just to let you know how I am. I need to be alone and not see that pain in your eyes every time I look at you. I have cleaned out my car and left the signed title and keys with a letter to Alice. Please let her have my car."

Grace gets up and starts to pace. "Nick, you want us to sever all ties with you?"

"Yes, Mom, for now. I need that. Please say you understand and honor my wishes."

As Grace was about to argue, a horn blew outside and Nick says, "That's for me. I called Charlie to come pick me up and take me back to the rectory."

Nick hugs both his parents, picks up his carton of treasures, and heads out the door. Grace breaks into tears and Mark, with his arm around his wife's shoulders, stands at the door watching their son walk out of their lives. He, too, has tears in his eyes.

CHAPTER 17

Luke and Cully head out with Cully riding shotgun. Cully is a bit intimidated being with Luke. Luke is a top-notch detective, and Cully feels inadequate.

"Hey, Cully, this your first really big case?"

"Yeah," says Cully. "I'm really excited, but I hope I don't hold you back."

"Naw, kid, don't worry about that. We all have to learn sometime and I've been watching you. You got some good instincts, and the Chief sure has lots of confidence in you."

"Thanks, Luke," says Cully as he becomes more comfortable in his seat.

On the way to the flower shop to interview Mrs. Reilly, they stop along the way for something to eat. Luke doesn't like to eat in his car, so they take their food to an outdoor table.

Cully asks Luke how long he's been a detective.

"About eight years now. I was a street cop first. I was a no-good hustler banging a different girl every night. Hanging with my also no-good hustler buddies. No future, no plans and then wham! One day my ma says she has cancer and is going to die. Now, Cully, you got to understand about Italian mothers. They are the salt of the earth, and their boys never do anything wrong. But I heard the tears and saw the sadness in her eyes when she looked at the bum I was turning out to be. That's when I saw a piece in the paper when I was twenty-two, it was a recruiting ad for the police department. So I went to the place, filled out an application, was interviewed, and hired. Had to do some schooling, on the job training they called it, and at twenty-three, I was a police officer. Worked my way up the ranks, and when my ma died, there was no longer sadness in her eyes."

"Wow, that's some story, Luke."

"Yeah, it the truth. Now let's get going and see what we can get out of Mrs. Reilly."

Their appointment was at 2:00 P.M. They drove through town looking for the shop when they saw this huge daffodil in a colorful pot sitting on the pavement and knew they found the flower shop. It was 1:45 P.M. when they arrived at the Daffy Daffodil Flower Shop. They sat for a few minutes. Luke explained to Cully that it was important to take in the surrounding whenever you are in a strange place.

Luke asked Cully, "What do you see?"

Cully looked around. "I see a small town, some other businesses. People going about their tasks. No children, so I guess school is in session. A town bank, quiet, peaceful community."

Luke says, "Know what I see?"

"What?" asks Cully.

"See those two old men sitting on the bench outside that barber shop?"

"Yeah."

"Well," says Luke, "they already pegged us as cops. They are veterans and they don't miss a trick."

"How do you know that? Are you busting my chops?"

"No, look at their hats. Both are wearing service hats. One looks like Navy, the other might be Marine. Now look over at that restaurant across the street. See that lady pacing back and forth. She has been doing that since we pulled in. Either she's meeting a lover and she's married, or she knows her husband is in the restaurant with his lover and she's not sure if she wants to confront him."

"Shit," says Cully, "you don't miss too much, do you?"

"No, Cully, I try not to, but you did good, too. Just remember, what's around you just might save your life someday. Come on, let's talk to our Mrs. Reilly."

Luke pushes open the flower shop door and looks around in wonder at the variety of flowers. The odor is unexpected. He assumes it will be clawing, but it's not. You can almost smell every individual flower. They look around and cannot find anyone when up pops this head filled with braids piled on top of the most adorable black woman Cully has ever seen.

Luke asks, "Mrs. Reilly?"

"Yes, but call me Betty. You must be the detectives here to ask about Candy?"

"Detective DeAngelo and Officer Anderson," states Luke.

Betty is about 5' and so very tiny. Luke figures her to be about thirty-five. She pulls off her garden gloves and shakes hands.

Betty asks, "Will it be ok if we talk while I work? I have a wedding in two days."

"No problem, what can you tell us about Mrs. Upkoff?"

"Oh my, where to begin," says Betty.

"Just start where you feel the most comfortable," says Luke.

"Well," Betty says, "Candy was so popular in school. We were the best of friends in high school and stayed that way up to her death. She'd sometimes bring Billy, that's her little boy, into the shop and help me arrange flowers when I got really busy. She had an eye for design, but she also had an eye for men. Candy was so blunt. Always teasing guys, promising what she never intended to give. She met her husband, he is in the service, when he came home with one of the neighbor boys for the weekend. I think Jesse is from Tennessee. He met Candy at a dance and that's all she wrote. This was around Easter, about five and a half years ago. By the summer, they were married. Jesse had to go overseas, so Candy stayed here."

Cully asks, "Was Candy a religious person?"

"No, she was raised Catholic but always told me she shocked the priests too much in confession, so she quit going to church. Although before her death, she mentioned having met a gorgeous priest she hoped she could seduce."

"Did she seduce men while her husband was away?" Cully asked.

"Unfortunately, yes, I know of several affairs, one night stands actually, they were never permanent. I think she really loved Jesse, but she missed sex."

Cully asks if she had any one special buried in the cemetery where she was found.

"No one that I know of, but that's where she liked to go to engage in her extracurricular activities. She'd tell me only the ghosts could see her sin."

"Betty, do you know of anyone who would want her dead? Someone who really hated her."

"No, Candy was a party girl, everyone liked her."

"What about a woman, maybe the wife or girlfriend of a man she went after?"

"No, she flirted with the local guys but had sex with only men passing through. But I am sure that her infidelities got back to Jesse."

"Where is her son?" asks Luke.

"I guess her parents have him. They lived with her parents, or maybe her brother and his wife took him."

"Oh," says Luke, "we didn't know there was a brother. Where does he live?"

"Just a town over. I don't think they were close. Jacob didn't like her wild side. Guess he was afraid she'd rub off on his wife. Look, fellows, I have got to speed up here and get these flowers finished. I don't know what else to tell you. She was my friend, and I am sorry for what happened."

"Thank you, Betty, I'll leave my card. If you think of anything, no matter how small, please call."

With that Luke and Cully walked out the door. Cully feels he has left a little bit of heaven behind. They get in the car and sit there for a while lost in thought.

Cully speaks first, "Well, Luke, what do you think?"

"I think it's a dead end. The men she had sex with seem to be the kind that enjoys a good lay, then moves on to the next. How about you?"

"I agree, but I was curious about this priest."

"A priest," laughs Luke. "Oh, Cully, you do have a lot to learn." He starts the car and heads out to the next interview. Mr. and Mrs. Langly, Candice's parents. Luke drives out of town while Cully finishes writing up his notes. They travel about ten miles and come to a lovely development called Sparrow Heights. Luke has no trouble finding the home, and when they pull in the drive way, they see Mr. and Mrs. Langly sitting on the porch playing with a five-year-old. One question answered.

The Langlys were in their mid-sixties. Fit-looking people with that sadness in their eyes that only the death of a loved one can bring.

They were very gracious and invited the policemen inside to the living room. It was a lovely home, and despite their daughter and grandson living with them, it was not intended to bring up a five-year-old. Knick-knacks and crystal items were placed around the room with care. Mr. Langly had a chess board set up, and it was obvious this was their retirement home. Books and puzzles could be seen in the dining area. They had little else to add to Betty's observations, although neither spoke of their daughter's infidelities. Again, the question was asked if they knew anyone who would want to hurt her in such a vile way. To that question, tears rose in Mrs. Langly's eyes.

"No", she said, "there was no one."

They thanked them for their time, and as they were leaving, Cully asks, "Do you know of any priests that Candy might have gotten to know before she died?"

Luke glanced at Cully and said, "Let it go, Cully!"

"Why, yes," said Mrs. Langly, "Candy mentioned meeting a priest and said maybe if he was her pastor, she would go back to church because he was so handsome."

"Do you know where she met him?" asks Cully.

"No, I am sorry. I assumed just in passing. Our parish has no visiting priests."

Luke was really annoyed with Cully for bringing up this priest again. Luke, being 100% Catholic, does not put up with anyone or anything that might smear his church and lets Cully know about it.

Cully defends himself, reminding Luke that the Chief said any little bit of information could be helpful.

Luke calms down and agrees with Cully but tells him again, "Lay off the priest angle."

CHAPTER 18

As Cully and Luke head home, Vinny gets ready to travel to Bucks County. He has an early appointment with Detective Arnold regarding the death of Suzanne Cunningham. He is puzzled by the ease of this killer in disposing of his victims. Vinny is frustrated. A crime like this with so many bodies should have some clues.

He has no trouble finding the police station, and as he pulls up, he sees an attractive woman exit the building. She is all business and walks with a purpose. The black slacks she is wearing fit snug, the dark gray corduroy jacket covers a white blouse. As she walks, the wind blows the jacket aside and he sees she is carrying. Short black hair with highlights of blond running through it. He cannot help but wonder, is she married?

As Vinny steps out of the car, the woman approaches him with her hand extended.

"Chief Miller, I am Detective Arnold."

"Good to meet you, Detective," says Vinny as they both size each other up.

Detective Arnold says, "I figured you would like to see the crime scene first. We can talk in the car on the way over."

Vinny follows her to her car and gets in.

"We don't get many homicides here, so this is a big deal to us," says Arnold. "We have exhausted all our leads and hope your investigation will help us find her killer."

Vinny asks, "What do you know about her?"

"Nothing really. She was new in town, had a small one-bedroom apartment over on Lexington. Opened a small bank account, about $800 at First

National. Her application for the apartment shows no living family, but she listed a husband overseas. No name, just husband. No previous address. She just showed up one day and got a job over at the EmergeCare Center and was to start in two weeks. The only personal information we got was she asked the landlord where the nearest Catholic church was."

Vinny asks if they had any luck tracking down her name.

"We tried tracking it, but no luck, and there is no Cunningham in the service married to a Suzanne. We think it was an alias."

"What about the men that found her?" asks Vinny.

"They're no help. Maintenance men for the town. Lived here all their lives. I have their interview notes in the file I made for you. I think it would be a waste of time interviewing them, but that is up to you."

"Did you do any analysis on the make-up that Ms. Cunningham was de-faced with? We are trying to see if it is the same brand that was used on the other victims. We believe he brings it with him." Vinny is quiet for a bit, then asks, "Detective Arnold, do you think a woman could of done this?"

Detective Arnold seems lost in thought, then says, "It would have to be a very strong woman. Our Ms. Cunningham was no light weight. Do you think it is possible?"

"I honestly don't know. The fact that these women were so humiliated and degraded but no sexual activity just baffles me. If it is a man, why not the ultimate act of defiling them more by raping them?"

"I appreciate your meeting with me, Detective," says Vinny.

As the car crosses the railroad tracks, Detective Arnold pulls into the clearing to lead Vinny to the spot where Suzanne Cunningham was dumped like a sack of garbage.

Vinny gets out, stands, and surveys the scene. A year ago, a young woman was left here to be found by anyone. Why? Why are all these women being killed and displayed? What is the murderer trying to say?

Vinny gets back into the car and they head back to the station. When they arrive, Vinny asks her to see if they can still do an analysis on the make-up to see if it matches. Detective Arnold assures him she will work the case with fresh eyes knowing now what she does. Vinny takes the file and after good-byes, heads to his car.

Vinny doesn't feel he has made any headway with this interview. He sits just watching the rhythm of this small town and knows that since his visit, Detective Arnold will start digging again for clues and information. He was very impressed with her. Vinny looks at his watch and it is only 9:30 A.M. He expected to be here longer.

It is a beautiful day and Vinny puts a call into Mary Lou at the station.

"Anybody back in the office?" he asks.

"No," says Mary Lou, "JJ called in and she is working at home until 11:00 A.M. She said she's following some leads. The others are all still out."

"Listen, Mary Lou," says Vinny, "I'm finished here, not much in the way of information that can help us right now. Detective Arnold is going to continue her investigation with some leads I gave her. With it so early and such a nice day, I think I am going to drive up to Williamsport and see what I can learn about our tattoo girl, Caitlyn Moore Thomas. Would you call the detective there, a Morrison, and tell him I am on my way and would appreciate his seeing me. I should get there by 1:00 P.M."

"Will do, boss, and don't forget to check in," scolds Mary Lou.

"I hear you, Mom..." laughs Vinny.

CHAPTER 19

The drive to Williamsport is very soothing to Vinny. The mountains are majestic, and in a few more weeks, the trees will be in full bloom. Vinny is wishing he would have invited Justice to ride along with him. As he drives, his thoughts are not on a serial killer. He is reliving his night of love making. Vinny actually is thinking maybe this could turn out to be long term. As he continues to enjoy the memory, he spots an advertisement for a restaurant at the next exit. Vinny detours and finds he is really hungry. He figures he has time for an early lunch. He notices several big rigs pulled into the lot around back and that leads his thoughts to the real reason he is on this journey. Not to reminisce about his love making, but he is here with hopes of securing a lead to catch a serial killer. He parks his Rover and sits awhile, taking in the scene. He spots a young girl dressed, or should he say more undressed, hanging around in back by the big rigs. She couldn't be more than eighteen or twenty. Short shorts, despite the crisp air, peasant blouse with the sleeves pulled off her shoulders low enough to show off her large breasts. Vinny continues to watch and, yep, pretty soon a truck door swings open and in she goes. Vinny knows what's going on but has no authority to interrupt. He wonders if this is what Ms. Thomas was doing. The name these girls have is "lot lizard." Vinny has sympathy for them but also disgust. For some reason, he has lost his appetite and pulls out and heads to his destination.

Vinny finds the police station with no trouble. After he parks, he calls Mary Lou and asks if she contacted Morrison.

"Yeah, boss, I called ahead, but Detective Morrison was not very happy to hear you were on your way. He really copped an attitude to think you would question their investigation," says Mary Lou.

"Damn it, Mary Lou, did you tell him I was just looking for information?"

"Of course, Vinny, I know how to deal with these egomaniacs."

"Ok, calm down," says Vinny. "I will try to smooth it over. I can be very diplomatic when I have to be. Talk to you later."

Vinny walks into the police station and greets the officer at the desk. He identifies himself and remarks that Detective Morrison is expecting him.

Officer Henry, Dwight to his friends, says, "Oh, right, you're that cop from the big city who is going to solve our crimes here in our backward town."

Vinny is taken aback, and instead of a confrontation, he again asks to see Detective Morrison.

"Have a seat," says Officer Henry. "I will let him know you are here. Have a seat over there." Henry points to a holding area where lawyers and their clients are waiting to see a judge or a magistrate.

Vinny tries his best to be the bigger man here. No fellow officer, no matter where he is from, should be treated like this. He takes a seat and waits.

After a half hour passes, he is finally summoned by Officer Henry and given directions to Detective Morrison's office by a finger point. Vinny knocks on the door and opens it, not waiting for an invite. He quickly surveys his surroundings. The office is like every other public official's office. Drab, cluttered and dingy. He approaches the Detective with his hand outstretched only to be told to have a seat, he'd be right with him.

Vinny knows how to play this game and takes time to scrutinize his enemy. Detective Morrison looked like an ex-army man gone to seed. A buzz haircut, graying on the sides, a ruddy complexion from being outdoors too much. His nose is bulbous, hinting at liking his booze to much also. Sitting on the chair, he looks huge. Arms showed a lot of time spent at the gym, but he also has a sizeable gut. Vinny decides his opponent (the way he thinks about him now) is not used to having his authority questioned.

Morrison puts aside the file he was reading and looks up at Vinny.

"So," he says, "what has happened in my town that brings you here?"

Vinny explains how they discovered the death of one Caitlyn Moore Thomas and how they believe it is linked to several other deaths of young women with the same M.O.

Morrison says, "Listen, Miller, this whore we found dead up behind the baseball fields was nothing more than a lot lizard who went with anyone, man or woman, for money or drugs. She was a tramp, lived up in the woods with her aunt in a filthy trailer. The aunt is no better. We didn't waste a lot of time on her. Figured one of her Johns wasn't happy with his service. Ha-ha, know what I mean? So you can waste your time but not mine. Have a safe trip home."

With that Morrison stood, ready to show Vinny the door.

Vinny was stunned when he realized that Morrison was no taller standing than sitting.

Vinny stood also and said, "Detective, I would appreciate looking at the file. I would also like to talk to the officers that were called to the scene and the person who found her. And if it is not too much trouble, directions to her aunt's filthy trailer."

"After your secretary called, I made a copy of the file, here, you can take it with you. It was kids that found her. They play up around the ball field and one of them called it in. I sent Officer Diaz up to investigate. You will find him over at Ruth's Diner over on Laurel Street having lunch right now. By the time Office Diaz got to the scene, these boys were poking sticks at her body. She was naked you know and some of the boys never seen titties before, nor pussy for that matter. I won't give you their names being minors and all. Now good day to you, Miller."

Vinny walks out into the light of day wondering how the hell does that little twerp get away with what just went down. A woman was murdered and he makes jokes. With as much conviction as he could muster, he vows to bring justice to Caitlyn Thomas.

Vinny finds the little diner, Ruth's, and as he walks in, he spots Officer Diaz at the counter.

Vinny approaches and says, "Officer Diaz?"

"Yes, that's me. What can I do for you?"

Vinny introduces himself and explains why he is here. Expecting a rebuff, he is surprised when Officer Diaz suggests they sit at a booth.

"What can you tell me about what you found at the scene of Caitlyn Thomas' murder?"

Officer Diaz blesses himself and says, "It was horrible, never seen anything like it, and these boys poking her and grabbing her breasts. Laughing and enjoying themselves. I chased them away and called for the coroner."

"Could you describe how she looked?" asked Vinny.

"Yeah," says Diaz, "painted with make-up to make her look freakish, an arrow sticking out of her chest, but the boys tried to remove it and it was broken. Something was attached at some point, but only fragments remained. One of the boys looked more guilty than the others, and before I chased them, I asked what was in his pocket. Finally, he pulled out a small statue of the Virgin Mary. I took it from him."

"What did you do with it?" asks Vinny.

Officer Diaz, reaches into his pocket and shows Vinny the tiny statue.

"Did the boy tell you where he found the statue?" asks Vinny.

"Yes, he points to her and says, 'Down there,' meaning her private area. I am appalled, Detective Miller. This poor woman. I shall never forget this."

"You've been most helpful, Officer Diaz," says Vinny. "Your Detective Morrison was rather blunt and offered no help."

"I know, he is not well liked but has friends in high places, so we all tread lightly."

"One more thing," asks Vinny. "Could you give me directions to Mrs. Thomas' aunt's trailer, and what is the aunt's name?"

Officer Diaz's directions are precise. "You go five and a half miles west and you will see a mailbox. It is pretty battered, but it is bright yellow with Moore printed in big, purple block letters. Turn on the dirt road right after the mailbox. You need to go slow. It's about a mile up that dirt road. You won't miss it. The trailer is the only thing you'll come to, but be cautious because Ms. Elizabeth Moore has a rifle."

Vinny thanks him, and as he leaves, he hopes that someday Officer Diaz will be in charge. He is one fine policeman.

Vinny sits in his car and goes over the file Morrison gave him. Certainly not much to go on, and the crime scene was destroyed by those boys. An autopsy was done but no toxicology report or follow up on the make-up. Although Vinny has not much to go on, he is certain of one thing: Caitlyn Thomas was a victim of their serial killer.

He puts the Rover in gear and heads west. It doesn't take long to reach the mailbox, and he turns right and heads up the dirt road. It is very isolated, and the road doesn't look like it's used much. Vinny swerves to miss a pot hole only to be attacked by tree branches encroaching onto the road. He breaks free into an opening and there sits a trailer. Vinny pulls up but not too close. He sits and watches. No one comes out, but he sees what looks like a towel covering a window, pulled aside a bit. Someone is watching. The trailer is more of a camper. Extremely small and is literally falling apart. He sees what looks like an outhouse off to the left behind some trees in the back. So no plumbing. He also does not see any wiring or poles, so no electricity. He does hear a faint humming that might mean a generator.

As Vinny gets out of his SUV, a window goes up and a gun comes out.

"Stop right there, mister. What do you want?" a voice asks.

Vinny holds up his badge and says, "My name is Vinny Miller, I am a policeman, and I would like to ask you some questions about your niece, Caitlyn. Are you Elizabeth Moore?"

"Yes, I am. People call me Bitsy. Now, Mr. Policeman, I want you to hold up that badge. I am going to check it out using the scope on this here rifle. Don't worry, I won't shoot you. Hold it up."

Vinny is not sure if he wants to trust this weird lady, but if he wants answers, he will have to do as she says, and with that, he holds it up in his right hand as outstretched as possible to the right.

She points the gun, he sees her using the scope, then she says, "Go sit over at the picnic table. I'll be right out."

Vinny goes over and sits. Soon the door opens and out comes one humungous arm and her right side. She turns her back to Vinny and squeezes herself out the door backwards. Vinny has never seen such a large woman. Has to be at least 400 pounds if an ounce.

Bitsy steps down, turns around, and makes her way to the table. Vinny stands up and introduces himself and shakes her hand. Bitsy is not only fat but tall, at least 5'8". She is missing teeth and has stringy, dirty red hair with graying streaks throughout. She has on a dress that is tight and shows her huge arms and tiny bust and an enormous behind. Vinny puts her age to be in the upper 60's.

"What do you want to know about Caitlyn?

Vinny says, "I'd like you to tell me about her. Did you see her the day she was killed? Why was she living with you? I thought she was married."

Bitsy eyes her company with some skepticism. "What is it to you?"

Vinny explains why he is here and the possible connection.

Bitsy starts, "Cailyn was such a sweet little girl. Her parents, my brother and wife, were killed in a car accident when she was only eleven. My other brother, Clarence, and his wife wouldn't take her. So she came to live with me here in this filthy trailer. I used the money I got for her from Social Security to send her to a Catholic school. Her parents were practicing Catholics, so Caitlyn was right at home there. I couldn't do much for her or with her beings as heavy as I am, but I loved her. We would sit and read together, play board games. She was learning to cook, too. Clarence's wife was our link to the necessary things. She'd bring our groceries and do my banking. Caitlyn and I were happy, but the child needed more. Long story short, at sixteen, she got pregnant by Forrest Thomas. He was almost nineteen and just graduated. I was surprised when Caitlyn told me she was pregnant and even more surprised to learn she'd been sexually activity since she was fourteen. But he loved her so much, so they got married. Four months into her pregnancy, Caitlyn lost the baby, and Forrest, well, he enlisted in the army and was going off to boot camp. His plan was to get housing on a military base and be a happy young couple. Caitlyn wasn't up for that now that she was longer pregnant."

Vinny asks, "What did she do?"

Bitsy continues, "Moved back in with me, finished high school, and got a job at that truck stop. She was eighteen by now, I no longer got any money for her, so she needed a job. Detective Miller, I could feel the ache inside that girl. She kept losing everyone she loved. So she turned to men. She went wild. Tattoos, drinking, and whoring around, and poor Forrest, no way to stop her."

"Did you know any of her friends?" asks Vinny.

"No, she stopped coming around much. Don't even know where she slept."

Tears started rolling down her cheeks, and Vinny felt the sadness in this woman. He says, "Bitsy, I am going to do my best to find her killer."

Vinny thanks her for her time, and as he was about to leave her sitting at the table weeping, Bitsy says, "You know, Detective Miller, I thought there for a while, she was straightening herself out. The last time I saw her, she was dressed nicer, spoke nicer, and when I complimented her, she said she met someone who understood her. I reminded her she was married, but she said not to worry. I asked why. Caitlyn said, two reasons, Auntie, one, he's not from around here, and two, he's a priest. Now what do you make of that?"

Vinny again thanked Bitsy for her time and headed to his car. Just as he was about to get in, he says, "Bitsy, I was told all this land belongs to your family. Why do you live like this?"

Bitsy looks off in the distance and says, "Chief Miller, see all those trees and bushes, the rocks jutting out the ground, little animals scuttling around. Not one of them makes fun of me."

Vinny nods as in understanding, gets in his Rover, and heads down the road.

On his way out of town, he stops by the crime scene. Vinny drives down an alley behind the score board of the baseball fields, where people from all over the world come to see youngsters play the great American past time. He can see that this would be a good, isolated spot to dump a body.

Vinny calls Mary Lou and tells her he should be back by 6:00 P.M. and that he would see her in the morning. Next, he calls Justice and she picks up on the first ring. Wants to know if she'd like a dinner date tonight. She would.

As Vinny heads back to the world he knows, he mulls over what he learned. This talk of a priest intrigues him. From the very beginning, his crew suggested a religious connection. Perhaps they have a good lead.

CHAPTER 20

SUMMER OF 2002

As Father Eric travels down the turnpike, he is looking forward to seeing Nick and to try to relieve this anxiety he has concerning Nick's emotions. In the back seat is a black valise, which contains a change of underwear and a clean shirt, his toiletries, and most of all his priestly garments. He is planning to stay the night and spend some time with his old friend Monsignor Timothy O'Reilly. Monsignor O'Reilly is the head of the Seminary and has promised to keep an eye on Nick. Father Eric had explained how terrible fragile Nick is and wanted special treatment for the boy. Beside the valise is a large, brown mailing envelope filled with letters to Nick from family and friends. Mostly just family. The only friend is Charlie. When Nick went away with Father Eric, he had made Nick solemnly promise there would be absolutely no contact with anyone from his hometown for at least six months. By the pile of mail he is bringing Nick, it seems he kept his promise, as well as did the family. It was important for Nick to immerse himself in his religious vocation 24/7 and rid himself of thoughts of Mary Ellen and his guilt.

Father Eric's heart swells and tears come to his eyes as he drives onto the Seminary's campus. So many wonderful memories flood back to him for this is where he gave himself up to God. As he parks his car and heads to the quarters of his friend, he hears someone call out.

"Eric, how good to see you," as Monsignor O'Reilly reaches the pavement to greet him.

"Timothy, you old goat," says Father Eric, as they embrace, so happy to see each other.

"Come in, come in," says O'Reilly. As they enter the rectory, O'Reilly calls out to his house keeper, Mary Elizabeth, to come please and take Father Eric's valise up to the guest bedroom.

The two priest settle into comfortable chairs in the study and O'Reilly pours them each a generous amount of Scotch over ice, they both start talking at once.

"So, Eric, how are things at St. Jerome's?" asks Timothy.

"Very quiet now that the scandal of Nick and Mary Ellen McGrath has died down. It seems like the young man that got her pregnant dumped her, and she moved to Oregon to be with her father."

"So sad," says Timothy. "So many hearts broken and families torn apart."

"Timothy, when can I see Nick,?" asks Father Eric.

"I have him scheduled to come here at 6:00 P.M. You will have privacy here in the study, and then when he leaves, you and I will enjoy a late dinner. Mary Elizabeth has prepared your favorite meal. Pot roast and mashed potatoes. I have no duties until morning. Although I do want to go around and check on the young men. Sometimes they need a lot of encouragement. I will take care of that while you meet with Nick."

"How's he been?" asks Eric

"Very sad at times," says Timothy, "but I hear him saying his prayers when I pass his door. I don't disturb him. Nick seems to have some very self-imposed guilt he is trying to deal with. His grades are excellent, and I got him into the Philosophy class despite the lateness of his arrival. He seems to get along with his classmates. I am sure you will get a better reading of his mental state when you see him."

Father Eric excuses himself after exhausting all the topics of conversation and goes to his room to freshen up. After several glasses of O'Reilly's excellent Scotch, a nap seems to be in order.

Nick is excited to see Father Eric. It will be the first familiar face he sees since that January night. Well, not the first. He kept his promise concerning his family but not his friend Charlie. During the six months he has been here at St. Borromeo's Seminary, Nick has managed at least five different times to travel with Charlie to Charlie's family cabin in the Poconos. Despite Charlie's wild nature in high school, he maintained a 3.80 GPA and was accepted into the Thomas Jefferson Medical College. He is in his third year, and with being in such close proximity to the Seminary, he picks Nick up late Friday nights and they spend the next day target shooting. Charlie has a gun range and an archery range. Nick finds there is such a relief firing a gun at a target, but he enjoys the quiet whoosh of an arrow as it meets the bale of hay. This time with Charlie is more therapeutic than any prayers. They drink, get drunk, and wail against women. By Sunday morning, Nick is back at the seminary ready to embrace his God that destroyed him.

Nick has no guilt of lying to Father Eric about having kept his promise. At this point in his life, the only person he trusts is Charlie.

The six o'clock hour comes, and Nick is very prompt. Mary Elizabeth escorts him into the Monsignor's study, and Nick is so happy to see Father Eric. After hugs and pats on the backs, the two men settle in.

"You are looking well, Nick. The food here seems to have help put some weight back on you," says Father Eric.

"Thank you, Father. I seem to be adjusting well, and yes, the food is great. My classes are going well, and I have made some friends among the other seminarians."

"Tell me, Nick, have you kept your promise about not contacting anyone from home?" asks Father Eric.

"I have, sir," says Nick. Nick feels it is not a lie because Charlie is no longer "from home," he's across town.

"Good, good, I am sure that has helped a great deal with your fitting in so nicely here at St. Borromeo's," says Father Eric. "Look what I brought you. An envelope filled with letters from your family and friends. Take them with you and enjoy them at your leisure. I am sure many of them are wishes for your success."

"Thank you, Father. I have missed my family (another lie), but you were right about not contacting them. I still harbor such awful feelings toward my mother. Not as my mother but as a woman. I saw so many similarities between her and that, you know, other girl and cannot help but wonder would she betray my father so easily? It is women in general that I loath," explains Nick.

"Oh, my son," says Father Eric, "this is the cross you must bear and only prayer, especially if you pray to the Virgin Mary, will help you to forgive. To be able to minister to others once you take your vows, you must forgive all, even that other girl."

"It's too raw right now, Father, but I am working on it," says Nick.

"Good, and I want to talk to you about something else. Being you got a late start, I would like to suggest that you continue classes during the summer.

I don't think you are ready for family yet, and this would help you catch up with what you missed starting late. Also, when you are not in class, Monsignor O'Reilly tells me he has a fall football program for underprivileged boys. You would coach them, have access to the seminary's van, and all the equipment is in storage. What do you think of this plan, Nick?"

"I will think about it so when the time comes for Monsignor O'Reilly to ask me, I will be ready with an answer. But off the top of my sinful head, I think I would love to do that."

Nick thanks Father Eric for coming, and with the envelope full of letters in his hand, he says goodbye and heads back to his room.

Father Eric is quite pleased with Nick and is confident that the boy is finally on the right track.

Nick gets back to his room and dumps the letters from the envelope onto his bed. He sorts them out according to sender. There are twenty-four from his mother. One every week that he's been gone. He pushes them aside. There are four from his father. My father, thinks Nick, and he lets his mind wander into his father's life. Why didn't his father warn him how women were? Was I so full of myself and my calling that my father just assumed I didn't need to know? I wonder how he kept my mother all these years. Perhaps his mother has been having affairs during their marriage. I certainly would not put it past her. Nick shakes himself out of his stupor and tosses his father's letters onto the pile with his mother's. There is one from Alice. She sent it from Paris. Nick forgot that Charlie told him his sister went to study cooking. That goes into the maybe pile. There are a few notes from his siblings, and he thinks those he will enjoy. Last but not least is one from Charlie. Charlie being Charlie is keeping up the ruse of not having any contact with Nick and has suggested a relaxing, fun-filled weekend of target practice and drinking as soon as possible. Nick will definitely see what he can do.

Nick gets his special box out from under the bed and plans on putting the letters inside. This is his box of treasures he has brought from home. When he opens the box, he gets a whiff of Mary Ellen. It takes him by surprise and he slams it shut, and tears come to his eyes.

"Damn, damn, that miserable excuse of a woman, even now she still torments me." He opens it back up to see what it is that tears at his heart. Ah, he sees her repair kit with her make-up. He must have kept it when he cleaned out his car. Nick picks it up and holds it to his nose. His mind is swimming with memories and he hates himself, his God, and the whole world. Something dark and vile starts festering in his very soul.

Nick puts the kit back, along with his family's letters. He wonders to himself, why don't I just throw it away? He cries out to God, why are you punishing me so...the mumbles that Monsignor O'Reilly hears at Nick's door isn't prayer but a damnation of the life he is now forced to live.

After a sleepless night, Nick gets up, dressed, and is ready for Sunday Mass. Father Eric will be participating, and this cheers Nick up. It was great seeing the good Father, and Nick is so appreciative for what he has done for him.

CHAPTER 21

The summer goes well for Nick. He is doubling up on his classes, going to his counseling sessions as required, and has fallen into a pleasant schedule. Coming back from his counseling session, he heads to his room. He finds a message on the door. Monsignor O'Reilly wants to see him at 3:00 P.M. Nick's one o'clock class is over just in time for him to keep this meeting.

Nick knocks on the Rectory door and Mary Elizabeth answers and directs Nick into the study.

Monsignor O'Reilly stands and says, "Good to see you, Nick, come in and have a seat."

Nick takes a seat and wonders what this is going to be about. Hope he has not learned of his secret trips to the Poconos.

"Nick, I have asked you here so I could ask you to consider doing something for me," says O'Reilly.

Nick flashes back to another request from a priest that put him in harm's way and smack in the middle of Mary Ellen McGrath's lap, literally.

Nick frowns from the memory and says, "How can I help you, sir?"

"We're coming into the fall, and there is a football program we run over at St. Elizabeth's for underprivileged boys, and I would like for you to work with them. Father Eric tells me you have younger brothers and this might help you miss them less. I know you are estranged from your family right now and perhaps this will soften you up a bit. What do you say?"

"I think I would like that. Do you think I have the time? What about transportation and uniforms, gear and all that is required?" asks Nick.

Monsignor O'Reilly says, "We have a van just for that purpose, and it will be signed out for your use only. Also, all the equipment you need is over at St.

Elizabeth's. Father Carney teaches fifth grade at St. Elizabeth's and he would be your partner in this. Ben's a fine teacher and priest. A bit older than you, but I think you would get on well with him."

Nick says, "When do I start?"

"Marvelous," says O'Reilly, "right after Labor Day."

Nick stands and thanks him for this opportunity, and as he is leaving, he turns and says, "Monsignor, you are wrong about my missing my family. As far as I am concerned, I have no family." With that said, Nick leaves the study and closes the door.

Monsignor O'Reilly, still standing, stares at the door and makes a mental note to talk with Nick's counselor. What a strange thing to say, muses the Monsignor.

Nick is excited to be part of this program. He loves being outside and working with kids. He lets his mind wonder back to his early days when he would play football with his brothers and Alice. He chuckles at how he remembered Austin, the kid next door, who would run across the street to see if he could play once he saw Alice was out. These thoughts all of a sudden disturbed him as his mind wonders if Alice is tormenting Austin like that bitch did to him.

Now Nick is in a foul mood. It happens every time he tries to bring up a good memory.

She is always there in the back of his mind, saying, "Oh, no, Nick, I want to be pure like the Virgin Mary." Nick sometimes wonder if she will ever go away. His counselor says he must first forgive her. That will never happen. No one on the face of the earth is more hated than Mary Ellen McGrath.

As Nick walks back to his room, he passes other classmates walking in pairs or groups. They are laughing and exchanging stories with one another as friends do. It is another reminder to Nick that he has isolated himself from the others. Yes, he has classmates and study groups, but his only friend is Charlie. He would be embarrassed if his peers knew what a fool he had been.

The fall football program is going exceedingly well. Nick is enjoying Father Carney. He has such a dry sense of humor that Nick enjoys, and his love of teaching shows on the football field. In contrast to Nick, Father Carney is a devoted, 100% priest. Something Nick sometimes finds annoying. In Nick's warped world of what it means to be a priest, unconditional love of man and the world around us is for suckers. Nick knows to keep his guard up and play the part.

After a gruesome practice, the young boys are exhausted. They are laying on the ground getting their energy back.

Nick knows what will energize them and says to Father Carney, "Ben, how about I treat and you take the boys down to the ice cream shop and let them all get some ice cream. I will clean up here and load the equipment into the van and will join you in about half an hour to an hour. I will even treat you." Nick playfully punches Ben on the arm and says, "You older guys need sustenance as well as the young." They both laugh as Ben is a good sport. Father Ben rounds up his young players and tells them if they can muster up enough energy to walk to the ice cream shop, Father Nick will treat them. The boys have no problem gathering around Father Ben, who gives them directions to stay together and comport themselves as proud young men. Once he counts noses, off they go.

Nick sits on the bench for a while and contemplates the gathering of the equipment. He is enjoying the peacefulness of the playground now that the boys are gone. As he sits there, a young man in a service uniform approaches him. Nick looks up and realizes this man is not much older than himself. Nick says hello, and the young fellow, so dejected, sits beside him.

"Sorry to bother you, Father, but could I have a word?"

Nick corrects him by telling him he is just a seminarian and has not yet taken his vows.

"My name is Cameron, Cameron Hyde, and maybe you are not a priest yet, but you must be able to help me. Please, may I just talk to you?"

"Sure, Cameron, just call me Nick. What do you think I can help you with?"

"It's my wife. I got home on leave for a few days, and I must report in by the end of next week. I will be gone for at least six months and today, Wren, that's my wife's name, Wren tells me not to come back. She says she doesn't plan to sit around and, as she puts it, twiddle her thumbs while I am gone for six or more months. She wants a divorce."

With that Cameron begins to cry. "Nick, I love her, what am I to do? I can't quit the service, she refuses to go with me and live on base, and I think she is seeing someone."

Nick's stomach begins to churn, and all he sees is Mary Ellen McGrath. Another faithless, lying, vow-breaking woman who has, or will, break this man's heart.

Nick says, "Cameron, have you asked Wren to go to counseling with you? Do you have children? What parish, I assume you are Catholic, do you belong to? Perhaps you could talk to your pastor. Cameron, I am only a student myself, and I am not equipped to help you."

Cameron responds to Nick, "But maybe you could talk to her. She goes to the gym every Tuesday night and takes a yoga class on Thursdays. She also works at the local grocery store. Maybe you could run into her by accident. Tell her I asked you to talk to her and tell her she is wrong. Nick, I love her so much. I can't imagine life without her. Please help me."

"I am so sorry, Cameron, but I am not able to help you. You must find faith in your pastor or perhaps her parents or friends. I am in no position to intervene." With that said, Nick starts putting the football equipment into the van and watches on as Cameron Hyde walks away looking like he has lost the battle.

Father Carney and the boys are waiting curb side for Nick, and as he pulls up, the boys say good-bye and head for their homes. Father Ben gets into the van and asks Nick what took so long. Nick told Ben he got hung up talking to a fan.

CHAPTER 22

A few weeks pass, and Nick has been consumed with rage against Wren Hyde. He tries to keep her betrayal out of his thoughts by praying, doing extra chores, studying even harder and longer, but at every turn, Cameron's words seep into his heart and brain. How can women be so callous and just dump their spouse with no regret, no consideration for what the other person feels. As long as they are enjoying themselves.

One day Nick's classes are cancelled due to a heating problem in the building where his classes are held, and Nick thinks this is divine intervention. He decides this has happened so he could check out Wren Hyde and maybe, just maybe, he can put this young couple back together. It is early morning, so he checks out the van and travels to the grocery store. As he wanders the isles, he keeps looking at name tags.

He comes around one corner and hears someone say, "See you, Wren, what time do you start tomorrow?"

A voice answers, "I'll be here by 9:00 A.M."

Nick hurries to the front of the store just in time to see a petite red head dressed in her store uniform head out the door to a small compact car. He abandons his cart and follows. He gets to the lot just as she pulls away. He now knows what she looks like. He follows in the van, and as she pulls into an apartment complex where she parks her car, Nick follows at a distance. Once she enters the building, he notes the name and address of the complex, plus writes down her license number. Nick then goes back to the seminary where not only God lives but also the devil who right now has Nick's heart in his grasp.

The weekend is long; Nick has spent most of it on his knees in prayer. The plan forming in his head is not very priestly nor God-like, and he is trying everything he's been taught to expunge his thoughts.

When Tuesday evening comes, Nick signs out the van using the excuse he needs to stock-up on snacks and drinks for the youth group. Nick drives to Wren's apartment complex and checking to see if her car is there, which it is not. He drives around looking for gyms where Wren goes on Tuesday's nights, per her husband. After circling several blocks, he is amazed at how many gyms there are. Nick has a flash of sanity and wonders what am I doing? He asks God to clear his sinful thoughts, becomes deep in prayer as he heads back to the seminary where, as fate would have it, he sees Wren exit a gym squeezed into a row of stores at the mall. He checks the time, 8:00 P.M., and he follows her. On her way home, she stops at a bar and goes in. The parking lot is not well lighted, and she is parking quite a distance from the door. He now has the information he needs and he checks the streets names, the name of the bar and the gym. His mind is whirling. He knows he cannot always count on having the van, so he begins to map out the bus routes and the distant from St. Barromeo's to this bar. He arrives back at the seminary by 8:45 P.M.

As Nick parks the van and heads to his dormitory lost in thought, he nearly runs into Monsignor O'Reilly.

The Monsignor sees it is Nick and says, "Mr. Dougherty, what has you out this time of night?"

Nick is startled and stammers, "Oh, Monsignor, I didn't see you. I am headed to the Chapel to pray before I turn in."

"Did you go off in the van?" asked the Monsignor.

"Yes, I went for refreshments for the football team's practice."

"Um, this late in the evening?"

"Yes, Monsignor."

"Well, off you go then, and Mr. Dougherty, after your classes tomorrow, please come by my office."

"Certainly, sir," says Nick, "is anything wrong?"

"We will talk tomorrow."

Nick hurries along no longer headed to the chapel. His encounter with O'Reilly has unnerved him. As he hurries off to his room, all he sees is a bar named The Pot of Gold that has ice cold beer and live music on Fridays, and he lets his imagination run to Wren Hyde, who is in this Pot of Gold tempting innocent men and leading them away from their commitment to their wives and families. At that moment, he takes this as a sign from God that he must confront her and bring her back to the vows she made to her husband. Nick is pleased with his decision and spends a very restful night.

The next day, after classes and his duties as a seminarian, he walks across campus to Monsignor O'Reilly's office. Nick is curious but not too worried what Monsignor O'Reilly wants with him. He greets Mary Elizabeth at her desk and says he is to see the Monsignor.

Mary Elizabeth asks, "How are you, Nick? Pretty soon we will have snow. It is getting so cold. Do you like snow, Nick?"

"Yes, it brings some fond memories of playing with my siblings and having snow ball battles, and we would even build forts and snowmen."

"Oh, that sounds wonderful. Do you still engage in these activities when you go home to visit?"

Nick looks at Mary Elizabeth, and she immediately knows she asked the wrong question.

Nick's eyes go empty, the smile goes away, and he says, "Families are for the weak and needy. My strength comes from God. I don't need anchors that weigh me down."

As Mary Elizabeth goes to reply, the door opens and Monsignor O'Reilly asks Nick to step in. He notices how quiet his usually over-bubbly secretary has become and wonders what just happened.

"Is anything wrong, sir?" asks Nick.

"Well, not really wrong. Just need to have a good talk with you. I have noticed you have been disappearing weekends, and I know you go out at night and don't get back to the dorm until late. Now I know Father Eric and I agreed to give you some lee-way on your comings and goings considering what you went through, but I am becoming concerned. Should I be?"

"No, sir," says Nick. "I just really need as much alone time as I can get without alienating myself with my peers. We spend so much time together in class, at pray, at meals, even in the dorm. I just need quiet and don't want to insult my classmates by being standoffish. So I go for long walks, talk to God, pray, ask for guidance, and I do this best when I am alone."

"That's all well and good but, Nick, it won't be long now that you will accept the Sacrament of Holy Orders, and I want to be sure and I want you to be sure this is what you want. Becoming a priest is a life time commitment. I don't want to see any doubt in you."

Nick says, "Sir, I appreciate the freedom you have allowed me to have, and I wish to continue. It is cleansing, and I really need it. Please don't forbid me to leave campus at night, nor restrict my weekends with my friend Charlie. It is every bit as important to my frame of mind as prayers and my duties as a seminarian."

Monsignor O'Reilly replies, "I don't want to restrict you, Nick. As long as I continue to see you making progress in healing your emotional pain and your commitment to the priesthood grows stronger."

"I am doing my best," says Nick.

"Fine, then go and continue to grow. You will make a fine priest, Nick, and I have confidence in you that you will soon be demon free."

As Nick leaves the office and says goodbye to Mary Elizabeth, she feels she needs to tell the Monsignor her conversation with Nick. You don't have to be a psychiatrist to see that that young man has serious problems. As she heads into his office, the phone rings. She stops to answers it. By the time she is finishing dealing with her office duties, Nick is no longer on her mind.

Nick walks back to his dorm and is relieved to get rid of the fake smile he puts on for the Monsignor and that silly goose of a secretary with her stupid comments about family. What does she know? She is just another dream-killing female. Pretending to be all sweet and caring while she plunges the knife into your heart. I would love to plunge a knife into her heart. Pox on all women. Nick starts to laugh out loud, that is what he and Charlie used to say about girls when they were nine or ten. Pox on girls! Haven't thought about that in a long time. Wait until I tell Charlie. He will get a kick out of that...especially since it is true.

As the week slowly goes from one day to the next, Nick has formulated a plan. He is going to go see Wren Hyde and convince her to stay with her husband who loves her very much. Each night in his room, he writes and rewrites what he plans to say. Page after page of writings goes into the waste can. He jots down ideas and makes notes, and finally by Sunday, he is satisfied with his approach and plans to confront her this Tuesday.

At Sunday Mass, he prays and asks God to let him succeed as a sign that he was indeed meant to be a soldier in God's Army.

Nick feels excited. He has not had this feeling since he began college. All of a sudden, he feels spiritual and powerful. He really does have the power to change people's lives for the better. Nick starts to believe he does have the calling and is beginning to have a better understanding of the role in his life.

CHAPTER 23

Tuesday. Finally. Nick is upbeat all day. Even some of his peers comment to each other the change in Nick. His teachers think Nick has finally seen the light as they like to say.

Dinner is over at 6:00 P.M., and after he eats, Nick goes back to his room to rehearse his speech and to wait till 7:30 P.M. when he heads out on foot. He is wearing all black with a clerical collar. He wants Wren not to fear him and to see he is clergy. He takes the buses, does lot of walking, and gets to the Pot of Gold by 8:15 P.M. It took him longer than he expected and is worried he may have missed her.

Nick rounds the outside of the bar and heads to the parking lot. Not very many cars, and Wren's is easy to spot. She has parked haphazardly at an angle by the dumpster. Typical, Nick thinks. He figures Wren is only concerned about Wren. He chides himself for his thoughts. He must believe Wren is just misguided, and once he shows her the errors of her way, she will fall lovingly into the arms of her husband.

Nick has no intentions of going into the bar and waits patiently by the dumpster. As he looks around, he sees so much trash, broken bottles, used condoms, scrapes of food people toss at the dumpster but miss. Over across the street are businesses shuttered for the night. All of a sudden, Nick hears a couple arguing. The sound is coming from an apartment. All the goings-on of life all around him. It is going on 9:00 P.M., and Nick is getting cold. He begins to wonder if Wren may have gone off with someone and left her car. Suddenly, the back door to the parking lot opens and out comes Wren Hyde. But she is with a man.

He grabs her by the coat collar and kisses her with passion and says, "Come on, baby. You got me so hot. We can do a quickie back here, no one will see us."

Nick steps back farther behind the dumpster. He has no desire to see this man take Wren.

Then he hears, "No way, Harry, I am a lady. If you want any of this, take me to a fancy hotel. Then and only then will I even consider sharing these goodies. Now let me go. I have to go home."

Harry grunts, "Go on then. You're nothing but a teasing whore." With that the door slams shut, and Wren stumbles to her car.

As she approaches her car, Nick steps out of the shadows and Wren yells, "Jesus H. Christ, am I seeing things? Am I really seeing a priest, or am I so drunk that I am having hallucinations?"

"No, no," says Nick, "Mrs. Hyde, I didn't mean to scare you."

"How do you know my name? Stay back, or I'll scream."

"Mrs. Hyde, I am Father Wright, I know your husband Cameron."

"How do you know my husband?" says Wren with apprehension.

"I ran into him on the subway. We got talking, and he asked if I would talk to you and perhaps help save your marriage," says Nick.

Wren chuckles and says, "Do you always do your sermonizing in bar parking lots, Father?"

"No, Wren, may I call you Wren? My schedule is so conflicted with yours, I decided I'd catch up to you here. Your husband said sometimes you stop here after your workout."

Wren is still not too sure she trusts him and says, "You certainly seem to know a lot about me."

Wren is starting to relax and starts to show more signs of her inebriation after the initial shock of seeing a priest and stumbles closer to her car.

Nick says, "I am very cold, Wren, could we maybe sit in your car and run the heater? Would you talk to me? Your husband is so sad and upset. Not a good place to be when you could be sent off to war at any given moment."

"Sure," says Wren, "I guess I can trust a priest. Especially such a handsome one. I will talk to you about Cameron, but it won't do any good. I want to have fun, and Cam is just so stuffy."

Wren weaves her way to the car and unlocks the doors. She gets into the driver's seat, and after Nick looks around the parking lot and seeing it is deserted, slides into the passenger's side.

Nick is getting all his memorized thoughts together and starts asking Wren questions. He asks why she things her husband is stuffy, taking a lead from her.

Wren starts the car and gets the heater running.

"Well," says Wren, "he doesn't ever want to go out and have fun. Sits in front of the TV all night when he is home. I am pretty, don't you think so, Father Wright? I want to go places where men will admire me and Cam will realize how lucky he is to have me."

As the car gets warmer, Wren unbuttons her coat and turns to Nick and says, "Look at my breasts, Father, even if you are a priest, you have to think they are amazing."

"Please, Wren," says Nick, "stop that. I'm here to see if you and Cam can fix what is wrong between you."

Wren's in a zone now, thinking maybe she should have had that quickie with Harry. As she rubs her own breasts, her hand goes between her legs, and she starts stroking.

Nick almost yells at her to stop but tries to keep his voice calm, "Stop what you are doing," he says and pulls her hand away.

"Oh, what's the matter, pretty priest? You want some?" And she reaches over and grabs Nick's crotch. "Oh," says Wren, "maybe you're not so much a priest. Make love to me. I need it so bad."

Nick is in turmoil, this is not how this was to go. Good God, what was he thinking? This tramp is beyond salvation. He needs to leave but that quick, she saddles him and starts kissing him and he tries so hard to push her away.

He grabs her wrists, and as he pushes her to the side, he looks up and sees Mary Ellen.

"Mary Ellen," he cries, "yes, I want you, but you deceived me." He takes her by the throat and squeezes and squeezes until her face fades and slumped beside him is Mrs. Wren Hyde, wife of Cameron, and she is dead. The life squeezed out of her.

Instead of panicking or feeling frightened or remorseful, Nick calmly pushes her back behind the steering wheel. Reaches out carefully with a hand covered by a handkerchief and shuts off the engine. God has finally spoken to Nick, and he now knows his calling. It will be to rid this world of lying, cheating whores. Nick quietly removes himself from the car and wipes off the door handle.

Nick feels no need to check to see if anyone saw him, Nick knows he is invisible and will continue to be so as he goes about his calling. His heart is light, he has done good work tonight. He starts to whistle as he finds himself heading back to school.

Tonight, a serial killer has been born, and his name is Father Nicholas Dougherty. He has just answered his calling and all in the name of God.

Nick woke with a start. As he sat up, the thought of what he did last night engulfed him. A smile broke out on his face. He felt supreme, untouchable. He had to get to a newspaper to see if the authorities found that deceiving tramp yet. He hurried and showered, got dressed, and headed for Mass.

Where can I find a newspaper, thought Nick. I never bothered before, but surely the library or maybe someone left one in the cafeteria. Perhaps it didn't get into the paper yet.

When Mass was over, Nick joined his classmates on the walk to the cafeteria. He was chatty and animated. Clark and Chad, two of the seminarians, exchanged glances.

They shrugged their shoulders and Chad mouthed to Clark, "What's with Nick?" Clark just raised his eyebrows. When they got to the cafeteria, Nick searches for a paper but finds none. He enjoys the banter with his peers, and as they leave the dining area on the way to class, Nick spots a paper in the trash. He quickly grabs it and puts it with his books.

Clark says, "Goodness, Nick, I never saw you interested in the paper before? Did you win the lottery or something?"

Nick laughs and says, "No, I thought there might be an article about my friend, Charlie."

"Charlie," replies Clark. "Does he go here? I never heard you mention him."

"Not important, I'll check it out after class," says Nick.

When Nick has a chance, he scours the paper. Nothing, nothing. He assumes if she wasn't found until later, it wouldn't be in the paper yet. Nothing to do but wait.

This new euphoria Nick is experiencing is so strange, and when Nick joins his friends in the TV room, most are shocked to see him. Nick never fraternizes, but his peers are so happy to see him. Being such pious, compassionate young men, they are ready to embrace him after his solitary months. They all seem to think that whatever crises Nick was dealing with has come to an end.

While watching TV, the new comes on, and there it is...

The camera showed a car, parked in the lot of The Pot of Gold, and the news reporter was saying, *"A young woman was found strangled to death in her car early this morning when Keenan McShay opened his restaurant. He was taking some trash out to the dumpster when he spotted her car. The woman was identified as Mrs. Wren Hyde. According to McShay, who knew the woman, Mrs. Hyde was the loving wife of Cameron, who is in the service. He is overseas and was notified late today and is expected home sometime tomorrow. The couple have no children, but friends say they talked about it, and Mrs. Hyde was excited to expand her loving family. The investigation is ongoing."*

Nick just stares at the TV and feels this anger boiling inside him. Loving wife, loving wife he keeps hearing over and over in his mind. Nick has gone silent.

His friends notice a bit of a mood change, and Clark asks, "Is everything alright, Nick?"

Nick snaps out of it quickly and says, "Oh, yeah, all of a sudden I remembered I have homework I didn't complete." With that said, Nick leaves the room.

On the way back to his room, Nick is so angry that they are portraying her as a loving wife. That is not right, Nick thinks. Perhaps I should have done something to her to show the world what a Jezebel she was. Once Nick gets to his room, he gets onto the floor and pulls out from under the cot the box he brought from home. As he digs around in it, he knows what he is looking for.

"Ah, I found it," says Nick out loud. In his hand, he holds the make-up Mary Ellen left in his car.

Nick says again out loud, "Perfect tools to show the world what a fraud these women perpetrate against guileless men."

CHAPTER 24

PRESENT

Vinny got back into town and has time to check into his office, get home, shower, and change before he will pick-up Justice for a late dinner.

Mary Lou looks up as Vinny enters the office. "Hey, Vinny," she says, "did you find out anything up there in Williamsport?"

"Yes, Detective Morrison is a dick!"

"Whoa," says Mary Lou, "what happened?"

"It seems our victim was not held in high esteem," says Vinny. "Detective Morrison considered her trash, seems she was a prostitute working the truck stops. He has no intention of any further investigation. Mary Lou, he was truly an asshole, treated me like dirt on his shoe. We'll get no help from him. Listen, I just stopped in to see if there were any leads and to ask you to notify the team that I want everyone in the squad room by 9:00 A.M. tomorrow morning."

"Will do, Chief. I'll get right on it."

Vinny is looking forward to seeing Justice and takes care in getting ready. He leaves the house and drives to her house to find her ready and waiting. He cannot believe how lovely she is and wonders why she would want to date him. Although he has no intention of asking.

"Hi, Vinny," she says as she tip toes up to give him a kiss.

"Um," Vinny murmurs, "that's nice. Perhaps we should skip dinner."

Teasing, Justice says, "Not on your life, mister, but if you're good, really good, I just might invite you in for dessert."

"Sounds like I'd better be on my best behavior," laughs Vinny.

Vinny planned on taking Justice to a popular restaurant two towns over. They chat comfortably with each other, and before long, they are sitting at a table dining. Vinny feels so at ease, and when Justice asks about the case, he tells her the sad story of Ms. Caitlyn Moore Thomas and the sorry condition of her aunt. How she owns all that land and could be wealthy but prefers a life of solitude, so no one bullies her.

"Vinny," says Justice, "I remembered I was at a funeral about a year ago. A friend of mine, Amy, lost her brother."

"Oh, I am so sorry," says Vinny.

"Yes, thank you, but what I am getting at is they were very devout Catholics, and when I viewed David's body, there was what looked like a greasy spot on his forehead. I found it awful that the people at the funeral home didn't clean him up better. When we were at the reception afterwards, I just had to voice my feeling to Amy. Then Amy told me no, it was at the family's request. It was the oil a priest uses when performing the Sacrament of Extreme Unction. They wanted him buried with the Sacrament fresh to his face. It got me thinking the other day, didn't you tell me your Jane Doe has a strange substance on her face? Could it be the sacramental oil? Vinny, I don't mean to step on your toes here, but I see you went very quiet. If I am out of line, please tell me."

"Oh, my God, no," says Vinny. "Justice, you are a genius. With the priest sightings we are getting, it just might be exactly that, and don't you ever hesitate to share your ideas. I love that I can talk to you about my case."

Vinny is now more than ever anxious to get to that squad room tomorrow. He thinks they have finally got a break in the case. Although as anxious as he is, he still finds time for dessert.

Vinny arrives early and heads to his office. He places a call to Will at the coroner's office but has to leave a voice mail. He asks Will to call him as soon as possible.

Vinny is excited about this possibility, and perhaps the oily substance on the victim's forehead is nothing more than a dab of oil from a pizza parlor that uses a secret blend. But he really feels this could be a break in the case.

Vinny thinks of that woman laying on a cold slab and wonders who she is. He promises himself that he must make that the highest priority.

He goes into the crime room and starts the coffee pot, secretly wishing someone brings donuts. If not, perhaps he could send someone for them.

As he stands staring at this crime board, he keeps reflecting on the comment made by Ms. Moore's aunt. She told me that Caitlyn said she met a priest.

Could he have been her killer instead of her savior? He heard them before he saw them. All of his team were on time, even J.J., and hallelujah, Cully, his most inexperienced, was carrying a box of donuts. Vinny could have kissed him. Luke looked like something the cat dragged in. Much too much partying going on there. But as long as his works stays where it should, Vinny decided to stay mute. C.J. stretched his tall body and worked some kinks out of his back while the remainder of his team were getting coffee and donuts.

After they finally settled in and finished with their jabs at each other, Vinny said, "People, we may have finally gotten a break in the case."

The detectives all perked up, and Mickey says, "Yeah, boss, about time. What happened?"

"It was suggested to me that the oily substance found on our Jane Doe's forehead might be Holy Oil that Catholics use in blessing the sick and dead. I have a call into Will already and I am waiting for a call back. Do you see what this means? If it is indeed Holy Oil? Add that to the religious statue, the fact that the women were not sexually abused, and several of our witness' commented, off handedly, that their murdered victim had recently come in contact with a priest. Detectives, I think we have a serial killer who is a God dammed priest."

There is a lot of mumbling going on among the detective and Vinny asks them to be quiet.

"Ok," says Vinny, "let's put our heads together and see what we have. Does anyone have anything they can update us on?"

J.J., who has outdid herself today with a black blouse that has a ruffle collar, ruffles at the end of her sleeves, a handkerchief skirt that is cream in color, and seems to be made of silk. High old fashion shoes with a heel and black textured stockings. Her hair is piled on top of her head with old fashion hat pins holding it in place. Vinny tells her she is looking rather elegant today.

J.J. blushes and pushes away from her computer and says, "I've been trying to track down those statues. So far I have located three distribution centers that sell these statues in bulk. I have contacted each of them and the one company, T.M. Bortz, ships to the parishes' right here and in Philadelphia. The other companies ship all over the U.S. and has shipped a few orders to some of our local parishes. But Bortz seems to have the lead here in our area. Unfortunately, we don't know where our killer is from."

Just as Vinny is about to ask more questions, Mary Lou pops her head in and tells him Will is on line two. Vinny quickly answers and relates his suspicion to him. Will tells Vinny that is something he can test in his lab and will not have to wait for results and that he will get right on it.

Will asks Vinny, "Any idea yet who our Jane Doe is?"

Vinny replies, "Not yet" as he hangs up the phone.

"Chief," says Max, "yesterday I took a call from a Ms. Rosemary McDermott, she is the CEO of the Joyland Cosmetic Company. That's the company we traced the make-up to, remember?"

"Yes, go on, what about it?"

"She said this Rosemary McDermott, that after I called and made inquiries, she got to thinking and she told me back in 2012, one of her customer service reps got a call from a man wanting to know where he could buy those two very same items I asked about. Once she got thinking about it, she thought it strange that here we are asking about the very same colors and products. The reason it stuck in her head was that one of her members of the company talked about bringing back the shades and it was voted down. There had been a much-heated discussion about it at their meeting."

"Did they get a name or a number, would they still have it?" asks Vinny.

"Ms. McDermott said no name was given, and if I felt the information was important, she would try getting the phone records from that year and see if she could be of more assistance. I told her yes, I would be most grateful."

Vinny says, "It seems our killer must be running out of make-up. What a break that would be to get a phone number and maybe even a location from where the call originated. It would probably give us a county in which to start looking and how did he end up here or did he start here and has come full circle. Max, excellent work. Follow up and keep at it. Get that list of phone calls. I know it may be a lot of grunt work, but it just might pay off," says Vinny.

"Mickey, I want you to work with J.J., follow the leads on the little statues. The lead may go cold, but perhaps the orders fluctuate and one parish may have ordered more than necessary or more than usual. See what comes up. Stay within this company Bortz' territory for now."

As they are discussing these ideas among themselves, Will Strauss from the coroner's office comes hurriedly into the office by passing Marylou, who is trying to stop him, and he pushes past her.

"Out of my way," says Will, "I have information your detective may find interesting."

Marylou is not one to mince words and says, "Listen, Dr. Strauss, you may 'think' you're some little god from your hellhole of a morgue, but around here we follow protocol. I'll let Chief Miller know you are here."

Will is stopped in his tracks. To think someone low on the totem pole dare talk to him like that, and before he can come back with a stinging remark, Marylou is telling him the chief will now see him.

Will goes huffing and puffing into the crime room ready to unleash his disdain for Marylou but stops short when all eyes are on him. He mumbles under his breath about not sinking to the level of these peons and proceeds with his temper in check.

"Well, Vinny," says Will, "now that I am permitted into this inner-sanctum by your devil dog, perhaps I have some good news."

"Have you tested the substance on our Jane Doe?" asks Vinny.

"Yes," replies Will, "and you were right. It is definitely the sacred oil used in that barbaric ritual by Catholic priests."

"That's good news, Will, but why barbaric?" asks Vinny.

"Just another misguided rule to let Catholics think all is forgiven, and off to heaven they go. Just misleading as penance for their confessed sins."

"Thank you for your commentary on Catholic practice," says Vinny. "We can do without your opinions. We just want facts. Also, tell me what you found out about the puncture wound on our girl's neck?"

Will looks around the room and is amazed to think this straggly group of people could have one intelligent thought among them, as he says to Vinny, (while being careful not to touch anything for fear of being contaminated by their ignorance,) "The puncture wound was caused by nothing more than a branch. I removed tiny particles of wood. Seems that perhaps as she was being dumped and posed, she got stuck with a branch or some sharp bush that caused it. No, your Jane Doe died of nothing more glamorous than affixation. She was strangled, pure and simple, by someone with a lot of anger and strength. And now if I can get passed your devil dog at the entrance of your liar, I have a luncheon engagement." Will leaves with a dramatic flair, and it seems everyone in the room starts to breathe again.

"Ok," Vinny says, "we now have more to go on. Cully, I know you devoured the information on those autopsies reports of our other victims, but I want you to go over them again. Also, the police files on all the dead women. Use a fine-tooth comb. Anything that strikes you as unusual, flag me immediately. C.J., you and Luke work the priest angle. Contact the diocese and get lists of visiting priests. See if any name keeps popping up. Let's get going, we seem to have gathered some really good clues and information. Good work, really good work," says an optimistic Chief of Police.

The team gathers their belongings and begin their tasks.

CHAPTER 25

EARLY SPRING, 2003

Mark pulls into his driveway, turns off the ignition of his car, and just sits quietly for a while. For a few years now, he has dreaded coming home to a wife who is sad and burdened by the feelings of failure in raising his precious first born. It seems nothing can take that sorrow from her eyes. Oh, there has been lots of good months and years, but always just under the surface lies the blame. Mark doesn't feel this way. He believes Nick is just immature, will grow out of this despair and loathing toward women. Surely, if the priesthood can't do it, then nothing can.

With a heavy heart, he heads for his front door, and just as he is about to reach for the knob, the door is thrown wide and their stands Grace, tears in her eyes, waving a letter. Mark's heart stops, and for that split second, he is terrorized. What now?

"Mark, oh, Mark, look! We got a letter from Nick. From Nick," shouts Grace as she waves it in front of Mark's face. "It's very short but look, read it, he wants to know if he can come home for Easter. My baby, he wants to see us. Do you think he has worked out his problems with us? Rather with me? His letter sounds so upbeat, no accusations, he just wants to be with family. Oh, Mark, we can tell him of Alice's upcoming marriage and Patrick's choice of college. Catherine will finally see and get to know a brother she only hears us talk about. Tristan remembers Nick, but Catherine only has our memories. I am so excited."

As Mark reads Nick's letter, he sees no underlining animosity. He seems to truly want to fix what's broken. He says although he wants to see his family, he will be staying at the rectory with Father Eric. Mark thinks that is a great idea. It has been a long time since he has seen his mother. Perhaps this cloud of doom that has hovered over their lives will finally be lifted.

Meanwhile Nick is wondering if his parents got his letter yet and if he will be accepted back into the fold by his parents and siblings. He has treated them shabbily, but now that he has a clear vision of the work God has chosen for him, a great burden has just poof, disappeared. Of course, he will not share his path that God has shown him, that is just between him and his Savior. But he will do his best to make amends to his family. He begins thinking of his sister, Alice. She must be twenty-one by now. The last he heard she was in Paris. Patrick will be graduating high school. Oh, how much I have missed. I really need to see Charlie, too. I have even been negligent with my best friend.

As soon as time allowed, Nick places a call to Charlie.

Charlie was thrilled to hear from Nick. "So how goes it, old friend?" says Charlie.

"Going really well, Charlie, I have had a burden lifted from my shoulders and I am now following a clear path. I have even contacted my parents. I want to spend Easter with them."

"Nick, Nick, Nick, so good to hear that. What happened to you that you have finally seen the light?" asks Charlie.

"Lots of prayer and meditation, lies, Nick. I was wondering if you could get free next weekend. We could get together up at your cabin at least one more time before I take my vows."

"Nick, old buddy, I would love that. Listen, let me see if I can shift things around here at home and at the hospital. I am still only a lowly intern, but I will let you know, ok?"

"Sounds great. Charlie. I will wait to hear from you," says Nick and hangs up the phone.

Nick is in a hurry. He awakes early, realizing what a busy day he has ahead of him. Mass, breakfast, classes, an appointment with his psychiatrist, then a dry run on conducting Confessions, plus spring means baseball. A new batch of boys will be eagerly looking forward to signing up to play. That means he must get the equipment out of storage and prepare the van. And most of all, gather up a dozen or two of his small Virgin Mary statues to give to the boys as a reminder of what a good woman represents. He must remember to order more. Nick also has another use for his statues, but if he thinks about it too long, he gets lost in the sheer pleasure of what he plans to do. It didn't take long to come up with a plan after he punished Mrs. Hyde. He will do better next time to show the world evil, conniving women. Perhaps I will put that plan to work this Friday night before my trip to Charlie's cabin. I will go up to the cabin, even if Charlie can't make it. I will get there late, but no harm in that.

Life for Nick has stabilized. He is comfortable with his seminary duties and extra volunteer work with the kids from foster care. One day as he is driving over to the school for practice, he hears something rolling in the back of the van. Concerned something came loose and might cause damage, he pulls over and goes to the back to check. As he is lifting baseball equipment and snacks looking for the culprit, he discovers one of the arrows that he and Charlie use to practice target shooting at the cabin. Nick sits on the rear bumper of the van holding the arrow, being careful not to hurt himself with the still, very sharp point and is transfixed at how God works. Here, by some miracle, is God showing him what the final act must be to show the world how hearts are broken. An arrow through the heart with a note attached to show why this woman has been silenced. He offers a prayer to God to thank Him for showing him the way and is confident he will know what message to attach to the arrow.

Friday finally comes and Nick has heard from Charlie. He will visit Nick Saturday morning but will have to get back to the hospital by noon on Sunday.

Friday afternoon Nick is preparing himself for his second kill. He has his gym bag with the make-up and arrow with his message already attached. His plan is to stop at some rather seedy bar along the way to the cabin and see if he can identify, lure, and kill an unworthy wife.

It is dark when he sets out, going on 7:30 P.M. It doesn't take him long to come across the perfect dive. Nick is dressed casually, jeans, a gray wool turtle neck sweater and a jacket. He is a very handsome young man and gives off the air of having money. Nick knows faithless wives love men with money. The bar is called The Quickie. A double entendre, meaning come in for quick drink and a quick fuck. A perfect place for Nick to troll.

As he enters the bar, he takes in the smells of beer, sweat, and cheap bar food. The Quickie is oddly shaped. There is a small horseshoe-sized bar, a few tables randomly placed as though the patrons can put the tables wherever they please. Things look grimy and dirty. A woman, old and tired-looking, is behind the bar washing glasses while the bartender, just as old and tired-looking, is reading a newspaper. Nick assumes they are married and the owners of the bar. They are as seedy as the pub. Nick is so disappointed. Sitting at the bar are only eight people, all men, and all but two are sitting by themselves. Nick grabs a bar stool and the bartender asks him what he is having.

"Just a beer, whatever is on tap," says Nick.

Nick nurses his beer for over a half hour and not one woman makes an appearance. He slaps down a ten and leaves.

He gets into his van and sits there thinking perhaps he is being too anxious. Mrs. Hyde was a spur of the moment, dropped in his lap, meant to be. I am being arrogant, and God will do the choosing. Nick feels satisfied with this thinking and starts the van.

Nick does not stop at any more bars and pulls into the driveway of the cabin around 10:30 P.M. After he opens up, gets the heat on, and puts away the groceries he brought, he goes out to the shed where Charlie keeps the archery supplies. Nick needs more arrows. He only has a flashlight with him, but he manages to find some old arrows that he and Charlie no longer use. He scoops them up; he has found at least six in the dark shed and takes them to the van. He wraps them in an old towel and puts them into the gym bag, along with the other arrow. He goes back into the cabin, undresses, and goes to bed.

Sometime around 5:00 A.M., Nick is awakened by some noises and gets up to investigate. As he sneaks down the steps he is startled to see a shadow out by the kitchen counter.

Nick shouts, "Who's there? I have a gun, identify yourself."

There is a burst of laughter and Charlie says, "Nick, you old fake, I know you don't have any gun."

Nick is so relieved and continues down the stairs to greet his one and only true friend. Nick is so happy to see Charlie. He goes and gets a pot of coffee brewing and helps Charlie get his stuff into his room.

Charlie is really surprised that he can actually see and feel a change in his friend.

Charlie says, "So, Nick, have you heard back from your parents about Easter?"

"Yes," says Nick, "they are really excited and seem genuinely happy that I made the gesture towards healing our differences."

Charlie comments, "I never did understand why you shut them out. Want to tell me?"

"After Mary Ellen, God, I hate even saying her name, betrayed me like she did, I guess I became unbalanced. I believed all women are like that, even my mother. I tried remembering insults she may have inflicted on my father. I blew everything out of proportion. Small comments that I guess husbands and wives say to each other are done so without malice. I really needed to cleanse my mind and heart. So it won't be long now that I will be entering the place I was always meant to be."

Charlie is happy for Nick and asks him, "So what happened that has undid your hate?"

"I cannot tell you, Charlie, but believe me when I say I have been called to perform a much needed deed and I have already begun," smiles Nick as he remembers the life going out of Wren Hyde's body.

Charlie looks at Nick and thinks, I believe, he is unstable but perhaps I am reading too much into this affect is he showing.

Charlie pushes his thoughts aside and says, "Ok, Nicholas Dougherty, soon to be Father Dougherty, I, too, have some wonderful news. Seeing as you have made the first move to seeing your family, I feel confident in telling and asking you something so very important."

"What, Charlie?" says Nick.

"Are you ready for this? Maybe you should sit down."

"I am sitting, Charlie, out with it."

"Here goes…I am getting married."

"MARRIED," shouts Nick.

"Yes," Charlie says cautiously.

"To whom, when, where did you meet her?" says Nick

"Nick, I am going to marry your sister, Alice, and I want you to be my best man. Will you?"

Nick's face goes ashen, "My sister," he whispers. "How did that come about?"

"I don't know, Nick, but I do know there has always been such a sexual tension between us ever since high school. Oh, I was jerk in high school, laid every girl that said yes, but Alice, oh, Alice. She wouldn't even look at me. Then when you took off and became cloistered, Alice and I started writing to each other. At first, about you, then it morphed into us. I think I always loved her, and when she got back from Paris, we met and that's all she wrote. Please, Nick, be happy for us."

Nick's emotions were in turmoil. His best friend and a sister he loved dearly, getting married.

Nick looks at Charlie, who looks like maybe he shouldn't have told when Nick says, "It isn't every day when your best friend becomes your brother. I would be honored to be your best man. But, Charlie, just so you know, being a priest, I will not have strippers at your bachelor party."

Charlie breaks into a huge smile, comes around the counter, and hugs his new brother.

CHAPTER 26

Grace is in the laundry room folding wash. She wonders why with two children gone from the nest, she still has so much laundry. As she folds a shirt of Patrick's she realizes it is one of Nick's old shirts. Grace is excited and scared, all in one. With Palm Sunday just this past weekend, that means Nick will be coming home any day now. What will I say to him? I never did know why all of a sudden I was banned from his life, not just me but all of us. Father Eric says he needed space. Space from his family.

Doesn't want pity Father says, or those looks that silently say, "See, I told you so."

Grace shakes off her doubts and finishes up with the wash. She needs to gather up Catherine and head to the store. Grace has a list of all Nick's favorite foods and also what she needs for Easter Sunday dinner. It is going to be a houseful, and Grace is in her glory. Alice is bringing Charlie, and Patrick is also bringing his girlfriend of the moment. Grace is relieved to know that Charlie told Nick about the engagement. Alice says he was thrilled.

It is early afternoon on Wednesday. Grace and Catherine are at the grocery store when Nick rings the doorbell of his old house. It feels strange not to just go bursting in through the front door like he did when he was in school. But he isn't sure that he should just walk in. The door opens, and there stands Tristan.

"Yes, can I help....Oh, Nick," yells Tristan and flings himself into Nick's arms.

"Wow, buddy," says Nick, "now that was a welcome."

They stand back from each other and Nick says, "Tristan, you have grown so much and you look so much like Mom. Is she here?"

"No, but she should soon be home. She went grocery shopping and the size of the list she is probably buying out the store. Come in, come in."

Nick enters his home, and as he looks around, he notices some changes. New furniture, family photos with him, but one thing is constant. The smells. It still smells like home.

Nick follows Tristan and is sad in a way at having missed out on seeing his brother grow up.

'Why aren't you in school?" asks Nick.

"Something to do with too many snow days not being used, so they tacked it on to the Easter holiday. Say, Nick, I hear you know about Alice and Charlie. Isn't it great?"

"Yes, T., it is. I just hope she stays true to him. He's a good guy. Whatever happened to Austin? I thought she would end up with him. He sure did love her. Did she dump him?" His eyes cloud over, and Tristan notices a change in Nick. All of a sudden, he seems angry, and then that quick, it was gone.

"No," says Tristan, "Austin was killed in a freak car accident. He goes off to war only to be killed by a car. Marcelene and the family were never the same. They moved about a year later."

"Good God, I never knew," says Nick.

"Yeah, there's a lot of things you missed, Nick," says Tristan with a bit of sarcasm, "but I am so glad to see you. You can have your old room back. Patrick can bunk with me."

"Slow down, brother. First of all, I am staying at the Rectory with Father Eric, and second of all, I must return to school by Monday. I have a lot of cramming to do and rituals to go through if I am to take my vows at Christmas. I worked so hard and don't want risk not getting my reward."

As Nick and Tristan are still catching up, in runs the prettiest little girl Nick has ever seen. Bouncing curls of pure gold with red highlights, the brightest green eyes, and so full of energy.

She runs into the kitchen and stops dead at seeing a stranger sitting with T. She stopped so quickly, Grace near trips over her.

"Catherine, what's the matter with you, stopping like that," says Grace a bit harshly, then she, too, stops abruptly and looks over to her number one son sitting at the counter as though he never left. "Nicholas," she barely breathes his name. With that Nick gets up and comes over to hug his mother.

Grace breaks down in tears and just holds on tight. Her thoughts are loving and nurturing, his thoughts are, perfume. Anything to entice a man. One of women's tools.

Nick gets to see a lot of his family during his visit. He got caught up on all the goings on. He is amazed at how beautiful Alice turned out and how happy she makes Charlie. Mark was in his glory when all his boys rallied around and got a game of hoops going in the driveway. Then, as soon as they were a family again, it was over. Nick had to return to school. He promised to stay in touch, and it was agreed they would all attend his ordination in December. And just like that, he was gone. And as he intended, his family is convinced they have their Nicholas back. Little did they know. It is not the first time Nick takes advantage of his role as a priest to get over on people. He is getting very good at it.

CHAPTER 27

The following months, Nick devotes himself to his studies. His plan is to have his training and schooling finished, so he can be ordained this coming Christmas.

As winter turns to spring and the trees begin getting that green sheen, which give the earth a soft, pleasant feel, Nick's peers seem to enjoy the changing season, and in keeping with his charade, he, too, speaks of the earth's renewal. Only his private thoughts go to that harlot Mary Ellen and the bastard child she gave birth to and praying she is miserable and not coping well as a single mother. The seed planted in her is tainted with the poison of deception.

Nick gets back to his room after his classes on Friday afternoon, and there is a written message from Monsignor O'Reilly with a day and time listed to meet with him. Nick knows this is a formality as all the Seminarians have received such a notice. His appointed time is not until the beginning of June. It seems he will have time for one more trip to the mountains to meet his best friend Charlie. He makes a mental note to contact Charlie and see when they can get together.

Nick sits on the edge of his bed and allows himself the memory of choking the life out of Wren Hyde. He does this often, and it fills him with such joy to think God has chosen him, Nicholas Doughery, for this spiritual, powerful calling, so he can continue God's work of cleansing mankind. As he drifts deeper into himself, he is feeling his hands go around her neck, he sees in her eyes that those big breast don't matter much now. He senses the smells coming off her as fear takes over the satanic desires she tried to entice him with. He sees in his mind her black soul and condemns her to hell. All of a sudden, he tumbles to the floor where he loses the memories and is jolted back to reality.

As he lays there on the floor, his breathing becomes steady, and as he looks down his body, he realizes he has the biggest hard-on he has ever had. He quickly gets onto his bed and takes advantage of this throbbing appendix that seems to be the root of all man's ills. Nick pleasures himself, and when he is finished, he falls asleep. Content and satisfied.

The next day, he marvels at how good he feels. It is Saturday, and after Mass, he returns to his room and calls Charlie. He gets voice mail and leaves a message. Nick has some studying to do and laundry, so goes about his tasks. Later in the afternoon, he sees some of his classmates out on the grounds playing a game of football. Nick decides to join them.

It is three days before Charlie gets back to Nick, and unfortunately Charlie cannot get away but encourages Nick to use the cabin if he wants. Nick is disappointed but declines the offer, stating he should use that free time to once again visit his family. Charlie is suspicious of Nick's willingness to visit his family because if anyone knows the depth of Nick's pain, it is Charlie.

Charlie says, "Well, Nick, how is it really going?"

"What do you mean, 'really' going?" says Nick.

"You seem different."

"In what way?" asks Nick rather curtly.

"Hey, man, don't get mad, I'm just sensing a change in you. After all I am your best friend and I know you," says Charlie.

Nick backs off and says, "Sorry, Charlie, it's just that I finally found my calling. God showed me the way, but now it seems He has forgotten me again and hasn't wanted to lead me to another sinner."

"What did God show you, Nick?"

Nick knows he cannot share with Charlie this special gift God gave him of being able to zero in on these wayward women, so he says, "He showed me evil and how to deal with it."

"That sounds ominous, Nick. So you think you can see evil?"

"Oh, yes," says Nick. "Now let's talk about something else. How's that sister of mine? Wedding plans going well?"

"Alice is driving me crazy but crazy good. I love her so much. Are you still going to marry us?"

"Sure will," says Nick.

They chat on for a while longer, then say goodbye.

When Charlie hangs up, he has a bad feeling. Something is just not right with Nick. He gets busy wrapped up in his own life and soon forgets his concern for his friend.

June arrives, and the schedule at the Seminary does not let up. Classes and training are still being held in anticipation of a New Year ordination of several young men, including Nick.

As Nick crosses the campus on his way to his meeting with the Monsignor, he is excited. He is anxious to see what plan the Monsignor has for him for these few more months of schooling and training.

He enters the office expecting to see Monsignor's secretary, Mary Elizabeth. Instead sitting in her chair is an attractive woman. She appears to be mid-thirties. Her hair is done in braids wrapped around her head. She has diamond earrings and is wearing a wedding band. She is dressed very modest but very colorful.

"Oh," says Nick, "I am sorry to act surprised, but where is Mary Elizabeth?"

The young woman stands, holds out a tiny hand, and says, "Hello, I assume you're the soon to be Father Dougherty. I am Tansie. I am filling in for Mary Elizabeth temporarily while she is on vacation. Ireland I believe the Monsignor mentioned."

Tansie sits back down, picks up the phone, and notifies the Monsignor that his appointment has arrived.

As Nick enters the Monsignor's office, he notices a white board had been set up off to the right of the Monsignor's desk. At a glance, he sees names of classmates and destinations.

"Come, come sit, Nicolas, and don't look so apprehensive. I am not about to send you off to kill anyone, ha-ha," laughs Monsignor O'Reilly.

Nick feels himself turn white and grabs a chair before he faints. He thinks, does he know, does this man know God's plan for me?

"Nicholas," Monsignor says, "what is the matter? You look like you are about to faint. Are you surprised that a stuffy, old Monsignor can have a sense of humor?"

Nick sputters a no while shaking his head. "Just didn't expect that, I guess," says Nick.

"Now that your heart is beating again, let's get down to why you are here. I am sure you are aware that at this point in your calling it is customary to send you to one of our parishes to train under the guidance of a seasoned priest. Now you have no say in this matter, but with much prayer and many conversations with Father Eric, I have decided to send you to the Parish of St. Anthony. St. Anthony's is down by the Navy Ship Yard. St. Anthony's priests deal with many service men. It is a unique parish. Some of these men and women have done tours and have settled here when they came home. A lot of their conflicts are of a different nature than you would find at let's say St. Jerome. I think you would be a great asset at this parish and it should expose you to another side of humanity with which you have no understanding. Father Wilber Jones is the Pastor and it will be to him that you report. Alright, time for questions."

Nick sits up in his chair while looking at the white board and says, "Is that an assignment board? Is that the name and place my classmates are going?"

"Yes," says the Monsignor, "and I shall now add your name and the name of the Parish."

"When do I report to Father Jones?" asks Nick.

"Right after Labor Day," replies the Monsignor.

"How will I get there?" asks Nick, "Will I still have use of the van?"

"No, we will need the van, but we have a special funding where we lease vehicles for just this purpose. Come September 1st, you will be able to choose a suitable vehicle for your journey. Now that will be all for today. Our temporary secretary, Tansie, will give you a folder on your way out with all the necessary information you will need. I will be talking to you again in late August to see if all is going as planned. I am very proud of you, Nicholas, you have come a long way since you began, and I can see that you are going to be very special in God's eyes. He will lead you to an amazing vocation. Now off you go. Enjoy these wonderful summer days."

With the summer months passing by, Nick no longer is involved in helping the sports program over at St. Elizabeth's. His heavy class schedule and preparations for his ordination is consuming his time. After a rigorous three-hour class in Philosophy, Nick feels he needs to clear his head. He still has the van and decided to visit Father Carney over at St. Elizabeth's. He wants to say thanks for mentoring him while he worked with the youth sports program. He signs out the van, and on his drive, he hears the rattling of his arrows. He had forgotten them. He sits up in the driver seat as a cold sweat breaks out.

How could he be so thoughtless, he thinks. I need those arrows to fulfill God's plan. He pulls into a parking lot of a big Box Store and just sits there for about fifteen minutes. Out loud, Nick starts talking to himself.

"Stupid, stupid, stupid," he berates himself and pounds on the steering wheel. "I must find a place for my arrows, God led me to them and I ignored Him. How can I be worthy of this vocation when I can't keep the simplest item in check?" Nick is flailing his arms and tearing at his hair and face. Almost screaming now, "I am not worthy, God!" Nick is getting very loud, and soon a passerby stops and stares.

"How's it going there, buddy?" the stranger yells, not wanting to get to close.

Nick realizes he has drawn attention to himself and says to the stranger, "Oh, I'm ok, just had some bad news. I'll be alright. Thanks for asking."

The stranger notices the wild look in Nick's eyes and how worked up he is, hair a mess from pulling at it, and he saw that this young man is wearing a clerical collar and the van had a I.D. hook identifying it as belonging to St. Borromeo.

The stranger says, "Ok then, are you sure I can't help?"

"No," says Nick, "thanks for your concern," and drives off.

This stranger, a young man coming from his job as a cashier at one of the mall stores, says to himself, "Wow, wait till I tell my friends about this wacked out priest. He looked insane."

Many years later when a story breaks about a priest serial killer, this young man will recall his encounter with a priest he thought was a whack job.

Now Nick is no longer in the mood to visit Father Carney. He needs to get himself calm and he continues to drive and think, of course, such a simple solution.

Nick says out loud but much more calmly, "I will just wrap them in a towel and keep them in the bottom of my gym bag." And with such clarity, he knows not only the arrows but his small statues of the Virgin Mary and that whore's make-up will fit in his gym bag, too. Finally, Nick sees he had to have this failing, so God could put him back on track. "I was getting too arrogant," says Nick. But this time he says it to himself, not out loud.

Nick continues driving and finds himself in the Vicinity of St. Anthony's.

"This is where I will intern," says Nick, again out loud. "It seems I have more conversations with myself," chuckles Nick, "I will have to keep that in check. Don't want people to think I've lost my marbles. Ha-ha."

On the drive back to his dormitory, Nick feels content. He has learned some things today, and one big thing is he must ready his gym bag. Nick is sure God is waiting for him to be better prepared before sending him another harlot.

CHAPTER 28

The summer months pass by uneventful. Nick keeps his guard up around his teachers and peers, but when he is in the seclusion of his room, he finds his anger and frustration take hold and he rants against God for giving him this cooling off period. Nick lays naked and prostrates himself on the cold floor while he pricks himself all over with sharp needles, even trying to inflict pain on his manhood. He believes this is the cruelest joke that God uses to punish him. His fantasies often brings him to a sexual climax, and he despises himself for this.

He calls out to God that he is ready to fulfill his mission. He curses God and sometimes even beseeches the devil to help him find these sinners.

His classmates often hear his muffled cries, and even though they cannot hear his words, they know he has a crisis not to be solved, and they avoid the passing of his door whenever they know he is in his room.

Sometime in August, Nick asks the Monsignor if he may have permission for a visit to St. Anthony's to see where he will be interning (He has not mentioned to the Monsignor that he had already been there once). The Monsignor gives him permission but only to tour the streets and location. Nick has strict orders not to engage in any meetings or visits. It is important he goes to meet Father Jones as an absolute stranger come September. There must be no preconceived opinions on either part. Nick certainly agrees as he is not really interested in meeting yet another priest who has not been chosen by God for great things, such as himself.

Nick chooses the second to the last Saturday in August and heads over to the garage to sign out a car. As he approaches the office, he sees that Tim

Weatherly is on duty. Tim is in his late 60's and has been a permanent fixture at St. Borromeo's for over thirty years. He is dressed in his trade mark outfit. His slacks are black and holds a fine crease. When one looks close, you could say they are "priest" slacks. Tim always wears a white shirt with a string tie. His coloring is like waxed paper and the few hairs on his head are snow white. It is said that years ago, Tim came to study for the priesthood all the way from Kentucky. Unfortunately, Tim found the bottle and loose women too much of a distraction and one night tried to hang himself. Fortunately, one of the seminarians found him before he could do too much harm and the staff and diocese put him rehab. When he was released, he begged the officials to let him stay on in some capacity. So led to the occupation of Tim Weatherly.

"Howdy there, young fella," drawls Tim. "What can I do fer ya?"

Nick is fond of Tim, after all, they have a lot in common because of loose women, and he engages in one of his few conversations with others.

Nick says, "Tim, old man, how's things going?"

"Don't old man me," laughs Tim as he bobs back and forth feigning a boxing stance. "I can still mess up that purdy face of yours anytime I want, and don't you forget it.

"Oh, no, sir," says Nick laughing and doing a bounce on his toes, too.

Nick stops and looks at the fleet of cars and says, "Tim, I need a vehicle for the day. How about a van or an SUV?"

"Oh, looky here, boy, I got a beauty in bay number four. A large SUV, washed, gassed, and ready to taken for a ride."

"That sounds perfect," says Nick. "Will you get me the keys?"

As Tim brings the keys to Nick, he says, "Say there, Cowpoke, what's in the gym bag? Most of youse youngens carry nothing more than a bottle of water. You planning on being out overnight? Gotta log that in, you know?"

"No," says Nick. "Just need the car for the day. As for the gym bag, that's my sinner detector."

"Sinner detector, what a crazy idea you young men come up with. I think all this God stuff gets into your brains far too deep and turns them into mush."

Nick laughs, takes the keys, and says, "You could be right on the money with that statement, Tim. See you sometime later."

Tim says, "You know what to do and where to leave the keys if you come back by the time I'm gone. Have a fun day."

Nick gets into the SUV and backs out of the garage. His sinner detector is placed directly behind him on the floor. Nick is excited.

He has prayed and suffered enough to have won God's guidance to find another deceitful woman posing as a loving, nurturing liar. He feels his temperature rise just thinking of the pleasure and self-importance he felt as he rid the world of Wren Hyde. Now he is better prepared, and he is certain today is the day he will start in earnest. Today will be the day that everyone will know the name of the sinner and why she had to die. Deceitful women everywhere is on notice.

CHAPTER 29

Nick begins to relax and is enjoying this leisure drive. He is even singing along with the radio. So sure that today he will be rewarded by God to do what he is meant to do. The sun is shining, the sky is blue, and Nick believes if he looks long and hard, he will see the face of God in the clouds.

Nick has already done a dry run to St. Anthony's, so he takes a route which will lead him into the Lancaster area with its wide open spaces and the Amish region.

"Now there," say Nick aloud, "are God fearing, pure, and holy people," as he is driving along some of the back roads having left the congested main roads for a more delightful drive. He spots a sign telling him of a road side stand and a small eatery up ahead. This pleases Nick, for he sees this also as a sign from God that he needs to fortify himself with nourishment. He is going to have a job to do. Nick can hardly contain himself. In his mind, he sees his sinner detector glowing bright, and his tools of slaying evil jumping for joy. It is a sign.

Up ahead he sees the eatery and pulls in. What a rustic, attractive way station out here all by itself, Nick thinks. The pretty Amish girls are working at the fruit stand. A young family emerges from the store. A little boy, around four, licking an ice cream cone as big as he is. They head over to a picnic table and sit down. The father and mother are chatting and holding hands.

That could have been me, thinks Nick, and just as quickly, he washes the thought from his mind.

Seated two picnic tables over, closer to where Nick is parked, is a young man in uniform and a young woman. Nick zones in on them and can hear some of their conversation.

The woman is crying, and says, "But, Gabe, I don't want a baby."

"Marissa, you can't mean that," says the young man. "Remember the joy we felt when you were pregnant before and how sad and heartbroken we were when you lost the baby? This is our second chance. Marissa, please don't do this."

"Gabriel," says Marisa, "how am I to raise a baby when you don't even know if you will be in the states? I don't want to have to raise a baby by myself."

"You won't be by yourself. There's my mom and both my sisters. They'll be glad to help. You can even stay with my mom."

"Does she know I'm pregnant? Gabriel, does she know?" panic in her voice.

"No, not yet," says a dejected man.

Nick sees another man being manipulated by a woman. They seem to have all the power, thinks Nick. Is this where my sinner detector has led me, wonders Nick.

Gabriel gets off the bench just as another car pulls up and a man in uniform jumps out the passenger side.

The two men greet each other, and Gabriel calls out, "Come on, Marissa, I'll drop you off at home."

"No, I don't want to go with you. I'll walk."

"Don't be like that," say the man. "It's a long walk."

"I don't care. I have nothing else to do."

The other soldier looks at his watch and says something to Gabe. Gabe looks wistfully at his wife, gets into his car, and the two men drive off in the opposite direction.

"Now what do you think of that?" says Nick softly to himself. "A mother not wanting her child. Denying the father of an heir. I think God has chosen my next sinner."

The woman sits there for a while and is trying to get herself together.

Nick decides he needs some refreshments, so he gets out and goes into the little store. He buys a cold drink and some chips, as well as a sandwich. He goes and sits at the picnic table this Marissa lady has just left.

As Nick fortifies himself for the task ahead, he watches the young woman head on down the road.

About a half hour later, Nick heads out. He has no doubts that he will find her, for God has plucked this sinner out of thin air to lay her in Nick's path of righteousness.

He drives for perhaps ten minutes on a dusty, unpaved side road and spots her in the distance. He reaches into the glove box and takes out his clerical collar and puts it on. As he approaches her, he slows down and stops a few feet ahead of her.

Marissa is cautious; perhaps, she thinks, this walking home to spite her husband was not a good idea. She crosses to the other side as a man steps out of the SUV. She sees he is wearing a collar. Could this be a priest? Marissa relaxes some when the man calls out to her.

"Miss, may I offer you a ride? My name is Father Wright. I saw you arguing with a man back at the food stand. Perhaps I could help. I see you've been crying."

Marissa is still not sure if she trusts this man but hell, a priest, and if you can't trust a priest, who can you trust? So she crosses back across the road and extends her hand.

"Hi, I'm Marissa."

Nick suggests they get into the air-conditioned SUV and she can tell him what's wrong.

As she climbs in, she burst into tears. "Oh, father, you can't believe what a mess I've made of my life."

"Oh, yes, young lady," says Nick, "be assured that I am all too aware what women can do. Now tell me."

Marissa blurts out, "I'm pregnant and need an abortion. I told Gabe, that's my husband, that I don't want a baby, but that's not true. You see, Father, it's not his baby."

"Oh, Marissa, you can still have the child. It could be his, couldn't it?"

"No, father, it's not, and as soon as I would give birth, he'd know it. You see, I had an affair with a co-worker. All the time Gabe was away. Father, my lover is black."

"Dear, dear, dear," says Nick. "Don't you think your husband would forgive you?"

"No, you see, I already betrayed him before. I told him I was pregnant and he had to marry me. But I wasn't. I just wanted him so badly, I tricked him. Then pretended to have a miscarriage."

"Well, young lady, you've been busy. Are you at all sorry for all these deceptions? What an awful way to send off your husband. I noticed he is in the service."

With this statement, Marissa bursts into tears yet again, and as Nick reaches for her, she thinks he is about to comfort her, only his arms do not entwine her, but his hands go around her neck, and as he chokes the very sinful life out of her, he watches her eyes. The eyes are the window to the soul, and in Nick's twisted mind, he sees the devil doing a happy dance just as her eyes go dead. He pushes this putrid, dirty, soiled woman aside and looks at her in complete disgust. The anger rises in him to the point he can hardly control his emotions. He tries to sit quietly in his seat and waits for his heart to quiet while thanking God for this mission.

As Nick sits there in the cool SUV, with a dead woman beside him, he spots an old barn out in a field sitting all by itself. Aha, thinks Nick. God has shown me where to dump this piece of shit. He drives to the back of the barn and parks. First, he gets his gym bag from behind his seat. He pats it gently and tells it what a good job it did detecting. He puts it in the back of the SUV. Next, he lowers the back seats to give him more room to prepare his Satan's whore. He carries her into the back and places her on the floor. Not once does he check to see if he is being observed. This is how sure he is that he is invisible when doing God's work.

He begins to undress her, taking his time, for he hates even to have to touch this sinful human. As he removes her clothing, he folds them neatly and places them in a plastic bag. Next, he lays her out, so he can see where to paint her so she looks like the whore she is. First, he closes her eyes and puts the Vixen Green eye shadow on her eyelids. Satisfied with that, he smears on the Poppy Paradise lipstick. Going wide all around, so she looks clownish and vile. Nick lifts her breasts and on each side tapes them up, so they look (as Mary Ellen would say) perky. Nick seems to think all women have perky breasts just to entice the unsuspecting man. He then lifts her out of the van and places her on the ground behind the barn.

He returns to the SUV, takes out a scissors, an arrow with his note attached, and the most important object, the statue of the Blessed Mother.

As Nick approaches his handiwork, he is just so happy and excited that he does a little happy dance of his own. He bends down by her head and savagely chops off her hair in ragged snips. He then takes his arrow (with a small thank you to Charlie) and plunges it into her heart with all his might, making sure his message is there for all to see. He takes her legs and pulls them up, so her feet are flat on the ground and pushes her legs out by the knees, exposing her "hell's pit," as Nick like to think of it, and with a violent thrust, pushes his statue of the Blessed Mother into her as far as he can.

He leans back on his heels as he admires his work and says, "See, Mary Ellen, see how pure you are for the next man."

Nick walks away, taking with him his scissors and tape. He puts his seats back up, puts his sinner detector back on the floor, gets into his SUV, and drives away. His work for today is done, and when the farmer finds her body, everyone will know she was a sinner.

On his way back to the Seminary, he stops at a place that has a donation bin for clothing and he drops off the last essence of Marissa.

Nick stops along the way and has dinner. He has removed the clerical collar and looks like just another nice college lad on his way home. He gets back to the garage after Tim has left. He grabs his gym bag, checks the back of the SUV to make sure he has not left any reminders of his work. He is sure God wants his missions to be between just God and himself. Nick deposits the keys and heads to his dorm, feeling such a thrill at his accomplishment. He must thank God extra tonight.

Unfortunately for Nick, no one ever finds Marissa, and over the years, her body turns to dust, her bones are scattered and dragged off by animals deposited throughout this farmland. The arrow gets twisted and broken, the message just a scrap of paper blown in the wind. The only thing left is a small statue of the Blessed Mother.

CHAPTER 30

As the team begins to gather their belongings, Cully says, "Chief." No one hears him, so he tries again, this time louder. "Chief."

Vinny is startled and looks over the room wondering who yelled his name when he spots Cully standing, looking rather embarrassed.

"Cully," says Vinny, "did you just call out?"

"Yes, sir," says Cully, and he gathers his courage and says, "Chief, it was my idea about a priest angle, and everyone here thought I was grasping at straws, too green to have a working theory, but it seems I may be right, and I respectfully request that I accompany Luke in following that very same theory." With that the office goes quiet and all eyes are on the Chief to see what he will do. Phones are ringing in the outer offices, you can hear bits of conversations, and when Vinny finally realizes all are waiting to see what he will do, he says, "Well, Detective Andrews, I see you found your voice. I was not aware that you had that theory."

Luke speaks up, "Chief, that's my fault. After we interviewed Ms. Reilly in connection to our victim Candy Upkoff and she mentioned Candy having talked about meeting a good-looking priest, Cully here came up with the idea that maybe we should be looking for a priest. This was not the first reference to a priest we had come across. So yes, in my opinion, Cully should take the lead on this."

"Cully, I am glad you spoke up," says Vinny. "C.J., if it's ok with you, I will have Cully and Luke do the priest follow-up."

C.J. just nods and says, "Plenty of other tips and clues to check into. Not a problem, boss."

As the team is getting ready to dig deeper into their ideas as to where leads will take them, Mary Lou knocks on the open door.

"Mary Lou, what it is?" asks Vinny.

"Detective Miller," Mary Lou says quietly, "I think we may have identified our Jane Doe."

The room suddenly became noisy, chairs being pushed back, papers being shuffled, voices asking all at once, who is it?

Mary Lou has a note in her hand. "We just got a call from missing persons. A Mrs. Warner from Ohio called. It seems her daughter Sara Warner Woodbury had come east to attend a reunion at St. Jerome's Catholic School. It is a reunion for all graduating classes. St. Jerome is celebrating its fifty-year anniversary. Sarah was a 2000 graduate. She left home around the beginning of November. Mrs. Woodbury told her mother she would be staying with friends. The reunion was a three-day celebration over the weekend of November third, fourth, and fifth. Mrs. Warner last heard from her daughter on Wednesday the first. She said she got to her friend's house with no problems. The drive was pleasant and she was happy. Enjoying her friends, getting re-acquainted, and looking forward to Friday. Mrs. Warner has not heard from her since."

Vinny asks, "Do they know why the mother waited so long to report her missing?"

Mary Lou says, "Seems Sarah is somewhat of a free soul since her divorce. She often meets a man and goes off for extended periods without telling her mother."

"What makes you think it's our Jane Doe?" asks Vinny.

Mary Lou replies, "Just the timing and where she was found. Only someone from this area would know about that make-out spot." Mary Lou puts her hands up before Vinny could ask. "Yes, they are sending dental records and DNA samples. They are being sent overnight express. Should arrive sometime tomorrow."

Vinny literally plops into his chair. Seemingly stunned. Could this really be our Jane Doe, he thinks. Everyone in the crime room is speechless. A calm has settled over the room. Finally, Vinny leaps out of his chair, his thoughts and actions back to the problem at hand.

"Ok, team, looks like we may be on our way to solving this crime spree. Luke, Cully, you two get over to St. Jerome's and see if you can get a list of the people who attended that reunion. Find out as much as you can about this Sarah Warner and who was the friend she stayed with and her movements. C.J., you and Max go back to the crime scene where it all started. First, track down what kind of car she was driving. Then get a hold of our diving team. All those quarries out there in the Blackwood area must be searched for her car. Mickey, I want you to come with me. We are going to go see Will down in the morgue. Give him a heads up and tell him what we have learned and that he should be ready for the overnight package. Then we will start interviewing the people from the reunion once Cully and Luke secures a list. Jet, use that computer and get everything you can on our Sarah Warner Woodbury. When she left the area, when and to whom she married, divorce date, and the where about of her husband. If he's also a local lad. He could be the prime suspect. Ok, people, let's move."

As Luke and Cully get into Luke's car, Cully says, "That was really straight of you Luke to tell the Chief about my theory."

"Cully," says Luke, "you have good instincts, and it's important to me that Vinny knows that. I am sorry for ignoring your theory. That was wrong of me, and I was so damn proud of you for standing up for yourself."

"Thanks," says Cully, "now let's get us a priest."

"Whoa there, big guy, if this is our Jane Doe, remember there's an ex-husband out there somewhere."

"Yeah, I know, but ex-husbands aren't usually serial killers, are they?"

Luke looks at Cully and says, "And priests are?"

CHAPTER 31

After Vinny and Mickey check in with Will and gives him the heads up, they meet up with Luke and Cully and find that the list is going to be harder to come by than they thought. Father Eric was not much help. It seems some of the alumni were in charge, and father had to go digging into his files to try to remember who it was. They promised to check back in the morning. Father promised to provide at least one name. Frustrated, they decided to call it a day.

Despite the antsy feeling everyone was having, Vinny and the team realize that this could possibly not be Sara Woodbury. Best to wait for Will to tell them Jane Doe's real identity.

Vinny got home about 6:30 P.M., and was thinking about a cold beer and calling Justice in that order. As he popped the cap and took a long swig, his thoughts went over the day's events. Justice is from around here, perhaps working at the Yellow Tree House, she heard talk about this reunion. So after finishing his beer, he calls Justice and asks her out to dinner. He is going to pick her up around 8:00 P.M.

Justice is excited. She knows Vinny has been preoccupied with this case and hopes tonight he can relax. Justice is fairly certain she knows what to do to relax him. In anticipation of a night of love making, Justice goes to her closet to choose just the right outfit to help her help him relax.

The next morning, Vinny's team assembles in the squad room. Everyone is excited and believes they finally have some good leads. Their excitement is clouded by the fact they are not sure this is that Sarah woman and the wait for lab results is palatable.

Vinny is sitting on the corner of the desk with one foot on the chair looking over the crime board. He thinks, "All these women, could a priest really do this?"

As the team settles, Vinny looks at Cully and asks, "Did you get a list?"

"Yes, we did, Chief," says Cully as he opens his file laying on the table. "There were 538 people at the reunion. Taking away women and men over fifty-five, we have narrowed it down to 233 possible suspects. St. Jerome has graduated sixty-three priests over the years that fit our profile. We have not had the time to start sorting, checking the whereabouts or where they are stationed."

"Good work, Luke, Cully, keep at it."

"C.J., any luck with the car?" asks Vinny.

"No, the diving team cannot meet us until tomorrow around noon. They are clearing up other duties, so they can devote all their time to us starting tomorrow."

"Ok," says Vinny, and as he steps off the chair, Mary Lou is knocking on the door frame.

"Detective Miller, I have Dr. Strauss on line two."

Vinny hurriedly grabs the phone, knocking over his coffee in his haste and angry with himself, yells into the phone, "WHAT?"

"I don't know what bug is up your ass, Detective Miller," says Will, "but considering I am the one bringing you good news, you could be more civil."

"Sorry, Will, what do you have for me?"

"I just finished the results of the dental records, and I can say without hesitation, our Jane Doe is definitely Sarah Warner Woodbury."

CHAPTER 32

SEPTEMBER 2005

The time has come for Nick to join Father Jones at St. Anthony's. He will be away from the Seminary until the middle of November. Part of him is excited to become part of a parish but part of him is also worried that he will find so many sinners among the parish that he may lose control and try to eliminate all of them. He must try very hard to avoid the women. He is once again assigned a vehicle and stops at the Monsignor's office to let him know he is on his way.

"Nicholas," says the Monsignor, "I expect great things from you. Listen to Father Jones, soak up as much as you can on how to conduct yourself as a priest. There will be many temptations, and you need to remember that God has called you to do His work."

Nick does the obligatory sucking up and thanks the Monsignor for his words of encouragement. But Nick knows this is the speech all the Seminarians get, and little does the Monsignor know, Nick already knows how to use this clerical collar to do God's work.

Nick arrives at St. Anthony's and is greeted heartily by Father Jones. The Father introduces him to his house keeper, Martha Dunn. Nick does his pleasantries and thinks to himself, now here is a woman who could never do the devil's work. Ms. Dunn is mid-sixties, terribly heavy, has white hair that looks like a dandelion. Her face is wrinkled with heavy wrinkles around the mouth, which is a sign of a smoker. But she has the most beautiful smile. She greets Nick with a great big bear hug and promises to fatten him up. Nick immediately is drawn to her. He thinks he has just maybe finally met a woman he will not despise.

Ms. Dunn shows him to his room and lets him know that once he is settled, he is to meet with Father Jones to go over the routine and to familiarize himself on how this parish works.

For the next two and a half months, Nick is assailed with sin and sinners. Not yet allowed to absolve sin in the confessional, Nick sits in with Father Jones when he has group sessions with the service men to listen and guide their broken hearts and hear the cries and sees the tears in describing how their wife has committed adultery and has ripped out their hearts. It is all Nick can do to keep himself from getting his sinner detector and going after these whore-bitches, but he knows the time is not right but soon.

Nick works hard to follow the example and direction of the Parish Priest. He tries to keep the volume of his rantings down, but on occasion, Ms. Dunn hears him and wonders what devils this beautiful young man is trying to exorcise from his being. She speaks to Father Jones about it, but he assures her it is not uncommon for a young man on the threshold of his ordination to rile against God. It is their way to come into the glory and know they have made the right decision in choosing the priesthood.

Ms. Dunn accepts Father Jones' explanation, but never before has any of the seminarians acted this way.

CHAPTER 33

Nick's transitional period is over, and he heads back to the Seminary. He has learned so much and feels he is ready for the next step towards Ordination. The Monsignor is pleased with the way Nick has grown, and with his admittance to the Ministry of Lector, Nick will soon make a fine priest. The Monsignor meets with Nick and wants him to spend Thanksgiving with his family. Monsignor O'Reilly has asked Nick to spend time relaxing and praying for the time has come to accept, without conditions, his life as a priest.

Nick arrives home and is welcomed by his family. All his siblings and Charlie are together. It is pleasant time, and Nick plays his role to perfection. No one, not even Charlie, sees the dark side and guesses his intentions.

As they all sit around the table filled with good food and conversation, a SUV pulled up in front of the house. Nick asks if they are getting company.

Grace says, "Nick, come outside. We have a surprise for you."

The family all gets up from the table and goes outside. There sits a brand-new SUV with a sign in the window, which says, "Congratulations, Father Nicholas, love, your family."

"What's this?" Nick asks.

Mark steps up and hugs Nick and says, "This is your gift from all of us. We are so proud of you."

After everyone has examined the SUV and aw'ed and oh'ed, they go back into the house for coffee and dessert. While they are excited about the gift and talking about the upcoming ordination, Tristan and Patrick disappear. Soon they round the corner of the room with another gift in hand.

Patrick says, "Nick, all of your brothers and sisters, even Catherine, has contributed to this gift. We, too, are proud of you." They hand Nick the gift and wait with apprehension as he begins to open it. Inside is the most beautiful chest, and in that chest are all the tools of his trade, so to speak. A gorgeous, gold unadorned Chalice and Paten, a Scaple, a deep burgundy pouch that holds the Sacred Oils used in Extreme Unction. Everything a new priest will need. Again, tears well up in Nick's eyes and he gets up from the table and kneels before his siblings, gathering them into his arms.

CHAPTER 34

Nick is so confused as he heads back to the seminary. He asks himself how can he have such a black heart when he has the perfect family. Over this holiday, he has even found some residue of the love he used to have for his mother. He does not want to believe that she, too, is the worst of sinners. Nick starts to think that just maybe he could actually be a good priest. After all that is all he ever wanted before he fell for that evil bitch. Can't even say her name without bile surging to his throat. He will have to pray and see where God leads him.

During the next few weeks, Nick has some peace in his mind and heart. He and two other seminarians are excited and looking forward to their Ordination. They, too, will be ordained in St. Jerome Catholic Church with Father Eric presiding. All three are from this parish, so the Bishop has agreed to welcome the three young men into the priesthood where they were born and raised.

It is just before Christmas, and the three seminarians are housed together at the rectory. Father Eric is bubbling with pride knowing these are his three "sons of God."

The day has finally arrived, and St. Jerome's Church is filling up fast. The parents and families of the three young men have the front pews. Grace and Mark walk down the aisle with their heads held high, and their children fall in behind them on their best behavior. Charlie is with them, but Alice has been delayed. Grace is hoping she makes it on time to see her brother ordained.

Grace whispers to Charlie, "Where is Alice?"

Charlie says, "I just got a text that she was running late and to save her a seat."

Grace looks to the back of the church, almost willing her to appear.

It is time. A guest priest approaches the lectern and announces how today is another star in God's Crown. That three young men are about to give in to the burning need inside them to commit to the challenging work before them, to be unselfish, giving, and loving to all they encounter.

As the priest drones on, Alice steps in the door as quietly as possible. She is upset that she is late and does not want to walk down the aisle to the front pew to join her family. As she looks around for a seat in the back where she will be able to see, her eyes deceive her. She goes stone cold and starts to tremble. There in the back sits Mary Ellen McGrath. Anger wells up in Alice to the point where she loses all perspective. As Alice heads over to where she is sitting, she sees Mary Ellen has even brought her bastard child with her.

Mary Ellen sees her coming, and as she starts to smile, Alice grabs her by the hair, tells her not to make a sound, and pulls her from the pew and marches her outside.

Mary Ellen's little girl follows and cries, "Mommy, Mommy," and just as the door is about to close, Nick, along with everyone else, looks back and Nick catches a glimpse of that lovely mane of brown hair and knows in an instant he has just seen the devil.

Nick's heart races. How, after all this time, just the sight of her stirs so many feelings.

His hatred of her seems to want to release itself from his mouth, spew from his nostrils, and as he believes his head is going to explode, he hears the priest say, "I am sorry for the interruption, let us get back to why we are here." As he looks to the three young men, he says, "We shall begin." The priest does notice that one of the young men looks totally drained of color and remembers later that he had hoped the young man would not faint.

As Alice shoves Mary Ellen to the steps, still holding her hair, she gasps between clenched teeth, "What do you think you are doing?"

Mary Ellen says, "Alice, let me go, you are scaring my daughter."

As Alice looks down, she sees the sweetest little girl clinging to her mother's leg crying and seems so frightened.

"I'll let you go," says Alice, "but be thankful your child is here, or you would go tumbling down these steps." With that she releases her hold and says, "How could you show up like this? What were you thinking? Oh, that's right, you only think of yourself. You take this child and you go back where you came from. Leave my brother alone!"

Mary Ellen gets a superior attitude, and with a smirk, says, "This is my church. I have moved back, have an apartment, and a job. You will be seeing a lot of me. This Ordination is a big thing, and I wanted to see Nick take the plunge. He certainly isn't good at anything else. I am sure he will be a mediocre priest just as he was a mediocre boyfriend." With that she turns and walks down the steps, leaving Alice standing there stunned. As upset and as angry as Alice is, she hurries back inside and takes a seat just in time to see the actual ritual. Her brother, whom she loves so dearly, is now Father Nicholas, and she sends a prayer to God asking Him to have kept Nick from seeing Mary Ellen McGrath.

After the ceremony, families, Bishops, and priests all congregate in the school cafeteria to enjoy a meal and congratulations. Alice catches up to her family and joins in the celebration.

After hugs and well wishes, Grace takes Alice aside and says, "Alice, where were you? You missed your brother's Ordination."

"No, Mom, I was late, but I found a seat in the back. I saw almost all the Mass."

"What happened back there, there was some sort of commotion," asks Grace.

Alice leans in and whispers to her mother, "I removed some trash that happened to find its way into church. Its name was Mary Ellen McGrath. I will tell you about it later. I just pray Nick didn't see her."

CHAPTER 35

Food and festivities are over, and people are leaving the hall. Charlie tells Alice he will bring the car around and wait for her outside.

"Say your goodbyes and meet me out front." As Charlie sits in the car, people watching and listening to his favorite radio station, he sees Alice come out of the church and head to the car. He notices that she is certainly not smiling. Alice opens the door, literally throws herself inside, and slams the door so hard, Charlie's eye balls hurt.

"Whoa," says Charlie, "what is this all about? Alice, talk to me, what has you so upset? You just witnessed the Ordination of your brother, spent time with your family, and this should be a joyous day. What could be wrong?"

"Oh, Charlie, how could she? Of all days. What does she want?"

"Alice, you're losing me. Who and what are you talking about?"

Tears stream down Alice's checks, and upon seeing this, Charlie leans over and takes her in his arms.

"Alice, please tell me what has you so upset. My God, Alice, you are shaking."

Alice pulls away and says to Charlie, "She was here. She dared show her face with no other purpose but to humiliate and bring more sorrow to our family."

"Alice, who and what are you talking about?" whispers Charlie as he tries to calm her.

Alice sits back and says, "Mary Ellen McGrath, and the worst part, Charlie, is that she and her little girl have moved back to town and they are here for good. That means we will run into her at times and have to look at her and be reminded of that hurtful time. Charlie, I am so afraid Nick saw her at the church."

"No, Alice, I don't think he did. We had a long and fun-filled conversation. We rehashed all our stories of the trouble we've been in together, and he was so light hearted. In fact he asked if he could use the cabin next week. He has some time before he is assigned a parish and wants to go away by himself and reflect. He gave no indication that he saw her. Here now, let me wipe those tears and put all bad thoughts out of your head. It is late afternoon, neither of us must work, and I know a very soft, inviting place where we can forget Mary Ellen McGrath."

"Why, Charles Sullivan, are you suggesting a roll in the hay?"

CHAPTER 36

"Finally, quiet. I truly love Father Eric, but get a few shots of Scotch in him, and you can't shut him up. We got back to the rectory after our Ordination and Father Eric just would not shut up. He told stories of his days in the Seminary, how God had called him and blah, blah, blah. He finally shut both his mouth and eyes and was asleep instantly. It was then that I managed to get away to the solitude of my room, and I helped myself to that fine bottle of Scotch.

I had actually thought there for a while that I was indeed intended for the priesthood where I would be elevated to a higher platform and gifted with unearthly powers of love, forgiveness, humility, and all those other foolish attributes we strive to attain. What a fool to have been led astray from the very mission God Himself has bestowed upon me.

Yes, I saw her. Saw her wild hair, that porcelain complexion, and the flash of those brown eyes. Only for a second when I looked back to see what the commotion was about did I glimpse the devil in actual form. My body twitched as though God struck me with the knowledge that I have strayed from the real purpose. I don't know why God keeps by my side. I constantly disappoint Him. But not anymore."

As Nick props himself up in his bed with his glass full of Father Eric's fine Scotch, he lets his mind wander as to all the special abilities he has to rid the world of as many deceitful, whoring women as he can.

As he drifts off to sleep, he says to himself out loud, "I can't wait to get started."

The next morning, a little bit hung over but relishing the new day, Nick packs up all his personal items, including his priestly possessions. As soon as he can, politely, without raising suspicion, he will also pack his new SUV (thanks, Mom and Dad) with his sinner detector, his tools for eliminating this disease that has filtered into the world, and will head to Charlie's cabin where he will perfect his calling. Nick is anxious to get started.

Nick bounds down the stairs with his satchel in hand and is stopped short. Father Eric is up and about, fussing with the house keeper over wanting scrambled eggs or an omelet.

"Good morning, Nick," says Father Eric.

"My goodness, Father," says Nick. "I cannot believe you are up, dressed, and already giving Suzanne a hard time. We put away quite a bit of Scotch last night. I am certainly not as awake as you."

"Oh, my boy," says Father. "It takes practice…ha. By the time you are my age, you, too, will have it down pat. Come sit and let Suzanne make you breakfast. I know you are anxious to get on the road, but humor an old friend."

Nick's mind is swirling with the excitement of getting on, hitting the road, solitude, but knows he must not seem to anxious.

As Suzanne waddles around the kitchen in her moo-moo with an apron tied in front, she asks Nick what he wants.

Nick decides a hearty meal will last him all day, so he asks for eggs over easy, bacon, and toast.

Their chatter is pleasant and light. No more sermons or how-to. Nick is now on equal footing with Father Eric. Nick looks around at the kitchen in this rectory where he has spent so much time, and he has a feeling of nostalgia. He knows in his heart it will be the last time he will spend time here. He must not be burden with silly ideas of friendship or comforts of home. He has a mission. One God Himself has given him.

It is finally time to leave. Nick has his SUV loaded, and standing on the porch of the rectory, he hugs both Father Eric and Susanne.

The day is bright, cold but crisp, and Nick is on his way to the cabin. In his head, and sometimes out loud, he is going through the things he wants to accomplish while at the cabin. As he is driving, he remembers a sporting goods store a little off the beaten track and takes a detour to do some shopping. He arrives at the store a little after three and is happy the store is not too busy. The store, Rambo's Home, is a privately-owned sporting goods store with a small deli attached. Nick enters and heads directly to the hunting section where he finds the arrows. After all, this is what he is preparing himself for…hunting. His intention is to replace Charlie's old beaten up arrows with new ones. He will tell Charlie they are a gift for using the cabin, and he will take the old ones to drive into the heart of the ball-busting "ladies" he intends to eliminate.

He finds what he wants and then starts to shop for his other tools. He needs tape. He finds packaging tape (to enhance those perky breasts). He finds note paper for the message and locates some string and wire. Not sure which will be better, if he uses it at all. He finds a bundle of rags and cleaning supplies. After all cleanliness is next to Godliness. He suppresses a laugh at that one, and besides, he doesn't want to get his new SUV all messy and splattered with the filth that might leak from the bodies. When Nick feels he has all the necessary purchases, he pays with cash and heads over to the deli.

As he leaves, the young woman who waited on him kept her desires to herself. She thought this young handsome man is one delicious piece of manhood. But her boss was near her register, and she had already been warned twice about coming on to the handsome hunters who frequent the Rambo.

She would never know how lucky she was. This clerk is exactly who Nick is out to eliminate.

The deli is small but crammed with all kinds of food. He buys enough staples to last him a week. Even though he has two weeks before having to return to the Seminary for his assignment, Nick wants some time to impress on the faculty and staff of just how religious and eager he is to start his role as priest. Must give them the perfect Father Nicholas, so no one suspects his personal connection to God. Besides, one week will be more than enough time to perfect his methods.

Nick arrives at the cabin, and as eager as he is to start preparing, he takes time to enjoy the quiet solitude of his surroundings. He pops a beer, and with a bag of chips, he goes out to the deck and finds the perfect spot to sit and take in this beautiful world. The sun is setting and gives off a rich hue to the area. Birds fly high, catching the last glimmer of the day. Nick is feeling content, serene, and thinks this is how the angels must feel, so close to God to be at such peace. He then scolds himself for putting his mortal self in the company of angels and quickly asks God's forgiveness. He must remain humble and righteous if he is to fulfill his destiny.

As the week progresses, Nick spends his time writing out in cursive each announcement. He takes time writing, perfecting, wants each word clear and meaningful. Was going to go with "Jezebel the Whore of Satan" but decided that is too lengthy and just writes "Jezebel, Satan's Whore." After he has about twenty-five of his announcements, he gets his sinner detector's satchel out and caresses it. It seems almost sexual the way he lovingly strokes the leather. He removes the items and puts them on the table beside the notes.

Nick was so pleased when he went rummaging around the closets and shed outback to have found so many of the old arrows he and Charlie used for practice. He left the new arrows prominently displayed on the fireplace mantel for Charlie to find with a note thanking him for use of the cabin and to please accept this gift.

He lays out the notes beside the arrows, then he finds and lays out the statues of the Virgin Mary. Next, he gently opens the cosmetic bag that has the lipstick and eye shadow. He takes time to smell inside the cosmetic bag and again has flashbacks to (he thought) a wonderful time in his life. As he turns the tube of lipstick, he can almost taste that despicable excuse of a woman. Her lips so soft, the tongue flicking in and out, teasing. Nick's hand goes to the bulge in his jeans and rubs himself, making his instrument of desire bigger and bigger. When he realizes what he is doing, he leaps up, smashing the chair to the floor and runs to the door. He flings it open and runs down to the dock and hurls himself into the cold water of the lake. His only desire now is to end this useless, pitiful life. As he is sinking, cursing the God he thinks has given him a mission, he looks up through the water and he sees a cloud position itself in front of the moon. The cloud is in the shape of a cross. Nick cannot believe that God is giving him yet another chance, and he drags himself out of the water. The cold he feels is his punishment. He makes his way back to the cabin, turns off the lights, and falls into bed without even changing out of his wet clothes. As the cloud in shape if a cross moves away from the moon, its light shines through the window illuminating Nick's tools.

It is only 4:30 A.M. when Nick awakes. He lay on the bed thinking of last night and how weak he was. He rolls out on his knees and goes into the kitchen. Nick makes coffee and pours a cup. He sits back down at the table and reaches for the velvet sack that holds the statues of the Virgin Mary.

He counts them and has thirty. He stands and lines them up all in a row across the table, and one by one, he takes his thumb, and as if were shooting marbles, he flings them one by one across the room, howling with laugher and yelling, "Take this, you pure and innocent bride of God. Like all women, you, too, are nothing but a tease. Poor Joseph." Nick is laughing so hard, tears run down his cheeks but as he picks them up off the floor and he goes to a deep place and becomes somber and remembers why he is doing what he has planned to do. He has lost part of his sanity. He sees the rest of his tools are still on the table. The contents of the cosmetic bag have fallen to the floor.

As he stoops to pick up the items, he has managed to turn his heart to stone and very calmly says to himself, "Even though I need to make these 'ladies' look hideous, I must be sparing. Don't want to run out."

Once all his tools are assembled, he tapes his notes to the feather end of the arrows, and a rippling thrill courses through his body. He cannot wait. The image of his first kill shivers through his body like electricity. Nick believes this feeling is due to the hand of God touching his soul and has forgiven him his lapse in faith.

His first week is over, and he has accomplished his task. He loads up his SUV and heads down the road back to the Seminary to learn of his assignment. If anyone were listening, they would hear the powerful voice of a young man singing hymns he learned as a boy. A serial killer that sings hymns has been born and is looking forward to bringing the wrath of God down upon the heads of sinners. Women sinners.

CHAPTER 37

PRESENT

"Chief, I have a question," says Cully.

"Well, let's hear it, Cully. We are all in the same boat here, and we all have questions and very few answers."

"What I don't understand is why no other police department caught on to this series of murders. These murders span ten years. Why didn't anyone but us make the connection?"

"I think, Cully, first off, I have the best team in the state," says Vinny.

At this everyone lets out a howl and high fives float around the room.

"Seriously though I think every department is just overwhelmed with work. Take the two victims in Reading. Even though they were a distant apart and there were enough differences, they thought the second murder was a copy-cat because no statute was found. The woman found in Williamsport was a prostitute and that poor excuse of a policeman in charge just wrote her off as trash. So no one looked very hard."

"I think we are going to bring justice to these women," say Cully. "I just hope in time to prevent any more deaths."

"Ok, let's get back to business," says Vinny. "That list of prospects. Where are we on that? Luke, anything?"

"I went over to speak to Father Eric, and he has agreed to help me identify, which priest is located in what parish. He was not too eager to help, I would like to add. Once we connect those dots, we can start interviewing them. We do know most of them have families right here in the area, and we can start with parents and/or siblings."

"That sounds good, Luke, once you get addresses and location of all sixty-three, bring the list back to the station and we will divide it among all of you.

Jet, we will need you on the computer helping to track families and their whereabouts. Cully, I want you to take the lead on this. C.J., I want you to re-check and recheck that list of men that fits our profile. I am sure there were many young men who may have started out by wanting to be a priest but failed and dropped out."

C.J. goes over to Jet, and together they start working the list. Their goal is to identify any young man that graduated from St. Jerome's and dropped out of the Seminary.

"Cully, call Father Eric and see if he has the information yet. I want you to be assertive and push him on this. I am sure he will deny even the very thought of one of his 'boys' being a serial killer. Don't let him drag his feet."

PRESENT

Father Eric is beside himself as he wears a path back and forth in the rug of the parlor floor talking out loud to himself.

"I cannot believe what that police chief is insinuating. How could a man of God do something so vile? I don't want to help these policemen. Hasn't our church gone through enough humiliation with this sex scandal and now they are accusing one of MY priests of murder."

Father Eric stops his rant long enough to pour himself a shot of whiskey, and as he is sipping at it, Suzanne, the housekeeper, knocks gently on the door frame.

"Father Eric, there are some policemen here to see you. Should I show them in?"

"Yes, Suzanne, please, and this is a private matter. Please no interruptions," says Father Eric with his head held high. He planned on showing these policemen how wrong they are.

Suzanne shows the two young cops into the parlor and Luke says, "Father, thank you for helping us. I am Officer Marino and this is Officer Andrews. We appreciate your help with this,"

"Yes, yes, of course," says Father Eric, "but I assure you, you are barking up the wrong tree as they say. No priest would ever be involved in mass murder. Come, let's sit at the desk and go over these names."

As they start the process, Cully gets out a tablet and writes down the priest's name, family, where the family members live, and what parish they can find the individual. It is a tedious job and takes most of the afternoon into early evening. As they finish with the last name, Cully's hand hurts from writing, and they could both use a large dose of that whiskey Father Eric keeps sipping at. As they leave the Rectory, both men seem depressed. Each lost in their own thoughts, each wishing they are wrong, but in their hearts and minds, they know they are looking for a priest.

Back at the station, C.J. and Jet have found thirteen more prospects. Young men who thought they had the calling only to find out celibacy was not for them. C.J. placed the list on Vinny's desk.

"Mickey," calls Vinny, "I want you to devote your time tracking down these thirteen names. We need an alibi for all of them."

"I'm on it, Chief," says Mickey.

"The rest of you divide the list Cully and Luke brought back from Father Eric. Do it alphabetically, so there is no cross checking and duplication of work. Once the list is divided, I want all of you to call it a day and I will see you all at 8:00 A.M. in the morning. Someone, decide who's bringing the donuts. Good night."

CHAPTER 39

Vinny is up early and is anxious to get to his office. He is thinking maybe he should be the one that brings the donuts but then he remembers how tight his shirt felt as he was getting dressed. He chuckled to himself, since entertaining the lovely Miss Channing, he seems to have put on a few pounds. Vinny is feeling over the top this morning having spent a most delightful and fulfilling evening with Justice. As he finishes dressing, he puts aside pleasant thoughts and gets back to thinking about solving these murders. As he steps outside, he takes a few minutes to thank God for such a beautiful day and asks, in his own way, for help in stopping the death of any more women.

Vinny arrives at his office and is surprised to find a wonderful aroma of coffee greet his nose. Somebody's been busy. It is a slow connection to his brain seeing fresh coffee in the pot and not one but two boxes of donuts and Max sitting at one of the tables.

"Max, what has you here so early?" asks Vinny. "Are you responsible for the donuts and coffee?"

"Hey, Chief, yes, I wanted to get an early start, but I've been sitting here wasting time wondering if we are on the right track."

"What has you guessing, Max, talk to me. Sometimes saying things out loud puts a new perspective on things," says Vinny.

As Vinny pours himself a cup of coffee and looks longingly at the donuts, he thinks, aw, go ahead, one won't hurt. He grabs one of the glazed and sits opposite Max.

"Let's hear it, Max," says Vinny.

"Chief, I have been a Catholic all my life."

"I didn't know that," says Vinny.

Max sits back in her chair and looks at the crime board. She says, "I know priests are still people, don't get me wrong. They can love and hate, forgive or hold grudges, but I just cannot wrap my head around a priest who has gone through such rigorous training and cleansing of the lay world could do this. Not the killing part but the way it is staged."

Vinny too searches the crime board and says, "What has you so ruffled by the staging?"

"Boss, what I find hardest of all the evidence is the statue of the Virgin Mary. Even the most die-hard non-believer of any religion or Deity has nothing against the Virgin Mary and to display that statue like that just has me baffled. I cannot believe a Catholic Priest could or would defile her. He would have to be one sick son-of-a-bitch."

"You see, Max, I believe evil is everywhere, always ready to leap in and destroy even the most righteous given the chance. Look at our evidence. The Holy Oil on some of the foreheads and the cursive writing. Who teaches cursive all through twelve grades? The Catholic schools. And don't forget the sighting of a priest during the time of their deaths by a few of the witnesses. I believe we are definitely looking for a priest," sighs Vinny.

"I see the evidence, Chief. I guess I am being naïve. Thanks for letting me vent."

As Vinny gets up for more coffee and to refill Max's mug, the rest of his crew start showing up. After a round of good mornings, the clashing of mugs, and the devastation of the donut boxes, the team settles down.

Vinny starts, "Ok, who is up first?"

"That would be me, Chief," says Max. "I have separated our list of priest's names. If anyone objects, let's hear it after I tell you what I did. There are sixty-three names on the list, alphabetically I divided them this way. Luke and Cully will track down thirty-two names, alphabetically from A to L. C.J. and I will have thirty-one names from M to Z. Mickey will work his thirteen odd names of those who became drop outs. Anyone have a problem with this?"

Vinny has been writing this division on the board and tells Max she has done a great job. All the members of this team agree.

"Jet," says Vinny, "I want a separate chalk board brought in, and you will be in charge of dividing it into three sections. I want you to list the names according to the division, along with Mickey's suspects. That way as information on our priests come in, we can eliminate or highlight possible priests. I really hate calling them suspects or perps. You other four, I want you to be as thorough as possible. You will find these priests in many different dioceses. They have not stayed local. It is important that you contact first the Bishop in that diocese to let them know you are there. But remember we are not, and I repeat, not asking permission to interview these priests. You will explain to the Bishop that one member of the alumni was murdered during or after the reunion they attended, and you are only there to ask what might have been seen. At no time do you even imply that we are looking at the priest as a possible murder suspect. You will be respectful, but do not let the Bishop sway you away from doing your job. Is that clear?"

"Yes, boss," the group sang out in unison.

After some bantering back and forth as to who will be the better investigator and find the killer, they all settle into doing some serious work. Luke and Cully sit quietly with their lists and cross reference Father Eric's list as to where each priest is located. Max, C.J., and Mickey all have the same method. They will work with a map and strategize the route they will take and discuss between themselves how they will go about the interviews.

Cully asks, "Chief, some of these priests are scattered quite far from us. Will we be able to have a traveling budget?"

"Good question," says Vinny. "I will talk with Captain Ritter and see about getting traveling expenses. I see no problem with him approving it. But remember, no luxury hotels and champagne dinners, you hear me, peons?"

They all laugh, and for a few minutes, forget the sad and arduous task ahead of them.

CHAPTER 40

2006

Nick is in his room at the seminary and is packing up his few belongings. He arrived back last night and decided to wait until morning to pack up his SUV. He has an appointment with Monsignor O'Reilly today at 11:00 A.M. and is hoping he can sway the Monsignor to allow him to leave for his assignment early. Nick still has one week of respite before he must report to his assigned parish. Today he will learn where he is going.

Nick glances at the clock and sees it is 10:30 A.M. He gathers up his notebook and checks himself in the mirror. He certainly looks like a priest. He thinks black is most appropriate. Nick crosses the campus and enters Monsignor O'Reilly's office and is greeted by Mary Elizabeth.

"Good morning, Father Dougherty," says Mary Elizabeth.

"Good morning to you, too," says Nick. "That's quite a title I have, isn't it? Such a strange title for a man who will never have children."

"Oh, Nicholas," Mary Elizabeth exclaims. "You will be the father of so many souls throughout your priesthood, and of course, I am not speaking from experience, but I can imagine the rewards will be just as important in God's eye, if not more so."

Nick is feeling a bit exposed making such stupid comments. He has to do better in reigning in his true feelings. Play the part, Nick, play the part.

"Of course, Mary Elizabeth, you are so right. You must have seen so many young and some older men go off to be the Father of their flock. I shall be one of those and praise the Lord to have the opportunity."

Mary Elizabeth softens her look and says, "You will be a great Father, Father, and I am sure you will be remember long after you are gone. Come, Monsignor O'Reilly is expecting you."

Nick follows Mary Elizabeth through the hallway to the Monsignor's office.

"Nick, my son," greets Monsignor O'Reilly. "Come in, come in. Sit any-where, this won't take long."

Nick takes a seat by the window and relaxes. He is so grateful that this is the last time he will have to endure this old man's platitudes and syrupy words. It is all Nick can do not to shout out and tell the old fart to shut his mouth and go screw himself. Nick might be young, but God-damn it, he knows how this cruel world works and it isn't with sweet words dripping from a foul mouth. Nick knows he, too, must put on a smile, say all the right things, and play this game. Play the game, Nick, play the game.

"Well, let me find my papers here among this mess. I will let you know where you will call home. I am so proud of you, Nick," says the Monsignor.

Under Nick's breath, he says, "Yeah, yeah, let's get on with it."

"Ah, here we are," says the Monsignor as he pulls out a folder. "It seems you have been placed in a wonderful parish."

"Where will I be going?" asks Nick.

"You are going to the town of Selinsgrove," says O'Reilly. "Do you know where that is?"

Nick is pleased and says, "Yes, sir, I am somewhat familiar with that area. I have relatives that live not far from there in Williamsport on my mother's side."

"Wonderful, wonderful, that will make your transition that much more pleasant," says the Monsignor.

"Let's see here, you will be going to St. Mark's Catholic Church. The Pastor there is Father William McCoy, a fine priest. I know him well, and you will fit in there nicely. There is also Father Adam Lynch, Pastor Emeritus. He is retired but likes to say Mass on occasion, which will free up time for you and Father McCoy. So what do you think, my boy?"

Nick jumps right in with his request and says, "Oh my, I am really so excited and so ready to begin my priesthood. Would it be favorable for me to leave early? I really have no reason to remain here, even though I do have one more week of adjustment. I am anxious to get settled in and meet my colleagues."

"I don't see why not," says the Monsignor. "When would you like to leave?"

Nick says, "I am ready now, but how about I leave Wednesday morning?"

"That can be arranged. I will have Mary Elizabeth call Father McCoy and tell him to look for your arrival sometime Wednesday."

"Thank you, Monsignor. That will give me time to say goodbye to my friends, get my plans in order, and notify my parents where I will be going."

The Monsignor stands and offers his hand to Nick and says, "May God be with you, Nick, you have had a bad time, but I see you are full of forgiveness, love, and a commitment to your vows. Please keep in touch."

Nick shakes the old fool's hand and thinks to himself, yes, I certainly have a commitment to doing God's work, not your work, old man. But instead says, "Thank you, Monsignor, for all your help and prayers."

The rest of Nick's day is spent packing up his few belongings and reminiscing about his time at the Seminary. He has made several really close friends and will miss them. Some have already graduated and moved on and are serving in churches across the country.

When Nick finishes as much as he can, he sits at his desk and calls his mother.

The phone rings in what was once his home, and on the third ring, the phone is answered.

"Hello," says Grace.

"Hi, Mom," greets Nick. "Have I caught you at a bad time?"

"Never, ever," says Grace. "I always have time for you. Where are you?"

"I'm still at school, but I have been given my assignment, and I wanted you and the family to know where I am going."

"Oh, Nick, that's wonderful. Where are you going to be?"

For a split second, Nick wonders why he is calling with this information. He really doesn't care if his family knows where he is, but as he keeps telling himself, he must pretend, so he says, "I'm really excited, Mom, they are sending me to Selinsgrove. My parish will be St. Mark's. I leave on Wednesday. I probably will not be saying Mass until the following Sunday, but when I find out, perhaps the family could come and share my first Mass with me. You could meet my colleagues and we could plan dinner together."

"Nicholas, how wonderful would that be," says Grace. "Of course we'll be there. Just let me know the details. I will talk to your dad. We could get to visit with Aunt Lydia. I haven't seen her in so long, and according to her letters, she is doing well."

"We can talk later about plans, Mom, right now I've got to go. I am having dinner with some friends."

"All right, honey. We will look forward to your call once you are all settled in. Say a prayer for us. Love you."

"Love you, too, Mom," gags Nick, barely getting the words out.

After Nick hangs up, he goes to a very dark place. Lays on his bed and drifts off with visions of his hands, these consecrated hands, ringing the necks of all those wanton women, hundreds of them flash before his eyes as he falls into a deep sleep.

When Nick opens his eyes, it is very dark and very quiet. He has some trouble remembering where he is. Panic sets in, and he sits up. Ah, yes, he remembers. I fell asleep. He looks around his room and eyes the clock. It is 9:30 P.M. He has slept all afternoon and into the night. Nick is now wide awake and finds he is hungry. He has missed dinner, but that's ok. He lied to his mother about meeting friends. He grabs his keys and heads down to the garage area to see his friend Tim. He and Tim have a lot in common, loose women and booze. Perhaps he can get Tim to go with him for a bite to eat and a few frosty ones.

Nick greets Tuesday morning around 10:00 A.M. He had a really good night with Tim. They put away quite a few frosty ones, and Nick is feeling the pain. Tim is an old hand at out-drinking these "sissy boys" and he has already put in two hours of work. Nick gets dressed and heads to the cafeteria for breakfast. He sees his friend Chad and joins him.

"Hey, Nick," says Chad, "you look like shit."

"Yeah," mumbles Nick, "I tried to out drink Tim last night."

"Silly boy, silly boy," chuckles Chad, "Nobody puts Tim under the table. I learned that the hard way."

The young men fall into a comfortable conversation, and after they finish eating, they decide to go shoot some hoops. Nick enjoys the sport, and after a couple of games, they say good-bye and wish each other the best.

Nick goes back to his room, showers, and takes a nap. He is anxious to get going and feels antsy. After his nap, he going down to the common room and watches some TV. Later he has dinner, goes back to his room, and goes to bed.

Wednesday is finally here. Nick literally leaps out of bed, gets dressed in jeans and a sweatshirt, and starts carrying things down to the entrance. He piles his belongings by the door and heads to the garage to retrieve his car. Tim is not around, so he helps himself to his keys and drives up to his building to load up his belongings. He is so anxious to head out. He has three suitcases with his personal belongings, one case with his priestly things, and the most precious case of all, his sinner detector. That case goes up front. As he is loading, his car, one of his teachers, Father Parks, walks by.

"Hi there, Nick," says Father Parks, "I see you are ready to leave us."

"All set, Father," replies Nick.

"I see you are in street clothes, no collar for you yet," says Father Parks rather harshly.

"Not yet, Father, I am still on my free time, but I am heading to my assignment. I am sure my collar will still be in good shape when I am ready to put it on." Nick's look pierces the priest to the bone and he looks away.

As he hurries away, he says, "That's good, may God be you."

The priest stops and sits on one of the benches in the court yard and watches Nick. He shivers, as though touched by ice. He bows his head and says a quick prayer. Not for Father Dougherty but for himself. He has this quivering feeling that he has just been touched by pure evil.

Nick is finally on his way. He feels light hearted and anxious to begin his career as a priest/destroyer of unclean women. As he drives to his destination, he is really enjoying the scenery and quiet. The mountains are majestic, and everything is green and golden. He lets his thoughts turn to questions as why God has made such a beautiful world only to dirty it with deceitful beings. One thing Nick is so looking forward to is the "confessional." Here his hopes of weeding out the sinner is beyond expectation. Nick feels this will be a direct link to using his sinner detector.

As he approaches the small community of Selinsgrove, he is so pleased at the ease, which he finds his way around. He wants to tour the streets, check out the stores and restaurants, and try to get a feel for the place he will be calling home. He finds St. Mark's Church and is so surprised. He pictured a traditional church building probably built back in the 40's or 50's but instead sees a most modern building. Stained glass windows encompass all sides, modern architecture, a building of angles and sharp corners. Beside the church is a Rectory that has a porch with a railing all around holding pots of flowers. Nick even sees a garage. He circles around and heads back to a restaurant he spotted earlier. He is hungry, and a restaurant will give him a small taste of the kind of people he will be ministering.

The restaurant is not very busy, and after a few glances, people go back to their conversations and pay him no mind. He is surprised that a stranger would attract so little attention. Perhaps the people here are not so friendly after all.

Soon it is time for Nick to meet his colleagues and see the place he will call home for however long his assignment will be. Nick parks in the Rectory's drive way and heads up the steps. He rings the bell and soon hears footsteps. The door is opened by a very attractive black woman.

"Yes, may I help you?" she says.

"I hope so," replies Nick. "I am Father Dougherty and have been assigned to this parish. I am to meet a Father McCoy."

"How wonderful, do come in and I will let the Father know you are here. My name is Clara Kennedy, and you may call me Miss Clara. I am the chief cook and bottle washer around here, plus I wear many hats."

Nick extends his hand and says, "Well, Miss Clara, I am very pleased to meet you, and if judging by the smells of I hope cookies, you and I are going to be great friends."

Clara laughs and shows Nick into the study and says, "I'll get Father McCoy. Please make yourself comfortable."

Nick paces around the room and notices just how inviting the surrounding are. Soft tones of browns and grays, comfortable chairs, a desk, no two desks. One used regularly and another smaller one.

Footsteps coming down the hallway are loud and precise, and a booming voice calls out, "Where are you, my boy?" as Father McCoy turns the corner and joins Nick in the study.

"So glad to meet you, Nick, I am William McCoy. You may call me Bill or McCoy, unless we are at a church function then it is Father Bill or Father McCoy. What may I call you?"

Nick is speechless at first, then finds his voice and states, "I've never thought of it, Bill. This is all new to me. What do you suggest?"

"I think we can apply the same to you as me. In public you will be Father Dougherty or Father Nicholas. Here you will be Nick, how's that?"

Nick believes he is going to like this big Irishman. He is such an imposing figure. Must be at least 6'3" and 245 pounds. Barrel chested, sparkling blue eyes, and a bit of hair ringing his head.

McCoy gestures to Nick to take a seat, and he explains to Nick the working of the Rectory.

He says, "You have met Miss Clara, and believe me, don't get on her wrong side, she'll put you in your place, ha. I've been tongue lashed on many occasions, but she has a heart of gold. We would be lost without her, but I will let you come to your own conclusions about her. She is our most important person in the Rectory. She keeps us fed, cleaned, and on schedule. I know you will just love her as much as we do. We have a two-car garage, but Father Adam has one bay and I the other. You can park in the driveway. I am going to have Miss Clara show you your room and then I will help bring in your things. Enjoy the rest of the afternoon checking things out. Dinner is at six, and at that time, you will meet Father Adam. So glad to have you aboard, Nick. We are a growing community, and you are needed here."

The two priests get up, and Father Bill calls to Clara to take Nick and show him around. As Nick is following Clara out the door, Father McCoy call out.

"Nick."

"Yes, sir," answers Nick.

"Make sure there is a collar around that neck when you come for dinner."

"Oh, yes, sir," simmers Nick, "of course. See you then."

Clara and Nick proceed with the tour and Nick is impressed with the size of the Rectory.

Clara says, "I will show you to your room first. It is on the second floor. There are two other bedrooms, and they are the fathers. Please respect their privacy. I will only come into your room to clean and change the bed clothes. You will learn the schedule later. Each of you have your own bathroom off the bedroom, so you will have your privacy also."

Nick responds to her, "I am surprised how big this place is. Do you live here, too?"

"I have an apartment above the garage. It is quite comfortable and affords me my privacy as well, yet I am close to the Rectory."

When Nick sees his room, he is pleased. The room is huge and he loves the private bath.

He says to Clara, "I think I will be very happy here."

"I will leave you to it then," says Clara. "Feel free to roam around, and don't forget, dinner is at six. If you find the kitchen, there just might be a cookie or two for you."

Nick spends the rest of the day getting used to his surroundings. He indeed finds the kitchen, and as promised, there are cookies. He gets his suitcases from the foyer (Father McCoy must have brought them in) and returns to his room and is looking forward to dinner and meeting Father Adam.

Nick enters the dining room at 5:45 P.M. with collar in tack and is greeted by Father McCoy.

Not two minutes later, in comes an excited, happy, smiling priest who comes right up to Nick, grabs his hand and says, "I am Father Adam, but you can call me Adam. I am so glad to meet you."

Nick takes his hand and says, "I am pleased to meet you, too, Adam."

"Come, come, let's sit. Bill, get me a dash of that scotch and let's get acquainted with this young fellow."

Nick sits across from him at the table and answers all their questions. Nick observes this new acquaintance and is puzzled as to why he is retired. Father Adam is a very spry, thin man. He barely reaches six feet and has a full head of salt and pepper hair. Glasses he keeps pushing up on his nose, and he seems to actually have a twinkle in his green eyes. He seems to be full of energy.

When dinner is over and Clara has removed the dishes after serving coffee, Nick says to his new roommates, "Gentlemen, I am very tired. It has been a long day, and I am looking forward to trying out that bed. You have made me feel at home, and I thank you."

After Nick says his goodnight, the two priests go into the study for a night cap.

"Ok, Adam, what do you think of our new roommate?"

"You know, Bill, he seems like a nice young man, but there is something off about him."

"Off, what do you mean?" asks Bill. "He is fresh out of the Seminary, away from home, family and friends, so I would expect some shyness and restraint."

"I can't quite put my finger on it," says Adam. "There doesn't seem to be any light behind his eyes, like he's empty."

"Good gracious, Adam," says Bill. "I think you have had one too many glasses of scotch. He's a priest, he has the light of God in him."

"I hope you are right, Bill, I hope you are right."

CHAPTER 41

PRESENT

It's been five days since Vinny's team went out and about interviewing and eliminating priests from a list of possible serial killers. It has left a foul taste in Vinny's mouth, and his detectives have had understandable mood swings.

C.J. and Max are in the squad room working with Jet at the crime board. Max is giving names to Jet for her to check off the list. These priests are not suspects.

"Max," Vinny calls out, "how is it going? What have you and C.J. learned?"

"We were able to contact all thirty-one by phone. After a few well-placed questions and the cooperation of said priests, we feel we have narrowed it down to three that seemed suspicious. C.J. is still working on some of the alibis of those we feel are not involved, but we want to be thorough."

"Ok, sounds good, keep your names of suspects until Cully and Luke show up with their list," says Vinny.

"Where's Mickey?" asks Vinny.

Everyone shakes their head.

C.J. remarks, "Probably sweating some bird about sleeping with a priest, ha-ha. Hoping to find some lovin', too. You know Mickey."

"Hey, who's taking my name in vain?" says Mickey as he waltzes in the room.

"Only stating the truth, my man," says C.J.

"Enough. Were you as successful as C.J. and Max?" asks Vinny. "They have narrowed their list to three suspects."

Mickey says, "Yes, boss, out of my thirteen names, I narrowed my list to three also."

"Good," says Vinny. "Hold that thought until we are all together. I hate having to go over everything two or three times. But you can give your names to Jet of the ones you eliminated."

Mickey goes over to Jet and nuzzles her neck, telling her how good she smells.

Vinny sees this and shouts, "Mickey, do you want another lesson on sex discrimination in the work place?"

"No, boss," sighs Mickey.

"Well, then stay out of Jet's neck."

Jet giggles, and Mickey throws her a kiss just as Vinny turns away.

Max asks Vinny when he expects Luke and Cully.

Vinny has taken to staring at the list of priests' names and is lost in thought and does not hear Max. He wonders how could there be so many suspects among priests, or are we barking up a tree like Max thinks.

"Chief," calls Max.

"Sorry, I was lost in thought. Cully called and said they'd be back by six. Let's call it a day. Tomorrow will be an important day. We have names and we have opportunity. Now we must weed out saint from sinner."

The next day finds Vinny sitting at his desk in the crime room going over some notes and checking some facts. It is 8:30 A.M., and his team is trickling in. Vinny picks up on the looks Jet and Mickey are giving each other, and he surmises that the earlier neck nuzzling blossomed into some serious necking last night. He certainly wasn't upset by this, although he wishes they would wait until after this case is solved. He smiles to himself, remembering the neck nuzzling he did last night.

Cully and Luke are here also. They got back last evening, and now all members of his team seem anxious to report their findings.

"Alright, people, listen up," starts Vinny. "We all seem to be bursting with information, so let's get started. It's about time we put this killer out of business. Mickey, you start. Go up to the crime board with Jet and let's start laying out the facts."

Mickey meets Jet at the board and says, "As you know, I had the misfits. Out of thirteen names, I narrowed my field to three names. Everyone else had alibis and I eliminated them. My first suspect was Angel Torres, he graduated high school in 1993. Changed his mind about becoming a priest when his sister was raped and murdered. He is now a lawyer in Philly. My second suspect was Michael Schwartz, graduated high school in 2006, but it seems he is in jail. On the way home from the reunion, he got pulled over and ended up with a

DUI. He managed to slide on that only to get caught again last month and is now doing time. The third guy I suspected was Jake Sorenson. He was a drop out, and he is now working construction up in Lehighton. Those are my three prospects, but after checking them out, I am sure we can just check them off the list."

"Good work, Mickey," says Vinny. "And none of the other ten on your list sparked your interest?"

"No, they all checked out," says Mickey as he takes his seat.

"C.J., are you ready with your list?" asks Vinny.

"Yes, sir," says C.J. as he rises from his chair and goes to the board.

"This one here," he points to Robert Walbert's name, "is fifty-two and was ordained in 1998. His parish is in Shartlesville. When we interviewed him, he acted kind of squirrely. Was not forthcoming, sketchy about his whereabouts, and I think he is strong enough to pull this off. We'd like to keep his name open. Our second suspect is Samuel Pitts, forty-eight, and ordained in 1998. He's in Coatsville. Max and I got bad vibes from him, but we think he may have had a re-connect that night with a former love interest and was ashamed."

Max speaks up, "I think we can eliminate him."

"Our third guy is James Marsden. He is thirty-eight, ordained in 2008, and his parish is in Wrightsville. Max and I strongly believe he is capable of these murders. His background is one with violence and abuse, and even though he is only thirty-eight, he seems to harbor a lot of rage. He keeps it in check, but every now and then it shows through. He was not cooperative of his whereabouts at the time of the other murders and pretended insult when asked. Let's keep him up there until we do more checking on him."

"I am impressed, C.J., Max. You both have done a good job as well, and you also feel the others on the list are cleared?" asks Vinny.

"We do," says C.J. and Max in unison.

"Luke, Cully," calls Vinny. "Are you ready?"

They have their heads together seemingly arguing about something, and once again, Vinny calls to them.

"Fellows, it's time. What's the matter?" asks Vinny.

"Go on, Luke, you do it," says Cully.

"No, I'll take the last two, but you need to get up there and tell the chief what we found, now go."

"Come on, guys, you're wasting time," shouts Vinny.

Cully gets up reluctantly and approaches the board. He starts talking, and no one can hear him.

"Cully," says Vinny. "We'd all like to hear what you have to say."

Soon Cully finds his voice, and once he starts, he is thorough and precise.

"Ok, I'll start with Drew Frantzen. He is forty-four, ordained in 2002. His parish is in Mount Carmel. He claims to have gone to a private party after the dinner the night of the reunion. We are still tracking down his alibi. I don't think he is our guy, but until we clear him, keep him on the list. Our second suspect is Richard Hoffman. He is thirty-three, ordained in 2013. His parish is in Lebanon. We realize he is probably too young, but Luke and I feel he may have been doing this while in the seminary. He is rough around the edges, street smart, and extremely defiant towards the police. Keep him on the list. Our next priest is Nicholas Dougherty age forty-one, ordained in 2005 and his parish is in Selinsgrove."

"Wait a minute," interrupts Vinny. "It that Mark and Grace Dougherty's boy?"

Cully replies, "I don't know a Mark and Grace Dougherty."

"Sure you do, Mark is the weather man on the local TV station. Justice and I just ran into them at church not too long ago. We even asked about Nick."

Max asks, "What did they say?"

"Come to think of it, they were a little evasive," says Vinny.

"Well, chief, when we talked with him, it was like he wasn't there. He said all the right things but with no affect. Lights were out, no one was home. He claims he drove around all night after the celebration stirring up memories about his days at St. Jerome's. We did find out that our murdered victim Sarah Woodbury was Nick's date for the Winter Snow Ball Dance his senior year. He said he didn't know a Sarah Woodbury, but when we said that's a married name and her name was Warner, he admitted knowing her. I think we really need to focus on him. He gave me the chills."

Cully sits down, and Luke takes over, "Our fourth suspect is Thomas Hines, he is forty-four, ordained in 2002, and his parish is in Danville. I think we can rule out Father Hines. He is only 5'6" tall and 5'6" wide. A jolly soul if you will He was on our radar cause when we talked to him on the phone, he kept laughing at our questions. He claims he fell asleep in his car and doesn't remember much of that night, so we went to see him in person."

"Man, that must have been one hell of a reunion," says Jet.

"Our last suspect we feel could also be ruled out. We met Zachary Barbour in Mifflenburg. He is fifty-six and ordained in 1990. For as big as Father Hines is, the opposite is true of Father Barbour. If he weighs 110 pounds, he's lucky. Very tall and so slight. When we shook his hand, it was like a bird's claw. So let's take him off the list. He has family still in the area and was staying with them. Even though we are sure he is not involved, we will still check."

"Ok," says Vinny. "So out of the eleven names, we still have five names on our list. Let's start digging, guys."

CHAPTER 42

2008

Nick is settling into his new role as priest quite well. The Fathers are enjoying his youth and stories he tells, and Nick has learned early on that if you do not follow Miss Clara's schedule, you can end up hungry. He is learning that the schedule is her Bible. If you miss a meal, you will forage for yourself, and you had better clean up after as well.

Nick finds he really enjoys his life as a priest. The congregation has taken to him, and the only buzz through the community is his long sermons, which are always "fire and brimstone." Most wonder why such a young priest would be filled with this dark side of humanity. The other priests preach love, forgiveness, and acceptance.

Nick is beginning to wonder if his sinner detector is broken. Nothing is scratching his itch. Even confession is not sending him any signals. He keeps telling himself to be patient. God has His plan.

St. Mark's parish has a football program for its boys, and Father McCoy has set up a meeting between Nick and Joe Bradford, a parent whose summers have always been spent working with any boy in the parish community who wants to play. The team is a group of misfits, but they play their hearts out. Father McCoy wants Nick to become involved. Most of the players are students at the St. Mark Catholic School. They range in age from eight to twelve.

The meeting is set for Sunday afternoon. As Nick is in the study reading the paper, Miss Clara appears at the door with Joe Bradford.

"Father Nicholas," says Miss Clara, "this is Joe Bradford. He says he has an appointment."

"Yes, yes, Miss Clara, thank you."

Nick recognizes Joe from church and says, "Joe, so nice to meet you."

Nick figures Joe is around thirty-five and was probably a football player in his early days. Around six feet and still looks like a player. A head of blond hair neatly cut and soft, pale, blue eyes.

Once the introductions are over, the two men settle into a comfortable conversation. Miss Clara brings them a pitcher of ice tea and then leaves them alone.

"So, Joe, tell me about your football program," asks Nick.

Joe is eager to start and says, "I started this program several years ago. We call ourselves the Ruffians. I did it mainly to keep the kids busy and out of trouble. We have a network of churches and teams that we play and some are rather far from us, but we make it a fun filled day, not just the game."

"When you say far, how far?" asks Nick.

"Our first game is in Maple Glen. It is near Horsham, two and half hours away, but we have parents who chaperone, a team bus, and kids who are excited. I understand you played football in school," says Joe.

"Yes, and I am very excited about this," says Nick. "When and where do you practice? Have you a schedule yet?"

"Yes, I brought it with me. I can't tell you how happy I am to have your help, Father. It is just so important to these children."

"Looks like our first practice is two weeks from now. I look forward to meeting these kids and their parents and, Joe, don't hesitate to call about anything,"

CHAPTER 43

The summer weeks fly by, and Nick has become involved in helping to coach these boys. Working with Joe is easy, and they get along well.

Their first game is coming up towards the end of August, and the kids are excited. Joe reminds the kids to bring along their bathing suit.

Nick asks Joe, "What is happening with bathing suits?"

Joe replies, "Our first game is two and a half hours away. We leave around 8:00 A.M. The parents who come along provide the food, snacks, and drinks. Our game is scheduled for 11:30 A.M. but will probably not get started till noon. It's all very relaxed. After the game, we go over to the town's swimming hole. A beautiful place, it even has a sandy beach of sorts and a lifeguard. We let the kids swim and eat as they want. And by 6:00 P.M., we pack it in and head home. It's a great day, Nick. I am so anxious for you to experience the joy in these kids' faces.

The day finally arrives, and the boys are so excited. They have practiced so hard and are certain they will have a win under their belt when the day is through.

A huge bus arrives with Joe in the driver seat. There are eighteen boys, three sets of parents, Nick and Joe. Nick has learned that Joe is a widow. His wife was killed in a freak accident. She was a hostess at a restaurant and walking to the door a piece of the building came loose and crashed down hitting and killing her instantly. Joe got a large settlement from the restaurant and used the money to buy the bus and all the football equipment. It had been Joe and his wife's dream to have a slew of kids of their own. With that not happening, Joe has devoted his time to other people's children.

They arrive at the field in plenty of time, and as they are unloading the bus, the other team arrives. This team is from St. Joseph's, right here in town, and has more than once beaten St. Mark's. There is some playful taunting and many of the boys are glad to see their friends from St. Mark's.

The bleachers begin to fill up and there is a great turn out. The game gets underway. Nick and Joe are pacing back and forth watching and coaching from the side line.

There is one woman who is so loud and obnoxious, constantly yelling at her son Randy on the other team. The only time she's quiet is when she is lip locked to the guy beside her. Dressed in shorts and a crop top and her hair pulled into a pony tail, she is an embarrassment to her son.

Nick glances back at the bleacher several times and gets the feeling his sinner detector would be doing a jig right now. Nick looks to Joe as to say, who is she?

Joe says to Nick, "Don't mind her, she is always all about her."

Nick says, "She and her husband should be a little more discreet with the display of affection in front of the kids, especially their own child."

"Ha," says Joe, "That's not her husband. He is deployed overseas right now. Her husband is in the army."

Nick's head is now about to explode. "I knew it, I knew it," he says to himself. "A Jezebel, right here in the open. God has sent me here at this time and place to eliminate this sinner." Nick's eyes are on the field, but his mind is working overtime. He needs a name. He heard her call Randy. He will check the roster of the other team. Nick starts plotting the where and when and how he will make this town a much holier place.

Nick's thought are brought back by cheering and yelling of his boys. The Ruffians have beaten the Yellow Jackets. The first time ever.

They race over to their coaches with such joy and pride and Joe says, 'Father Nick, couldn't have done it without you. Thank you."

Joe was right about the swimming hole. A beautiful place, and the boys and adults are eager to get started eating and swimming. The other team shows up and there she is…Randy's mother. Nick needs to learn more, so he gravitates toward the group of men on the other team and introduces himself. He finds the men and conversation pleasant The man Randy's mom was all over is also there, and Nick notices she is gone.

Nick says to the man, "Where's your wife? She sure is a fan of football."

The man looks sheepishly at Father Nick and says, "She's not my wife, she had to go home to get her other two kids, so they can come and swim and picnic with their brother."

"Oh," says Nick. "What's her name?"

"Tammy Reed," says the man. "I am looking after her while her husband is deployed. Don't get the wrong idea, Father. Tammy just gets carried away sometimes. She doesn't mean anything by it."

"Of course," says Nick, "You know the saying, judge not, etcetera."

"Right," says the man.

Nick is just beside himself. God has sent him his next mission. He has a name and a place, and he knows he'll be back with his sinner detector in hand. He can't wait. It's been a long dry spell. He sends a quick thank you to God and joins Joe and the rest of his group.

Father McCoy notices the excitement in Nick and chalks it up to the fact that his football team won their first game, and Nick gives himself credit for the fine coaching.

The three priests are having a late Saturday evening dinner and Nick says, "Bill, I am going to be getting in late Tuesday night. I am planning on visiting my Great Aunt Lydia and some other cousins and relatives. I don't want you and Adam to worry. I may stay overnight."

"What a fine thing, Nick," says Father McCoy. "Nothing like family. I am glad to see you are appreciative. We lose members of our families far too soon."

And with that, Nick turns a deaf ear as Father McCoy drones on and on and on.

Tuesday finally comes, and during practice with Joe and the team, Nick asks Joe where he keeps the rosters of all the teams they will be playing.

Joe says, "They are in my office in the file cabinet. Why do you want them?"

Nick says, "Just wondering where we will be going and who we will be playing."

"Oh, Nick, I am sorry," says Joe. "I keep forgetting how new you are to the program. I will lay them out on my desk. Help yourself."

Nick thanks him, and after practice, he gets the rosters and looks up Randy Reed's address. He now has all the information he needs.

At dinner that evening, he reminds the Fathers of his plan to visit family.

By 8:00 P.M., Nick is on the road. He can hardly contain his emotions. As he travels down the interstate, he is singing his made up lyrics about Tammy Reed.

"Tammy Reed, Tammy Reed, you have become a bad seed… Here comes my sinner detector and the devil won't reject ya! HA-HA-HA! To hell, to hell, you're going to hell. Happy birthday to me."

Insanity is taking a hold on Nick. As each mile passes, he becomes more lost to reality.

CHAPTER 44

Tammy Reed is tired of being a mother and a part-time wife. She finally gets the kids to bed and the kitchen cleaned up. She is trying to decide if she wants to sneak away and go down to the pub. She knows if Randy wakes up and finds her gone, he'll take care of his siblings.

It's been a long day, and it took so long to finally get the kids fed and into bed. Tammy pours herself yet another glass of wine, gathers up her cigarettes, and goes on the back porch to wallow in self-pity.

Meanwhile, Nick has found the house where Satan's whore lives. He drives around the streets, checks the lay out, and sees there is a back yard, and knowing without any doubt that he is cloaked in protection from prying eyes, he parks his SUV and approaches the back area. And as God would have it, there sitting in the dark of night is Tammy Reed, smoking and drinking.

Nick walks right up the yard, and Tammy sees someone on her property. She gets up and heads in the direction of this intruder. Before she can register in her mind this is the priest from last week's football game, he slams a fist into her face and down she goes. Nick picks her up and carries her to his SUV, places her in the back seat, gets into the driver seat, and knows exactly where he is headed. The swimming hole.

Nick parks the SUV and opens the back door. Tammy is moaning and gaining consciousness, and as she starts to sit up, Nick wraps his hand around her neck and strangles her.

He carries her to the edge of the water where he places her and then proceeds to undress her. As he takes off the few clothes she has on, he neatly folds them and places them into a grocery bag. He goes to the rear of his SUV and retrieves his satchel. He places it carefully beside the dead sinner and begins his ritual. First, he tapes her breasts, so they look perky. Then he applies the make-up in such a way that Tammy Reed looks the part she was playing, a tease, an evil-doer. He grabs her pony tail, and with a quick snip of the scissors, he hacks off her hair. When Nick is satisfied, he takes one of his statues of the Virgin Mary and rams it into her well of deceit. As he looks down on her in disgust, he is so pleased with himself. He then takes an arrow and plunges it into her heart.

When he is finished, he does a little dance and sings, "To hell, to hell, you're going to hell, happy birthday to me."

On the way home, Nick flutters the pony tail hair out of his window where the wind picks it up and it disappears. Nick finds a shopping mall and detours into the parking lot where sits a container from an organization asking for clothing donation. Nick stops and places the grocery bag into the container and continues on his way. A job well done.

CHAPTER 45

PRESENT

Vinny is pacing back and forth in front of the white board where there are five names of priests who are suspected of being a serial killer.

His mood has darkened and says, "J.J., I want you to research the members of the Dougherty family. I am truly bewildered that Nicholas Dougherty is on that list. Find out where each of his siblings are living and their work history."

J.J. starts the fingers moving, and in no time, has what Vinny needs.

"Oh, boss," says J.J., "Patrick is thirty-two, not married, has an apartment in East Greenville. He graduated college with a Masters in finance. Works for a financial firm. Says here he is quite the playboy and an eligible bachelor. His brother Tristan is twenty-eight. He is married, has three kids, lives in Bethlehem, and teaches at DeSales University. His wife Annie is a stay at home mom. Alice, his sister, is thirty-six and married to Nick's best friend, Charles Sullivan. He's a doctor, she has the local restaurant here in town. The Sullivan Steak House. They have no children. Then there is a younger sister, Catherine. She is twenty-three and a student at Lehigh University and lives at home."

"That was fast and thorough," says Vinny. "Good work. All the other details we will take into account if need be. Right now that's a good start."

"One more thing, chief," says J.J., "looks like all but Catherine were at the reunion."

"That's good to know. Mickey, I want you to start digging into the alibis and background on Frantzen and Hoffman. C.J., Max, I want you to zero in on those two on your list. Cully, Luke, I want you two to interview and question relentlessly the two brothers Tristen and Patrick. See where they were that night, who they were with, and if they interacted with their brother, Nick. I am going to interview Mark and Grace myself since I am somewhat friendly with them. I want to keep Alice and this Charlie Sullivan's interview for last, and Luke, Cully, I will go with you for that interview. If this Charlie is Nick's best friend since high school, he may know things he doesn't know he knows. Once we get all the facts, then we will interview Father Nicholas Dougherty a little more in depth. One more thing people, as you learn facts about this case, I want you to update our crime board as you go. That way I will be able to see the progress without having to always meet."

Vinny gets into his car and sits for a bit, going over in his mind how he will handle Grace and Mark Dougherty. He puts his car in gear and heads out.

He finds their street, and as he slowly passes the houses, he is aware of the bomb he is going to visit upon the Dougherty's. It is a pleasant neighborhood. Trees line the street, many of the yards are landscaped with flowers and bushes. He spots the house he wants and sees a car in the driveway. Good, Vinny thinks, Mark is home. He pulls in behind the car and gets out and walks to the door. He rings the doorbell and waits.

Mark hears the bell and is annoyed. He just got home from the TV station and he is looking forward to some quiet time with Grace. With all his children grown and gone, he enjoys the empty nest.

As he opens the door, he sees it is the Chief of Police.

"Vinny, what a surprise," says Mark. "Can I help you with something?"

Vinny shakes Mark's hand and says, "May I come in?"

"Of course, of course. Grace and I were just enjoying some quiet time. Please join us."

Mark takes Vinny into the living room where Grace is seated having a glass of wine.

"Goodness, Chief Miller, what a surprise," says Grace. "Can we help you with something?"

"I am really sorry to bother you," says Vinny, "but I'd like to ask you a few questions about your son Nicholas."

"Nick, why Nick?" asks Mark.

Vinny replies, "I am sure you have been following the details of the death of a young woman that was found a few months ago by Jeb Landis."

Mark and Grace nod yes.

"We have identified the young woman as Sarah Warner. Her married name is Woodbury. She was here for the reunion St. Jerome held. I've been told Nick dated Sarah in high school, and I wanted to know if Nick might have said something to you about her when he was here for the reunion."

Grace blurts out, "We didn't even know Nicholas came to the reunion until Alice told us. He never even stopped to say hello. Nick seems to have issues with us, chief, he doesn't share anything with us, not since his ordination. Even when he baptized Tristen's three children, he was very distant towards us. Well, me really, chief. He seems to have an unhealthy view towards women since that McGrath girl hurt him so badly. And for the record, Chief Miller, he did not date that girl. He took her to the Winter Snow Ball dance and that was all. She would have liked more, but Nick was focused on his vocation, not some loose immoral girl."

Mark asks, "Why are you asking about Nick? Surely you don't suspect our boy."

"My officers and I are checking on everyone we can locate that was at the reunion. It seems that was the last time anyone saw Sarah."

"I'm sorry we couldn't be more help, chief," says Mark. "Perhaps Alice and Charlie could help more. I understand from Alice and my other two sons that Nick seemed to be enjoying himself. In fact Tristen mentioned Nick was extremely attentive towards his brothers."

"Thank you for your time, sorry I interrupted your day," says Vinny.

Mark and Vinny shake hands and Vinny heads to his car. Vinny makes a mental note to have J.J. research what happened with that McGrath girl. He could sense asking the Dougherty's would open some very deep wounds.

CHAPTER 46

2014

Over the next six years, Nicholas Dougherty has kept his promise to God to cleanse the world of evil-doing women. He uses family as his excuse to be away from St. Mark's, but never is he gone long enough nor does anything out of the ordinary to alert the Fathers that he is not this full of energy young priest out there in the world helping and administering to those in need.

When Nick gets his itch, he plans, and from Bethlehem to Philadelphia to Scranton, he moves without detection, hunting.

In 2014, Father Adam calls Nick to his study and informs him the Bishop has asked him to spare Nick for five or six months and have Nick reassigned to St. Peter and Paul in Reading. It seems Father Craig Evans is having some needed surgery, and his duties as pastor will be interrupted for at least five months. Father Evans is the only priest serving that community. Nick shows disappointment, but Father Adams assures him it is a wonderful opportunity and will give him the experience for when he will get a church of his own.

Nick accepts this challenge, and later that month, packs up and heads to Reading.

Father Evans is grateful for Nick's help. The two priests get along well, and Father Evans is anxious to get this over and back as the head of his church. Last Sunday of the month, Father Evans introduces Father Dougherty to the congregation, and that Monday enters the hospital, after which he will be in rehab for at least four months.

As the days pass, Nick fills his role beautifully. He has such an air about him that the congregation has fallen in love with him. Nick has been kept so busy he has little time to hunt. This parish has no housekeeper, so he also has to keep the Rectory clean and do his own chores. Sometimes there are volunteers who help out with meals and heavier cleaning.

One late summer evening, Nick must take some legal papers to the church's lawyer. He is to give them to Attorney Anna Serento, who is the church's representative. Nick drives into Reading to the law office and goes in search of Anna Serento.

Nick approaches the receptionist and asks for Attorney Serento.

The receptionist, an attractive young lady, says, "You're not Father Evans, are you representing St. Peter and Paul's Parish?"

"Yes, I am Father Dougherty covering for Father Evans while he recuperates from surgery. I have some paper work that I must discuss with Attorney Serento."

"It's nice to meet you, Father. I hope Father Evans is ok," says the receptionist. "Please have a seat, and I will find Anna for you."

As Nick goes to sit, a woman comes out of one of the offices. She is not very tall, maybe 5'5" at most, a bit on the chubby side, and very loud with wild blond hair. She is wearing a suit just a bit snug but shows an ample breast with a blouse open two more buttons than it should.

"Well, well, well, looky here," says this woman as she approaches Nick. "Aren't you just a delicious tidbit of manhood."

Nick is stunned. Doesn't this woman not see my collar? Doesn't she know you don't talk that way to a priest, for God's sake.

Nick is about to insult her when she reaches out her hand and says, "Hi, I'm Attorney Serento, but you, my gorgeous creature, may call me Anna. So you're the priest covering for Father Evans."

Nick shakes her hand, which she holds entirely too long but starts that itch that Nick is only too familiar with and says, "Yes, I am Father Dougherty."

"Come into my office and let's see what you have…Ha, don't look so shocked, I mean the papers you have in your hand. HA-HA! Besides, I am married. Here's a picture of my husband. He is a JAG with the Navy, never home, so I find my thrills elsewhere, know what I mean? HA-HA. Wouldn't mind thrilling you. Sit, sit before I attack you on the spot."

After forty-five minutes of listening to inappropriate comments laced through the legal discussion, Nick is more than ready to get out of there. Anna Serento has affirmed what Nick already knows about women, and this one must be sent to hell.

Nick is still stinging from the sexual verbal abuse he has taken as he sits in his car. His appointment lasted almost an hour and a half. Nick is hungry and decides while he is in the heart of Reading, he will have dinner here. With the luck of the Irish, there is a restaurant right across the street from the law office.

Nick is seated by window and has a clear view of the office building and an alley running between the buildings. Nick has finished his dinner, and it has now gotten dark. As Nick crosses the street to his car, he sees a flicker of light coming from the exit door to the lawyers' building. He stops to get a better look and sees it is that filthy-mouthed lawyer. She propped the door open, so it wouldn't close and lock on her, and she lights a cigarette. Nick can see her hiding behind a huge array of dumpsters. Odd that such a loud, obnoxious woman would hide her smoking, thinks Nick.

All of a sudden, the door opens a bit farther and out steps a well-dressed black man. He is tall, has the presence of an important man. He is dressed in black slacks and a white shirt opened at the collar. He begins a conversation with Anna. They are very animated, and Anna laughs at something the man says.

Nick watches assuming this man is also going to light up a cigarette when all of a sudden Nick sees the man's hand start to unbutton the already unbuttoned blouse and goes down on her with his mouth while taking both breasts in his hands and starts sucking. The lawyer reaches down and starts unbuckling his pants and before you can say hell's bells, he pushes up her skirt and is screwing her against the wall.

Nick watches with amazement. The adulterers finish up, arranges their clothing, and as the man steps back inside the building, Anna lights up one more cigarette before she steps back inside the door as if this was the most common behavior.

Nick now knows what he and his sinner detector must do.

For several nights over a two-week period, Nick cases the alley and watches. In both weeks, Nick sees this fornication taking place on Tuesday and Friday nights, just like clockwork.

The following Tuesday, Nick, dressed in street clothes, goes to the lawyer's office building, and parks his car out of sight at the other end of the alley. And, true to form, out comes Anna, smokes and fucks, and then the man goes back inside and Anna lights up another cigarette. Nick approaches her.

At first Anna is startled, no one can see you behind this cluster of dumpsters, and then she realizes that it is that gorgeous priest from St. Peter and Paul's.

"Are my eyes deceiving me?" asks Anna. "You're that scrumptious hunk of manhood I've been drooling over for the past two weeks. Are you here to have a taste of some forbidden fruit? I see there is no collar keeping you from what comes natural. And, baby, I can give you a taste, a big taste of what comes natural."

Nick smiles and reaches out and strokes her breast just to put her at ease and says, "What would your husband say if he knew you were seducing a priest?"

As Anna takes her hand and reaches for Nick's privates, that has actually started to react to the animal instinct, she says, "He'd say go for it, baby."

With those words still ringing in her ears, Nick reaches up and puts his hands around this wretched woman's neck and squeezes the life out of her. She falls down behind the dumpsters while Nick reaches over and closes the exit door.

He goes to the place beside the dumpster where he set his sinner detector and goes about his work. When Nick finishes his mission, he gathers his things and heads back to the Rectory where the first thing he does is take a shower and masturbate. It disturbs him that he enjoyed Anna Serento's breasts and hand on his joy stick. He wonders if he is starting to enjoy their debauchery.

The next day, late morning, a janitor comes out of the lawyer's office building to dispose of trash, and behind the dumpsters he finds Anna Serento, naked, made up to look like a whore and as dead as can be.

The police are called.

CHAPTER 47

PRESENT

The years start to blend together for Nick. He is having trouble separating his two worlds. He paces in his room, rummages in the refrigerator for food late at night. His personal appearance is suffering as well. He goes months without a haircut, then will go and have his head almost shaved bald. His SUV is dirty, and some parents are complaining to Father McCoy about Nick's sermons. Threatening to forbid their children to attend Mass when he is there. Not wanting their children subjected to the rantings of sermons nullifying women.

It is early September, and Father McCoy is in his study reading when Father Lynch knocks on the door.

"Bill, have you some time to give me?" asks Adam.

"Why, of course, Adam, come sit, what's on your mind?"

Adam closes the door to the study and sits opposite Father McCoy.

"Bill, we need to talk about Nick. I am becoming quite concerned about his behavior. He seems to be having some kind of a meltdown, even a mental break."

"Now, now," says Bill, "I don't think it is that bad, although I have noticed a few erratic behaviors. But nothing to worry about."

Adam says, "Even Miss Clara came to me about him. She told me that often times she will hear him ranting and raving in his room, and one day she was so concerned, she knocked to see if he needed help. When he opened the door, he stood there in his shorts, his hair all askew, and when she asked if he was alright, he told her he got carried away practicing a sermon. She didn't believe it for a second."

Bill says, "Adam, don't you think you're being melodramatic? He's young, full of piss and vinegar as my old man would say."

"No, I don't," says Adam. "Miss Clara also mentioned he has far more street clothes than his priestly attire that needs washing, and the other morning, I was up early and went out to the garage. When I passed Nick's SUV, it was warm. I touched the hood. He was out all night. Do you think he is seeing a woman?"

"No," says Father McCoy. "If he has a love interest, it won't be a woman. Over the years, he has made it quite clear he has no love for women. Why he doesn't even keep contact with his own mother."

"We have to do something, Bill," says Adam.

"Let's just give it awhile, and we can both stay alert and keep an eye on him. If need be, I'll have a talk with him. How does that sound?" asks Bill.

"Ok, but, Bill, a close watch. I am really concerned," says Adam. "And by the way, that Aunt Lydia he claims to be going to visit all the time…she died three years ago."

A few days later while having a marvelous dinner and a heated conversation over the condition of the world, Nick announces to the Fathers that he has received an invitation to an all school reunion at St. Jerome's.

"What do you think, Bill, should I go?" asks Nick.

Adam and Bill exchange glances, and Bill says, "Why, Nick, I think that's a splendid idea."

Nick says, "I really would like to go back and see my friends and especially Father Eric. I have had so little contact with anyone for such a long time. Even my best friend and brother-in-law Charlie. But could you manage without me for a few days?"

"When is it, Nick?" asks Adam.

"According to the invitation, it will be the third weekend in October. A weekend of activities starting Friday through Mass on Sunday. I could be back Monday," says Nick, "or try to make it back Sunday night."

"What do you think, Adam, can we spare the boy for a weekend?" asks Father McCoy.

"Nick, I think that will do you good. You need a few days from your hectic schedule. Why don't you accept the invitation and make your plans," says Adam.

The next few weeks go almost too smoothly. Father Lynch watches carefully, and Nick is the epitome of a devote priest. Even his sermons have been tampered down. Adam notices a spring in Nick's step but still a vacancy behind the eyes.

CHAPTER 48

Nick is beside himself with excitement. Although he has mixed feelings, he is sure he may find several wanton women left, by themselves, without their husbands, to tempt and tease and play with former boyfriends and even find new ones to destroy at this reunion. On the other side of the coin, he is excited to think he will reconnect with friends and is really anxious to see Father Eric. The one person who helped him get his act together, so to speak.

The weekend is finally here, and Nick has packed his public suitcase but also makes sure his private suitcase is well stocked. He must try to be more sparing with the make-up. He is running out. Nick remembers calling the company way back to see if he could get more, but unfortunately they no longer carry those colors. But right now that is not a concern. Getting on the road is. Nick has reserved a room at one of the local hotels. A bit farther out than where the other alumni will be staying, he wants his privacy.

Nick checks in, puts his things out, and takes a nap. Friday's events start at 3:00 P.M. at the local community park. There will be a cook-out with local bands and stands set up commemorating each class that has graduated from St. Jerome's. Pictures, memorabilia, and souvenirs to buy. At 4:00 P.M., Nick arrives and is immediately surrounded with old friends and acquaintances. He spies Charlie heading his way and his heart skips a beat...Charile, his one and only best friend in the world. The only person he can truly say he loves.

"Charlie," yells Nick, "come here, you old man, and give me a hug."

They hug, clapping each other on the back and then shaking hands.

"Where's Alice?" asks Nick.

"She couldn't make the cook-out, but she'll be at the dinner dance tomorrow," replies Charlie. "I saw your brothers over by the beer stand when I came in. Let's go see them."

The afternoon of food, beer, and comradery fills Nick's heart with joy. He is amazed at his brothers and has some twinges of regret not having kept in closer touch with them. It seems the only thorn in Nick's side, the only darkness that spreads through Nick's heart and mind, was when Sarah Warner sought him out and brazenly hugged him and kissed him on the mouth, telling him how much she missed him. Missed him? Nick hadn't thought of her once since that party where she practically raped him.

She was like a fly that wouldn't go away. She hung on his every word. Interrupted his conversations with his other classmates and followed him from place to place. Finally, she met up with some other girls from her class and she went away.

Now there, Nick thought, was a perfect candidate for elimination, but another saying came to mind, "You don't piss where you eat." There will be others just as deserving, just not here.

Nick has a good buzz on, and despite this, he drives back to his hotel. Nick always has this attitude of being one of God's chosen. Nothing and nobody will interfere with him. He is bullet proof. After all God has made him special and has given him special qualities. He falls into bed and sleeps the sleep of the dead.

It is almost noon when Nick wakes. He showers, dresses as a priest, and turns the TV on to catch his father doing the weather report. He is stunned to see how much older he looks. Perhaps he should visit his mother and father while he is here. Once he is ready, he goes in search of lunch. He is ravenous. Beer always makes him hungry. Maybe that's why the Fathers always drink scotch.

He finds the restaurant in the hotel and sees several other alumni he recognizes from yesterday. No one he knows. He was really surprised at the number of priests that were there. St. Jerome certainly has its share.

After lunch he decides he really doesn't want to see his parents and even though he enjoyed his brothers last night, he has had enough of family for now. Besides, he'll see them tonight at the dinner dance. Nick decides to just drive around and check out all his old haunts.

As Nick drives through town on his way back to the hotel, he is feeling tranquil. He has enjoyed reminiscing when he sees the ball field and the corner ice cream shop where they all hung out, plotting their futures.

"No," Nick shouts out loud and quickly pulls over to the curb. "It can't be, oh, God, don't let it be," cries Nick as tears roll down his cheeks. He says, still talking out loud, "Yes, yes, it is, it's Mary Ellen McGrath." She is standing in front of the post office. The sun glistening off those curls, the curve of her back, just as lovely as if she was seventeen again.

He puts his head on the steering wheel and curses her soul to hell while he feels the stirring of lust for her. When he looks up, she is gone.

He wipes his eyes, goes to his dark place, and heads back to the hotel.

CHAPTER 49

Slowly, Nick opens his eyes. He is not sure where he is. Nothing smells right, nothing feels right, and it is dark. Slivers of light shine through a slated blind and there are unfamiliar noises.

He sits up with a start and the memory of seeing Mary Ellen rushes back to him, and now remembers where he is. After seeing that witch, he came back to the hotel, and after an exhausting tirade of pacing and throwing the few things not nailed down, he fell asleep.

As Nick sits on the edge of the bed, he contemplates packing and heading back to St. Mark's. He cannot risk running into her. What if she shows up as a guest at the reunion? Nick believes he would lose what is left of his sanity.

Nick wrestles with this dilemma and decides the hell with her. "I am going, and I am going to enjoy myself," he says to no one in particular.

Nick arrives at the Convention Center, and the music is already streaming out through the doors and windows. Laughter can be heard, clinking of glasses signaling toasts among friends.

As he enters the center, he spies Charlie and Alice, drinks in hand talking with his brothers. He joins them.

"Nick, old buddy, was worried you weren't coming," says Charlie.

"Almost, Charlie, almost," says Nick.

Alice grabs Nick by the arm and says, "Come on, brother, dance with your sister while Charlie gets you a drink."

Nick gets caught up in the moment and says, "Why not, let's show these old alumni how it's done." And off they go.

When they come back to the group, Charlie hands Nick his drink, and Nick swallows it in one gulp, turns to Annie, his sister-in-law, and says, "How about dancing with a priest? Charlie, would you get me another one of these," and hands Charlie his glass.

As Annie and Nick are dancing, Annie says, "Nick, it is so good to see you. I don't think we spent time together since Colleen's Baptism."

"I know, I've been very busy, Annie, it's a priest's job to rid the world of evil, and I have been working long and hard at it."

"My goodness, Nick, you make it sound like you are a super hero," laughs Annie.

"You'd be surprised. I am a super hero, and my special power is invisibility," chuckles Nick.

The dance ends, and Annie is relieved. She likes Nick, after all he is her brother-in-law, but he is so strange.

When Nick and Annie rejoin the group, Alice says it is time to find their table. They will soon be serving dinner. Alice tells them she has been able to arrange for a table of eight, which will accommodate Tristen, Annie, Patrick and his date, Nick, Charlie, and Alice. She is not sure if anyone else will be joining them.

They find their table, and as the others find their seats, Nick goes to the bar for another drink. On his way back, he stops to chat and say hello to old classmates. When he gets back to his table, he sees that someone else has indeed joined the Dougherty table. It is a woman.

She is standing with her back to him, talking to his family, and as he approaches, she turns and says, "Nick, how wonderful to see you again." It is Sarah Warner.

"Sarah," says Nick. "Nice to see you, too, and you look lovely." Nick gives her his full attention and let's his eyes wander over her body, noticing the sexy red dress, the tight way it clings to her body, and how wonderful she smells.

"Thank you, Nick," says Sarah as she smiles her most beguiling smile. "I am at your table. I have no date, so I have been asked to help fill in any vacancies. I hope no one minds."

Alice speaks up, "Sarah, of course we'd be happy for you to join us. Come sit by Charlie and me." Alice knows Sarah is still hot for Nick and doesn't want any awkward situations.

"No, no," says Nick. "This lovely lady must sit by me. Perhaps after we eat, we could share a dance or two."

Charlie looks at Nick as if he has two heads, and as Nick orders another drink from one of the servers passing by, he wonders just what is Nick up to. He's getting smashed, and I've never seen him so, so what, so flirtatious?

Conversation around the table is both fun at time and serious at times, but at no time is it strained with Sarah sitting beside Nick.

Sarah is in her glory. She can't believe how nice Nick is being to her. She has longed for moments like this, and now it is happening.

As the evening progresses, Nick and Sarah have many dances. Each time Sarah gets bolder as Nick holds her in his arms and soon she becomes brave enough and just tipsy enough to suggest that maybe, just maybe, they could go somewhere else.

By the time Nick has had his share of booze, danced with former classmates, and has yet again ended up with Sarah, Nick heard her suggestion and at first says, "Sarah, you know that cannot happen."

"Why, Nick," pleads Sarah. "Can't we just be alone, even for a little while. Just to talk, just to reminisce. Nothing else."

"You are a tease, Sarah," slurs Nick, "but what the heck. Yes, let's go somewhere, where we can just sit and talk without all this noise and people."

"But, Sarah," whispers Nick, "we cannot leave together. Why don't you leave first and park in St. Jerome's school parking lot and wait for me. Then I will come and pick you up. I must remain here for at least a half hour after you leave."

"Oh, Nick, I'll go right now,"

When Nick and Sarah get back to the table, Sarah sits for a few minutes and then says, "Well, friends and classmates, I must be going." She looks at Nick and says, "Nick, you have made my night. Thank you for being so attentive. Good night, all."

After Sarah leaves, Nick becomes very animated and tells jokes and seems to be enjoying himself. Charlie is surprised at how Nick has opened up; he figures it is the booze but is happy to see that Nick treated Sarah decently.

Soon the convention hall is emptying out and people are leaving. Nick stands, sways a little, and announces he is leaving, too.

Alice asks if he plans to be at Mass in the morning to end the reunion's celebration, and Nick says yes. Father Eric is including all the priests on the alter that has graduated from St. Jerome's.

"Wonderful," says Alice. "We will see you tomorrow. Are you ok to drive? You had a lot to drink."

"Yes, I am fine. Good night."

CHAPTER 50

The cool air hits Nick and sobers him up just a bit. He has told Sarah he'd meet her but is now wondering the wisdom of that decision.

"Oh, well, what can it hurt," he asks himself as he drives off to meet Sarah Warner.

Sarah has been sitting in her car waiting. She is sure Nick will not show up and is just about to leave when she sees headlights enter the school's parking lot.

"Yes, yes, yes," she screams out loud. "He did come."

He pulls up beside her car, and she gets out of her car and enters the domain of her one and only love. Now if she can only entice, sweet talk, or if need be, beg, get him to make love to her.

As she enters the car, she says, "I was afraid you weren't coming."

"No, Sarah, a promise is a promise," says Nick. "Where do you want to go?"

"Where are you staying?" she asks.

"Well, I have a hotel room but, Sarah, it wouldn't look good for a priest to bring a gorgeous woman back to his hotel room, now would it?"

"Gorgeous, Nick, you think I am gorgeous?" asks Sarah, not believing her ears.

"Yes," says Nick as he leans over toward her and says, "you smell good, too."

Sarah leans over into Nick as he smells her, and as one to take advantage of a situation, kisses him on the mouth. Stars and fireworks go off in her head.

Nick does not retreat but returns the kiss, and she says, "Please let's find somewhere quickly."

Nick says, "I know, let's go to the old haunt where we went as kids to make-out. Blackwood."

"Perfect," sighs Sarah. "Do you think it is still a hot make-out place?"

"No, not anymore, but let's find out. Kids now a days don't go parking. At least from what I hear in Confession."

They ride in silence for a bit. Sarah is beyond happy, and Nick seems to be really going to be good to her. Sarah's definition of good is Nick will make love to her.

Nick says, "How long are you staying before you need to go home?"

Sarah replies, "I'll stay as long as you want me to, Nick."

"We'll see how tonight goes," says Nick, "before we make other plans."

Sarah is so impatient to get to the make-out spot. These consoles on SUV's do not make for snuggling. Sarah reaches over and takes Nick's hand. He is so willing, and as Sarah holds his hand, it is all he can do to keep from gagging and pulling away. He thinks to himself, she is making me dirty.

They finally arrive and see at once that the lover's lane has not been used in a long time.

"Oh, Sarah," says Nick, "look, no one has been here in a long time. We should be safe from prying eyes," and he reaches over and cups her chin in order to kiss her.

Sarah is so warm and wet in anticipation of having Nick, she kisses him and whispers, "Let's get in the back seat."

They move to the back, and Nick slides in with ease and has opened his shirt. He knows he must play this part and finds Sarah gross, but maybe a little bit of the flesh will do him good. Sarah's red party dress rises above her thigh, and Nick gets a glimpse of red thongs. He finds his own desires getting stronger.

Sarah has nothing on except her dress and under pants, and soon Nick has pulled down the straps and has exposed her breasts. He gently, at first, cups one breast with his hand and leans in and kisses and teases her nipple with his tongue while his other hand slides under the dress to find her sweet spot.

Sarah is groaning, never has she felt this way. This is Nick Dougherty, the only man she ever truly loved, the one she always compared to every man she ever met, and he is finally going to make love to her.

Sarah reaches down to unzip Nick's pants while she is delirious and in the throes of passion as he works magic with his mouth and finger.

As she takes out his member and whispers in his ear, "Let me take you in my mouth," when Nick says, "Oh, Mary Ellen, I love you so much."

Sarah jolts back, pushes Nick's hands away from her, and says, "What did you just say?"

Nick looks bewildered. What's happening?

Just like Mary Ellen, as soon as he thinks she's going to let him slide into her, she backs off and reminds him what a pure virgin she is...well, enough is enough and he slaps her and says, "Mary Ellen, you can't keep teasing me like this."

"Nick, Nick," shouts Sarah, "I am not Mary Ellen. Mary Ellen does not love you, how dare you use me like this." This is déjà vu all over again.

Nick's eyes come into focus and stares at Sarah and says, "You're not Mary Ellen, you are that slut of a Sarah Warner. What are you doing to me? For God's sake, cover yourself."

Sarah is stunned and says, "Oh yeah, oh, holy one. A moment ago, you couldn't get enough of me and now I'm a slut."

Nick's itch is back full force, and he remembers he is here to do God's work. He is sure God will forgive him for enjoying the prelude, and with that thought in mind, he reaches up and strangles the life out of Sarah Warner. As she lays there in the back seat, Nick arranges himself and zips up his pants. He is exhausted. Where did Mary Ellen go, and how did Sarah take her place?

Nick sits still for ten to fifteen minutes, trying to find his right mind. He finally realizes he has completed a mission and is puzzled at how it happened.

As Sarah lay there, already practically naked, Nick removes her dress and panties and must remember her shoes and purse in the front seat.

Nick gently lifts her out of his SUV and places her in a nest of leaves. He removes her jewelry, goes to the back of the SUV, gets his sinner detector, and proceeds to show God how he takes care of the evil lurking at every event. When he is pleased with his work, he takes her hair he has chopped off and lets it float away in the night's wind. He gathers up his things, takes Sarah's keys from her purse, and drives away, leaving behind Sarah Warner, cast away yet again by Nicholas Dougherty.

Nick remembers an old junk yard not far from the school where Sarah has left her car. He drives to the junk yard and parks his SUV behind some old train cars. He hikes back to the school yard and drives Sarah's Ford Focus back to the junk yard where he hides it among all the old abandoned cars and rusted out trucks. Knowing he has the cloak of invisibility, he walks away in no great hurry. He gets into his SUV and drives back to the hotel where he admires himself and the work he does.

Sunday morning finds St. Jerome's parking lot filled to capacity. Everyone has come out to celebrate Mass with the priests who attended the reunion. The church is filled with family and friends. The Dougherty family is well-represented. Mark and Grace file in with their children and grandkids. There is Tristen, Annie, and the three children, Patrick and Catherine, and just a bit late comes Alice and Charlie. Mass begins with Father Eric leading the parade of priests, two by two up onto the alter. It is a magnificent sight. So many priest from one small community.

After the Homily, Father Eric introduces each priest with their name, year they graduated from high school, and where they are ministering.

Grace is bursting with pride. Her boy, her sweet, gentle boy. She wishes her relationship with Nick was better, but at least he is now talking to her. Grace wonders what happened that turned him away from her. She knows it has to be something connected with that awful girl Mary Ellen.

Thinking of her, Grace scans the church, praying she had the decency to stay away.

After Mass Nick joins his family in the parking lot, and despite Mark's insistence that Nick come back to the house for a feast and some family time, Nick feigns his need to get back to his Parish. He has already stayed too long and has put a burden on the Fathers.

He says his goodbyes, and says to Charlie, "If you see Sarah, tell her I enjoyed our time together."

"I will, Nick," says Charlie. "Wonder why she is not here. Sarah wouldn't miss any chance to see you, even if it to say goodbye."

As Nick drives back to Selinsgrove. he detours into a mall parking lot and disposes of the last remaining memory of Sarah Warner Woodbury.

He arrives back at the Rectory late evening. He is happy, content, and anxious to get back into his routine.

CHAPTER 51

For the next few weeks, Father Adam keeps a close eye on Nick and is surprised to see that he appears calmer.

One morning at breakfast, Father Adam says to Father Bill, "Where's the young lad this morning?"

Bill replies, "He has Mass this week for the school children. He left early this morning."

"I've been watching him, Bill, and I think that reunion trip did him a world of good. He doesn't seem so haunted, and I think he's been in every night since he's back," states Adam.

"I told you, Adam, you worry too much, but I think you are right. Nick has been back, what, four, five months now, and I, too, see a big change in him. Although I am not sure what he means when he says his time here will soon end. Have you listened to his sermons lately?" asks Bill.

Father Adam says, "Yes, he is obsessed with the Resurrection."

"Perhaps he is preparing his sermons and the congregation for Easter," suggests Bill.

"It certainly is better than his fire and brimstone against women," chuckles Adam.

Nick is indeed a changed man. He is still savoring his experience with Sarah and how tempted he was, but God prevailed and brought him to his senses. He never felt this content after any other mission and is beginning to believe that perhaps his specialness is ending. God has tested him, and by all accounts, he has served Him well. Besides, he is running out of his tools. Nick sees this as another sign that his mission is near completion, and God is almost ready to reward him.

When the Fathers are content in their appraisal of Nick and have left down their guard in monitoring him, Nick again seems to have become agitated. He flares up for no reason, and towards the end of summer, they are again on high alert. Father McCoy shares with Father Lynch that he plans to discuss Nick with the Bishop.

In the meantime, Nick gets a call from Father Evans in Reading. While Nick was transferred there, he worked with many groups of children.

Miss Clara calls to Nick that he has a call on the house phone.

"Hello," says Nick.

"Father Nick, this is Father Craig, from St. Peter and Paul. How are you?"

Nick is hesitant and says, "Why, I'm just fine. How good of you to call."

"I'm calling with some bad news, Nick, and thought you should know. Remember Ms. Eberhart and her son? You were really taken with the child, and I know you were fond of him."

"Yes, I remember," says Nick, "His name is Stevie, about eleven or twelve. From what I remember, his mother really neglected him. Is he ok?"

Father Craig says, "Yes, yes, the boy is ok, but word came through that his father was killed overseas. Remember his father was serving in Iraq. The funeral is in two days from now. I thought you would want to know. Perhaps seeing you would ease the boy's confusion. His mother is no help, it seems she's not too upset. Making it all about herself, but in all fairness, people grieve differently."

"Yes," says Nick. "I will talk to Father Bill. I am sure he will allow me to come to the service. Thank you for calling, Craig, and God be with that child."

Nick gets permission, and in two days, heads to Reading to attend the funeral of Stevie's dad and hoping to be of some comfort to the boy. Stevie's father had belonged to a parish in Chester Springs, and that is where the funeral Mass is taking place.

Nick was a few minutes late and quietly finds a pew. Other than service people in uniform, there are very few mourners. Nick sees an older couple, presumably his parent, and a few other possible relatives. Sitting in the front row is Ms. Eberhart and Stevie. The child is almost invisible, and Nick's heart breaks a little.

As the Mass is over and the family moves down the aisle, Stevie spots Nick, and he breaks out in a big grin. Nick waves a small wave, and once outside, tries to catch up, but mother and son are already in the car. Nick follows the possession to the cemetery. It is a small cemetery on the outskirts of town. It is tucked away behind large trees, and if you didn't know it was there, you would never find it. Despite its location, it is well-attended. Grass is mowed, flowers are neatly placed, and it has the feeling of a sacred place.

After the coffin is lowered, Nick sees Stevie sitting alone in the row of chairs meant for family. His mother is off to one side talking animatedly with three young, good-looking soldiers. Everyone else has gone. She has no concern for her child.

Nick approaches Stevie, whose whole face breaks out in a big smile and he races to Nick and hugs him.

Nick bends down and says, "Stevie, I am so sorry about your dad."

Stevie says, "Mom says I'm better off now because I really didn't know my dad, do you know your dad, Father Nick?"

Nick takes his hand and leads him back to the chairs while still keeping an eye on his mom.

"I could kidnap him," Nick thinks, "and she would never bat an eye. What an awful mother," and he feels an itch, small but an itch.

He sits beside the little boy with his arm around him and tells him that his father was a brave, brave man. Like a super hero, and Stevie must always be proud of him, and when he is older and needs guidance, Nick tells him to come here and talk to him. That his father will always protect him.

"What kind of nonsense are you filling my boy's head with?" says Amy Erberhart as she approaches from behind.

"Stevie tells me you think you and he are better off now that he is fatherless," answers Nick rather sternly.

"That's none of your business, Father, come along, Stevie, we have things to do, and Father Dougherty is not welcome." She grabs her little boy's hand and walks off.

"Poor little boy, he has no power," thinks Nick. "He is already under the power of a wicked woman."

It is late afternoon, and Nick decides to hang around for a while. He drives around remembering his time he spent with Father Craig. He also remembers, with pure delight, that lawyer over in Reading, with torpedoes for breasts that he showed what fucking in alleys can get you, and with that, he laughs and laughs.

Nick finds a nice restaurant and decides to have dinner before heading back to the Rectory. While he is enjoying his dinner, his mind wanders to this beautiful child and tries to think what he can do to help him.

Nick decides to go and see if Ms. Eberhart will talk to him. Perhaps he can make her understand how much Stevie needs her.

He knows where they live, and it is going on 10:00 P.M. He is sure Stevie is in bed, and maybe his mother will talk to him. He arrives at the house and rings the bell.

Amy comes to the door, "Who is it," she says, noticing a collar which belongs to some priest. "Oh, it's you, what do you want?"

"Ms. Eberhart, I have come to apologize for sticking my nose where it doesn't belong. May we start again, and please may I talk to you about Stevie?"

Amy steps out of the door onto the porch and says, "Yes, ok. I guess we were all upset, but be quiet, I don't want to wake my son."

"Perhaps we could sit in my SUV? Would Stevie be scared to find you missing?" asks Nick.

"No, he often wakes up when I'm not home. He knows what to do," says Amy.

As they climb into Nick's SUV, he notices a change in Ms. Eberhart's manner. She has warmed to the idea of discussing her son, and Nick is so relieved.

As soon as they are settled she says, "What's it to you what happens to my boy?"

Nick says, "It's going to be hard on him not having a father, and it is important that you spend more time with him and tell him nice, good stories about his dad."

"Ah, hell, Father, Stevie has few memories of his dad. He enlisted right after I got pregnant, so he wouldn't have to deal with us. Why he never even married me. Every now and then he'd come home on leave, but everything was tense and I couldn't wait for him to go back. I have lots, and I mean lots, of other fish to fry. I am not letting some bastard kid stand in the way of my happiness."

Nick says, "Quiet down, someone will hear you."

"I don't care, and if they see or hear me, they will think I scored a priest, shall I tell them that?"

Nick is starting to lose it and tells her to shut up and slaps her. She fights back, slapping at him, calling him a faggot for not wanting a woman, and that sets him off. Nick punches her in the stomach so hard, she doubles over, the wind gone from her body, and Nick leans in for the kill. He grabs her neck, looks her in the eyes, and squeezes the life out of her while telling her she is nothing more than Satan's whore.

Nick did not plan for this kill. He feels uneasy. He did not have the fulfilling itch that comes before the kill. He sits there beleaguered and wonders who this woman is and what is she doing dead in his SUV.

All of a sudden, the mist in his brain clears and he remembers Stevie's mother. He's gained his senses now. What an awful person, surely she deserved to die, but why no itch? His sinner detector did not go off.

Nick panics and thinks maybe his power of invisibility is wearing off. He must dispose of her, but where?

Nick drives around the streets, down alleys, stays off main roadways, and finally it occurs to him. The cemetery, it worked before with the lovely Candy. He makes a few wrong turns but finally finds it. He drags her from the SUV, no gentle placing of this one, he is in a hurry and feels vulnerable. He just dumps her, and as he looks down on her, he realizes she is not one of the wicked that God sent him to destroy. He goes to his SUV and gets out his oils and anoints her and asks God to forgive him for making Stevie an orphan.

Nick gathers up his belongings and drives away. He has no feelings of elation like before. He is depressed, doesn't know why he is not pleased. Nick starts to think God was not happy with this one, and why did he anoint her?

Nick gets back to the rectory in the wee hours of the morning. As he sits in the driveway in his SUV, he has no memory of where he is or how he got here.

This is how Father Adam finds him at 7:00 A.M. Asleep in his SUV, looking like a truck ran over him. Father knocks on the window and Nick stirs. He looks at Father Adam with such a blank stare that Adam's heart skips a beat.

He opens the door and says, "Nick, are you ok?"

Nick staggers out, unaware of Father Adam, and goes to his room where he sleeps the entire day.

It is the third day since Nick is back at the Rectory, and he has not come out of his room since his return. His response to a knock on the door is go away.

The Fathers are so terribly concerned, and Father McCoy has asked his friend and personal doctor, Dr. Henry Mitchell, to see if they can help Nick.

Dr. Mitchell arrives, and Father Bill explains about Nick, his refusal to come out of his room, and his bursts of unintelligible rants.

Father Adam knocks on Nick's door and orders him to meet in the study immediately, or he will break down the door.

As the two priests and Dr. Mitchell wait patiently, the door to the study opens and there stands Nick. The Fathers are horrified at his appearance. He has not shaved nor bathed since his return. His jeans and t-shirt are dirty and Nick stinks.

"Nick, come in and sit down," says Father Bill, "this is Dr. Mitchell, he's here to help you."

"Don't need help," says Nick.

"Tell me where you are, Nick," says Dr. Mitchell, "do you know?"

Nick stares off in the distance and says, "Yes, I am on the verge of getting my reward for doing God's work."

"And what reward is that?" asks Dr. Mitchell, thinking he means his reward for becoming a priest.

Nick looks at him, suddenly with such an intenseness, and says, "Why, my Ascension into heaven."

Dr. Mitchell walks away and goes over to the Fathers. "Bill, I think we need to commit this boy. He's having some kind of mental breakdown. I will get the car, and you bring him out. We will get him to the hospital immediately."

Father McCoy goes over to Nick and says, "Come, my son. Let's get you some help."

Nick gets up and goes along with Father McCoy without incident.

As he walks to the car, he says to Father McCoy, "Sorry but you cannot go with me, Bill. God has chosen me, not you."

That night Father Nicholas Dougherty is admitted to the mental ward in the local hospital.

CHAPTER 52

Vinny arrives late Wednesday morning and is greeted by two of his team. He notices Mickey is up at the crime board and is making notes after the names of the priests he has interviewed.

Jet is at the computer looking as Victorian as ever. Vinny thinks she looks like one of those porcelain dolls sitting there. No wonder Mickey gets all hot and bothered.

"Hey, chief," says Mickey.

J.J. just looks up and waves her fingers.

"What do you have, Mickey?" asks Vinny.

"I am eliminating my two names, chief, Frantzen and Hoffman. Frantzen finally gave up his host's name where he was at some private party. It seems his conscience thought it was wrong to go off from the reunion. No S & M, just priestly guilt for having fun. As for Hoffman, he has the ability, he's defiant, and really rough around the edges but very devoted to his God and being a priest. I just don't see it."

"Good work, Mickey," says Vinny. "I see C.J. has also crossed Walbert but still has a question mark at Madsen."

As Vinny is immersed in the clues and information on his crime board, Cully comes bursting into the room, shouting, "Chief, chief, they found her car. They found our victim's car. It was in Clyde's Junk yard just beyond the school yard, hidden among other wrecks."

"Who found it?" asks Vinny.

"Some local kids, they were looking for car parts with Clyde and came across it. Lucky for us, Clyde's an upstanding citizen. He knew it was not one of his, so he called our station. Mary Lou took the call, and I was already here, so she told me and I went to see. I had it hauled over to our garage to be gone over by our forensic team and look, chief, in the glove box was some sort of diary our victim kept. Seems she was obsessive about recording the details of her life. What she ate, when she slept, and, chief, who she was meeting that night."

"You gotta be kidding," says Vinny, "give it to me." And there in black and white, Vinny reads out loud…*"wish "N" would hurry up. I don't like this school yard, never did. Maybe he won't show. What do you think, people?"*

Mickey looks up and says, "It seems it's time for a warrant for Nicholas Dougherty."

Vinny calls Mary Lou into the office and instructs her to call the DA's office and secure a warrant for the arrest of Nicholas Dougherty. Then get on the phone and connect him with the person in charge of the Selinsgrove Police Department.

In about a half hour, Mary Lou tells Vinny she has Sergeant Tucker Dunn on the line.

Vinny introduces himself, fills him in on what's going on, and asks the Sergeant if he and his men would pick up Father Nicholas Dougherty at St. Mark's Rectory and hold him on suspicion of murder. Vinny takes time to elaborate on the crimes and will fax the warrant.

As the rest of Vinny's crew arrives, they all sit around, waiting and pacing to hear that Father Dougherty is in custody.

Luke finally says, "I can't wait any longer. Let's just head up there."

"No," says Vinny, "let's wait."

Fifteen long minutes later, Sergeant Dunn calls back.

"Chief Miller, my men went to the Rectory but Father McCoy, the Pastor, told us a rather bizarre story. He and a Doctor Mitchell had Father Dougherty committed to the mental ward at St. Jane's Hospital two weeks ago."

"Mental ward, what's going on? Did you see him, is he lucid?"

"I'm really sorry, Chief Miller, but when we got over to the hospital, got through all the doctors, all the stalling, and waiting for approval, we learned that Father Dougherty signed himself out. Just up and left, and no one was told. He's in the wind Chief. We were just a few hours too late."

"This is very disturbing. Does he have a car? If so will you please put out an alert. We have to find this priest."

While Vinny is trying to get his head on straight, wondering how they could have been so close and now are so far away from arresting a serial murderer, Vinny gets a call from Dunn telling him the SUV is gone from the Rectory. The priest must have come back to the Rectory when the other priests were at the school and the housekeeper was out shopping. Some of his street clothes are missing, as well as some snack type foods.

"Ok, people, listen up. Our Father Dougherty is in the wind. Luke, you and Mickey go see the parents. See if they know where he is. Do not, and I mean do not, upset Mrs. Dougherty. Find out if she knows he has left the hospital and where he might go. At no time are you to insinuate he is a killer. Max, you hit up the brothers and sisters. Same goes for you. No accusing, just more routine questioning. We don't know if they even know he is gone. C. J., you check out Mr. Dougherty. Cully, you come with me. We are going to see Dr. Sullivan. A best friend might know more than family."

Everyone piles out of the station. Vinny and Cully get to the hospital and asks to see Dr. Sullivan. After a short time, Charlie comes down the hallway.

"Chief Miller, this is a surprise. How can I help you?" says Charlie.

"Dr. Sullivan, thank you for your time," says Vinny. "Did you know your friend Nick was hospitalized in the mental ward at St. Jane's up in Selinsgrove?"

"Yes," says Charlie, "the doctor, a Dr. Mitchell, called my in-laws. Seems Nick had some kind of break down but assured us he just needs some rest."

"Dr. Sullivan," begins Vinny.

"Please call me Charlie,"

"Ok, Charlie, Nick walked out early this morning and no one knows where he is. I was hoping you could help me find him," says Vinny.

"Why, why is his whereabouts of interest to you?" asks Charlie.

"I need you to keep this in the strictest of confidence, but we have reason to believe that Nick is responsible for Sarah Woodbury's death."

"That's impossible," shouts Charlie, bringing attention to them standing in the hallway.

"Please be quiet, doctor. I assure you we have the proof. We also suspect him of multiple murders. Now please do you have any idea where he would go? Please, Charlie, time is of the essence."

Charlie paces back and forth, trying to absorb this information, and in his heart, he knows something has been off with Nick for some time.

"Yeah, Chief Miller," says Charlie, "I think I know exactly where he would go. I have a cabin up in the Pocono's. Nick and I have spent time there all our lives. He has full run of the place."

"Give me directions," says Vinny.

"Let me come with you, Chief Miller. If he is there, he'll respond to me. Please let me help my friend," begs Charlie.

"Ok, but we must leave right now," says Vinny.

Charlie says, "Give me fifteen minutes, I must clear my calendar."

"Meet us down front, you ride with me," says Vinny.

"Cully, radio our team and tell them to meet us here within ten minutes. They are to use one vehicle and, Cully, you and the Doc will ride with me."

Charlie meets the detectives in front of the hospital, and as he climbs into the car with Vinny and Cully, he asks, "Chief, may I let my wife know what's going on?"

Vinny says, "Absolutely not, let's see if he is at the cabin. Then we will make decisions."

It has taken them over an hour to arrive at the dirt road that will take them up to the cabin. Vinny pulls to the side and Mickey does the same. Vinny walks back to the car and instructs his team to be vigilant and as quiet as can be once we get to the cabin. "If he is here, we don't want to spook him."

As they drive up the dirt road to the cabin, they spot Nick's SUV. They pull behind it and in front, so there is no escape. As they emerge from the cars, Vinny motions to C.J. and Mickey to check the cabin. Luke and Max are to search the car.

As the detectives are performing their duties, Charlie walks around his cabin with Vinny and Cully.

C.J. and Mickey comes up to them and tells Vinny the cabin is clear, but he has definitely been here.

Vinny asks Charlie where the other paths lead and Charlie says, "One goes to the pond and the other just off into the woods. Sort of a hiking trail." Vinny motions to his team to follow. He signals Max and Luke to check out the pond, he and the others will follow the trail.

As quietly as possible, led by Charlie, they start off. After about 500 yards, they hear Nick's voice. Vinny indicates to his people to move slowly, and as they get closer, they hear Nick yelling, it seems at God. They follow the sound, and Vinny holds his hand up to stop them. Charlie starts towards Nick, but Vinny catches him and says no and holds him back.

There standing in a small meadow among the trees is Nicholas Dougherty. He is as naked as a Jay bird, standing with his arms out stretched, reaching for heaven. Rays of sunlight beam down on him, and he is begging God to take him.

The detectives watch and listen.

Nick is crying, begging, "Dear God, please take me up into your divine home. I've done everything you asked. I am yours, dear Lord. Let me ascend into your arms."

Nick has not moved. He is so intent in his pleas, he doesn't know anyone is near.

Vinny goes to move in, and this time Charlie grabs his shoulder, "Please, chief," he says, "let me go to him. You'll scare him. He'll trust me. Could you send someone back to the cabin for a robe?"

Vinny agrees and tells Cully to go back and see what he can find to cover Nick.

Charlie approaches Nick slowly and says, "Hey, Nick, old friend, what are you doing?"

Nick doesn't seem startled. He just turns toward Charlie and says, "Charlie, you came to see my ascension into heaven. How did you know?"

"Nick, why would you think God will raise you up?" whispers Charlie.

"Oh, Charlie, I have been chosen to do a special job for God. He even gave me super powers." And once again, he beseeches God to please take him.

Charlie says, "What special job did you do, Nick?"

Vinny and his detectives move closer very quietly, so they can listen to what is being said.

"I have rid the world of women. So many, Charlie. Because you know they are deceitful, dirty, they tease and promise you love only to laugh in your face. Surely you know that, too, Charlie," says Nick.

Cully arrives with a robe and hands it to Charlie.

"Nick, listen to me," says Charlie, "I want you to put on this robe and come back to the cabin with me. Will you do that for me?"

"But, but I am to ascend," mutters Nick so quietly.

"Not today, my friend, not today," says Charlie as he leads Nick back to the cabin.

As Charlie helps Nick get dressed, Vinny and his team stand around in silence, trying to absorb what they just witnessed. Instead of the vicious, hard-ass career criminal they all expected to one day catch, they instead find a gentle soul committed to God and thinking he was doing God's work.

Vinny breaks the silence and says, "Max, anything in the SUV?"

"Yeah, boss," says Max, "there is a satchel with the items he used. No more arrows but several copies of his message written in cursive. Remnants of the make-up, Vixen Green and Poppy Paradise. Not much left though. He probably thought his mission was done when he ran out of his tools. There are a few little statutes of the Virgin Mary still in the bag, too."

"So, people, we caught our serial killer. Somehow I don't feel as good as I thought I would."

Charlie brings Nick out from the bedroom, and they sit at the table. Nick grabs Charlie by the arm and whispers, "I think I know why God is mad at me. I should not have killed Ms. Eberhart."

"Nick," says Vinny, "who is Ms. Eberhart?"

Nick speaks so softly that the detectives have to strain to hear him.

"She's Stevie's mom; she's a vile creature and pays no attention to Stevie. She was not on my radar, but she made me so mad calling her son a bastard, she deserved to die, so I killed her. I think that is why God's mad at me, but He will forgive me, and soon I will be taken into heaven."

Vinny gathers his detectives together and says, "We need to get Father Dougherty back to our station, and people, this is a touchy one. Cully, you and Luke ride with me and Father Dougherty. C.J., Max, you take the doctor with you and Mickey, you drive the SUV. Once we get back, Mickey, you drop the SUV off at our garage, then go wake up Father Eric at St. Jerome's. Explain very briefly, very briefly, that Nick is being held on murder charges and he must contact the dioceses and get him a lawyer."

"What are you going to do with Father Dougherty?" asks Max.

"I am going to see he gets processed, finger printed, picture taken, read him his rights, although I don't think it will register, and then I will have Dr. Sullivan wait with me until I get a prosecutor to go with us to the mental ward at the St. Mercy's hospital and have him committed under lock and key. Any questions?" asks Vinny.

Charlie goes outside and calls Alice. He tells her briefly what is going on and asks her to gather the family at her parent's house, and as soon as he can, he will be there to explain what has happened. When he comes back in, Vinny explains the arrangements to him. Charlie approaches Nick, tells him they are leaving now, and helps to escort Nick to Chief Miller's car.

CHAPTER 53

Several months have passed, and the scandal that rocked this small community has died down. The Dougherty family, ever so strong in their love and faith, have endured the looks and the whispers of strangers but also the kindness of friends. Nick has been sent to the Institute for the Criminally Insane at Greystone Park in New Jersey.

A certain Mary Ellen McGrath has pulled up stakes and moved. She did not have the courage to face all the whispers and accusations directed at her for destroying a good man, a wonderful priest.

Nick would have been so pleased to see how this "love of his life" was shunned and that people now know what she did.

Mrs. Dougherty has been asked by the doctors at the institute to please not visit her son. It seems after a visit from her, Father Dougherty becomes violent and difficult to control. They have to sedate him to calm him down. Grace is heartbroken, but it is her love for him that she will consent to their wishes. Father Eric and Charlie are the only two people Nick recognizes, although he does not speak to them. He is often heard late at night begging God to give him his reward and cursing God for going back on His promise.

Chief Miller has Mary Lou write an official letter to all the heads of all the police departments where these particular murders took place, so they could close out their cold cases.

Vinny is in his office when Justice comes to visit.

"Justice," says Vinny, "look how lovely you look, all dressed up. What's the occasion?"

"Vinny, I am so excited. I found a house for us," exclaims Justice.

"You did, where?" asks Vinny as he encircles her with his arms and kisses her cheek.

"Well, since I am soon to be Mrs. Miller, and we don't want to live in your house, I have really been searching, and besides, don't you close on yours in a few weeks?"

"Yes, yes, I do, tell me what you found," Vinny says as he gets up to close the door.

Vinny's team is no longer a team, and they have all been assigned other cases and working with other detectives, but none of them will ever forget solving one the biggest case in their careers and working with Vinny.

Not wishing anyone ill, each secretly hopes to one day catch another big one, so they can again work together under the direction of Chief Vinny Miller.